As the bestselling New Jedi Order series approaches its epic climax, the secrets of the Yuuzhan Vong—who they are, where they came from, what terrible forces drive them—are at last exposed.

But will this knowledge aid the Jedi . . . or doom them?

Also by Greg Keyes

THE NEW JEDI ORDER

THE FINAL
PROPHECY

GREG KEYES

arrow books

Published by Arrow Books in 2003

1 3 5 7 9 0 8 6 4 2

First published in the United Kingdom in 2003 by Arrow Books

Arrow Books
The Random House Group Limited
20 Vauxhall Bridge Road, London, SW1V 2SA

Random House Australia (Pty) Limited
20 Alfred Street, Milsons Point, Sydney,
New South Wales 2061, Australia

Random House New Zealand Limited
18 Poland Road, Glenfield
Auckland 10, New Zealand

Random House (Pty) Limited
Endulini, 5a Jubilee Road, Parktown 2193, South Africa

The Random House Group Limited Reg. No. 954009

www.starwars.com
www.starwarskids.com
www.randomhouse.co.uk

A CIP catalogue record for this book is available from the British Library

Papers used by Random House are natural, recyclable products made from wood grown
in sustainable forests. The manufacturing processes conform to the environmental
regulations of the country of origin

ISBN 0 09 941043 5

Printed and bound in Great Britain by
Bookmarque Ltd, Croydon, Surrey

UNKNOWN REGIONS
SSI-RUUK STAR CLUSTER
BAKURA
ENDOR
BESPIN
HOTH
BORLEIAS
CORUSCANT
KOORNACHT CLUSTER
DEEP CORE
CORE WORLDS
FONDOR
INNER RIM
DURO
COLONIES
YAG'DHUL
TYNNA
CORELLIAN TRADE SPINE
RIMMA TRADE ROUTE
EXPANSION REGION
FALLEEN
RODIA
ANDO
NABOO
SULLUST
DAGOBAH
ELROOD SECTOR
KATHOL SECTOR
MINOS CLUSTER
CORELLIAN RUN

TINGEL ARM

EMPIRE · BASTION · BELKADAN
· HELSKA
· DUBRILLION
· DANTOOINE
· ORD BINIIR · BIMMIEL
AGAMAR
· DATHOMIR · YAVIN
· ITHOR
· WAYLAND MERIDIAN
SECTOR
· MYRKR OSSUS
· OBROA-SKAI · TION
CRON CLUSTER
HAPES CLUSTER DRIFT
· KASHYYYK CORPORATE
SECTOR
BIMMISAARI · · KUBINDI
· KESSEL
HUTT · YLESIA
SPACE
· NAL
HUTTA
RIM
· GAMORR

THE STAR WARS NOVELS TIMELINE

 44 YEARS BEFORE STAR WARS: A New Hope

Jedi Apprentice series

33 *YEARS BEFORE STAR WARS: A New Hope*

Darth Maul: Saboteur
Cloak of Deception

32.5 *YEARS BEFORE STAR WARS: A New Hope*

Darth Maul: Shadow Hunter

32 *YEARS BEFORE STAR WARS: A New Hope*

> **STAR WARS: EPISODE I THE PHANTOM MENACE**

29 *YEARS BEFORE STAR WARS: A New Hope*

Rogue Planet

22.5 *YEARS BEFORE STAR WARS: A New Hope*

The Approaching Storm

22 *YEARS BEFORE STAR WARS: A New Hope*

> **STAR WARS: EPISODE II ATTACK OF THE CLONES**

21.5 *YEARS BEFORE STAR WARS: A New Hope*

Shatterpoint

19 *YEARS BEFORE STAR WARS: A New Hope*

> **STAR WARS: EPISODE III**

10-0 *YEARS BEFORE STAR WARS: A New Hope*

The Han Solo Trilogy:

The Paradise Snare
The Hutt Gambit
Rebel Dawn

5-2 *YEARS BEFORE STAR WARS: A New Hope*

The Adventures of Lando Calrissian:

Lando Calrissian and the
Mindharp of Sharu
Lando Calrissian and the
Flamewind of Oseon
Lando Calrissian and the
Starcave of ThonBoka

The Han Solo Adventures:

Han Solo at Stars' End
Han Solo's Revenge
Han Solo and the Lost Legacy

 STAR WARS: A New Hope YEAR 0

> **STAR WARS: EPISODE IV A NEW HOPE**

0-3 *YEARS AFTER STAR WARS: A New Hope*

Tales from the Mos Eisley
Cantina
Splinter of the Mind's Eye

3 *YEARS AFTER STAR WARS: A New Hope*

> **STAR WARS: EPISODE V THE EMPIRE STRIKES BACK**

Tales of the Bounty Hunters

3.5 *YEARS AFTER STAR WARS: A New Hope*

Shadows of the Empire

4 *YEARS AFTER STAR WARS: A New Hope*

> **STAR WARS: EPISODE VI RETURN OF THE JEDI**

Tales from Jabba's Palace

The Bounty Hunter Wars:

The Mandalorian Armor
Slave Ship
Hard Merchandise

The Truce at Bakura

6.5-7.5 YEARS AFTER
STAR WARS: A New Hope

X-Wing:
  Rogue Squadron
  Wedge's Gamble
  The Krytos Trap
  The Bacta War
  Wraith Squadron
  Iron Fist
  Solo Command

8 YEARS AFTER STAR WARS: A New Hope
  The Courtship of Princess Leia
  A Forest Apart
  Tatooine Ghost

9 YEARS AFTER STAR WARS: A New Hope
  The Thrawn Trilogy:
  Heir to the Empire
  Dark Force Rising
  The Last Command

  X-Wing: Isard's Revenge

11 YEARS AFTER STAR WARS: A New Hope
  I, Jedi
  The Jedi Academy Trilogy:
  Jedi Search
  Dark Apprentice
  Champions of the Force

12-13 YEARS AFTER STAR WARS: A New Hope
  Children of the Jedi
  Darksaber
  Planet of Twilight
  X-Wing: Starfighters of Adumar

14 YEARS AFTER STAR WARS: A New Hope
  The Crystal Star

16-17 YEARS AFTER STAR WARS: A New Hope
  The Black Fleet Crisis Trilogy:
  Before the Storm
  Shield of Lies
  Tyrant's Test

18 YEARS AFTER STAR WARS: A New Hope
  The Corellian Trilogy:
  Ambush at Corellia
  Assault at Selonia
  Showdown at Centerpoint

19 YEARS AFTER STAR WARS: A New Hope
  The Hand of Thrawn Duology:
  Specter of the Past
  Vision of the Future

22 YEARS AFTER STAR WARS: A New Hope
  Junior Jedi Knights series

23-24 YEARS AFTER STAR WARS: A New Hope
  Young Jedi Knights series

 25-30 YEARS AFTER
STAR WARS: A New Hope

The New Jedi Order:
  Vector Prime
  Dark Tide I: Onslaught
  Dark Tide II: Ruin
  Agents of Chaos I: Hero's Trial
  Agents of Chaos II: Jedi Eclipse
  Balance Point
  Recovery
  Edge of Victory I: Conquest
  Edge of Victory II: Rebirth
  Star by Star
  Dark Journey
  Enemy Lines I: Rebel Dream
  Enemy Lines II: Rebel Stand
  Traitor
  Destiny's Way
  Ylesia
  Force Heretic I: Remnant
  Force Heretic II: Refugee
  Force Heretic III: Reunion
  The Final Prophecy
  The Unifying Force

ACKNOWLEDGMENTS

Thanks to Shelly Shapiro, Sue Rostoni, and Jim Luceno for holding this whole thing together. The rest of the *Star Wars* authors for giving me great books to follow. Enrique Guerrero, Michael Kogge, Dan Wallace, Felia Hendersheid, Helen Keiev, and Leland Chee for superior comments and editing. Kris Boldis for reality checks on the *Star Wars* universe. Finally, thanks to all my friends in Savannah for their support, especially Charlie Williams and the rest of the gang in the Savannah Fencing Club.

DRAMATIS PERSONAE

Corran Horn; Jedi Knight (male human)
Erli Prann; adventurer (male human)
Garm Bel Iblis; general (male human)
Gilad Pellaeon; Grand Admiral (male human)
Han Solo; captain, *Millennium Falcon* (male human)
Harrar; priest (male Yuuzhan Vong)
Jaina Solo; Jedi Knight (female human)
Mynar Devis; Interdictor captain (male human)
Nen Yim; master shaper (female Yuuzhan Vong)
Nom Anor; executor (male Yuuzhan Vong)
Onimi; Shamed One (male Yuuzhan Vong)
Princess Leia Organa Solo; diplomat (female human)
Qelah Kwaad; shaper (female Yuuzhan Vong)
Sien Sovv; admiral (male Sullustan)
Supreme Overlord Shimrra (male Yuuzhan Vong)
Tahiri Veila; Jedi Knight (female human)
Wedge Antilles; general (male human)

PROLOGUE

Three kilometers beneath the surface of Yuuzhan'tar—the world once known as Coruscant—the sound of chanting drifted up a shaft nearly as wide as it was deep, the melancholy strains yearning toward the few distant stars that could be seen from the bottom. In the pale blue light of lumen reeds, the faces of the chanters appeared ravaged, their bodies misshapen.

These were the Shamed Ones of the Yuuzhan Vong, and they chanted to their Prophet.

Nom Anor felt his bile rise at the sight. Even after all this time as the "Prophet," it was difficult to shake the long years of contempt he had held for them.

But they were his hope, now. They were his army. Once, not long ago, he had dared to dream that with them behind him he could pull Shimrra—Supreme Overlord of the Yuuzhan Vong—from his polyp throne, cast him into the pits, and assume his place.

But there had been setbacks. His eyes and ears within Shimrra's palace had been uncovered and killed. More of his followers were discovered every day, and fewer answered the call.

Their faith was wavering, and it was time to give it back to them.

"Hear me!" he called, his voice soaring above the Prayer of Redemption. "Hear the voice of prophecy!"

The chanting subsided, and an eager silence descended.

"I have fasted," he said. "I have meditated. Last night I sat here, beneath the stars, waiting for I knew not what. And in the darkest hours, a great light fell about me, a cleansing light, the light of redemption. I looked up and there, where the stars gaze down upon us, was an orb—a world, a planet in the skies above us. Its beauty made me tremble, and its power pressed down on me. I felt love and terror at once. And then those emotions subsided, and I felt—belonging. I knew that the planet itself was alive, welcoming me. It is the planet of the source, the planet of the *Jeedai*, their secret temple and fount of their knowledge and wisdom—and I saw us, the Shamed, walking with the *Jeedai* upon its surface, one with them, one with the planet."

He dropped his tone from singsong to a near growl. "And in the distance, I heard Shimrra's wail of despair, for he knows this planet—this living planet—is our salvation and his doom. And he knows it will come for him, one day, because it will come for us."

He lowered his hands, and for a moment the silence prevailed. Then a great roar went up, keen and joyful, and Nom Anor heard what he most wanted to hear—the sound of hope, the cry of the zealot—his name on the lips of a multitude.

What matter that he had put the story together from a few conversations and rumors he had collected from Shimrra's palace before his informant died? There *was* a planet, rumored to be alive in some unusual way. Shimrra *was* terrified of it, and had had the commander who brought the news of it slaughtered out of hand, along with all his crew. His story would give his people hope. It would encourage them to fight. And when they were captured, and told the prophecy to their punishers, it would get back to Shimrra, and bring his fear back home.

Better, Nom Anor had heard from old sources in the Galactic Alliance that the Jedi had mounted a search for just such a planet. What they wanted with it he did not know, but it seemed the planet had repelled at least one Yuu-zhan Vong battle group, so perhaps its people had potent weapons.

In any event, rumor would build on rumor, reinforcing the veracity of his vision, strengthening the resolve of his followers, knitting their single strands into ropes and the ropes into cables until they were strong enough to knot around Shimrra's neck and strangle him.

Strength swept through him as the sound of his adopted name built toward the heavens. He looked out over them, and this time was much less offended by their faces.

PART ONE

VISION

ONE

She was being followed.

She paused and wiped a damp wisp of yellow hair from her forehead, touching in passing the scars that marked her as a member of Domain Kwaad. Her green eyes scanned through the many-legged gnarltrees, but her stalkers weren't yet showing themselves to the usual senses. They were waiting for something—reinforcements, probably.

She hissed a mild shaper's curse under her breath and started off again, picking her way over moldering logs, through sluggish mists and dense brakes of hissing cane. The air was a wet fever, and the chirps and trills and bubbling gulps from canopy and marsh were oddly comforting. She kept her pace the same—there was no reason to let them know she was on to them, not yet. She did alter her path subtly—no point in going to the cave until this was dealt with.

Or I could lead them there, she mused, *attack them while they deal with their inner demons . . .*

No. That seemed somehow like sacrilege. Yoda had come here. Luke Skywalker had, too, and so had Anakin. Now it was her turn. Tahiri's turn.

Anakin's parents hadn't very much liked the idea of her coming to Dagobah alone, but she'd managed to convince them of the necessity. She believed that the human and Yuu-zhan Vong personalities that had once shared her body had become one seamless entity. It felt that way, felt right. But Anakin had seen a vision of her, a melding of Jedi and Yuuzhan Vong, and it hadn't been a pretty vision. She'd thought at first, after the joining that had nearly driven her mad, that she had avoided that outcome. But before she moved on, before she put those she loved at risk, she had to consider the possibility that the fusion of Tahiri Veila with Riina of Domain Kwaad was a step in the *fulfillment* of that vision.

Anakin, after all, had known her better than anyone. And Anakin had been very strong.

If the creature he had seen was lurking in her, the time to face it was now, not later.

So she'd come here, to Dagobah, where the Force was so strong it almost seemed to sing aloud. The cycle of life and death and new birth was all around here, none of it twisted by Yuuzhan Vong biotechnology, none of it poisoned by the machines, greed, and exploitation all too native to this galaxy. She'd come to visit the cave to explore her inner self and see what she was really made of.

But she had also come to Dagobah to meditate on the alternatives. What Anakin had seen was all of the worst of Yuuzhan Vong and Jedi traits bundled into one being. Avoiding becoming that was paramount, but she had a goal beyond—to find the balance, to embody the *best* of her mixed heritage. Not just for herself, but because the reconciliation of her dual identity had left her with one firm belief—that the Yuuzhan Vong and the peoples of the galaxy they had invaded could learn a lot from each other, and they could live in peace. She was sure of it. The only question was how to make it happen.

The Yuuzhan Vong would never create industrial wastelands like Duro, Bonadan, or Eriadu. On the other hand, what they did to life—breaking it and twisting it until it suited their needs, wiping it out entirely when it didn't please—was really no better. It wasn't that they loved life, but that they hated machines.

There had to be some sort of common ground, some pivot point that could open the eyes of both sides and end the ongoing terror and destruction of the war.

The Force was key to that understanding. The Yuuzhan Vong were somehow blind to it. If they could actually feel the Force around them, if they could feel the *wrongness* of their creations, they might find a better path, one less bent on destruction. If the Jedi could feel the Yuuzhan Vong in the Force, they might find—not better ways to fight them— but paths to conciliation.

She needed more than that, though. It wasn't enough to know what was wrong—she also had to know how to make things right.

Tahiri had no delusions of grandeur. She was no savior, no prophet, no super-Jedi. She was the result of a Yuuzhan Vong experiment gone wrong. But she did understand both sides of the problem, and if there was any chance she could help Master Skywalker find the solution her galaxy so desperately needed—well, she had to take it. It was a role she accepted with humility and great caution. Those trying to do good often committed the most atrocious crimes.

They were gaining on her, getting clumsier. Soon she would have to do something.

They must have followed her to Dagobah. How?

Or maybe they had known where she was going before she left. Maybe she had been betrayed. But that meant Han and Leia—

No. There was another answer. Paranoid reflexes were a survival trait growing up in a crèche, but even deeper instincts told her that her friends—adopted parents, almost— could never do such a thing. Someone had been watching her, someone she hadn't noticed. Peace Brigade maybe. Probably.

They would imagine they could curry a lot of favor by turning her over to Shimrra.

She twisted her way through a maze of gnarltrees and then clambered quickly and silently up their cablelike roots. They had once been legs, those roots, as she'd learned when she came here less than a decade and more than a lifetime ago. The immature form of the tree was a sort of spider that lost its mobility in adulthood.

She'd been with Anakin, here to face *his* trial, to discover if having the name of his grandfather would bring him the same fate.

I miss you Anakin, she thought. *More now than ever.*

About four meters off the ground, she secreted herself in a hollow and waited. If she could simply avoid them, she would. At one level her instincts cried out for battle, but at a deeper level she knew that her Yuuzhan Vong fighting reflexes had inevitable connections with fury, and she was here to avoid becoming Anakin's vision, not embrace it. There was a part of her plan that she hadn't told Han and Leia about—the part where, if the cave confirmed her worst fears, she would cripple her X-wing beyond repair and spend the rest of her life on the jungle planet.

Perhaps, like the spiders, she would sink her limbs into the swamp and become a tree.

She reached out with the Force, to better assess her pursuit.

They weren't there. And she suddenly realized that she hadn't felt them in the Force, but with her Vongsense. It had come so naturally she hadn't even questioned it.

That could only mean her pursuers were Yuuzhan Vong, maybe six of them, give or take one or two. Vongsense wasn't as precise as the Force.

She reached for her lightsaber, but didn't unhook it, and continued to wait.

Soon she actually heard them. Whoever they were, they weren't hunters—they moved through the jungle clumsily, and though they pitched their voices low enough that she couldn't actually understand what they were saying, they seemed to be gabbling almost constantly. They must be very confident of their success.

A dark shadow glided soundlessly through the undergrowth, and she snapped her gaze up in time to see something very large blot the fragments of sky not occluded by the distant canopy.

Native life, or a Yuuzhan Vong flier?

Pursing her lips, she waited. Soon the distant muttering became coherent. As she'd thought, the language was that of her crèche.

"Are you certain she came this way?" a raspy voice asked.

"She did. See? The impression in the moss?"

"She is *Jeedai*. Perhaps she left these signs to confuse us."

"Perhaps."

"But you think she is near?"

"Yes."

"And knows we are following her?"

"Yes."

"Then why not simply call out to her?"

And hope I answer the battle challenge? Tahiri thought, grimly. So they *did* have a tracker with them. Could she slip around them, back to her X-wing? Or must she fight them?

Moving very slowly, Tahiri shifted in the direction of the voices. She could make out several figures through the understory, but not distinctly.

"At some point we must, I suppose," the tracker said. "Else she will think we wish her harm."

What? Tahiri frowned, trying to fit that into her presuppositions. She couldn't.

"*Jeedai!*" the tracker called. "I think you can hear us. We humbly request an audience."

No warrior would do that, Tahiri thought. *No warrior would use such honorless trickery. But a shaper . . .*

Yes, a shaper or a priest might, a member of the deception sect. Still—

She leaned out for a better view, and found herself staring straight into the yellow eyes of a Yuuzhan Vong.

He was perhaps six meters away. She gasped at the sight of him, and revulsion jolted through her. His face was like an open wound.

A Shamed One, despised by the gods. He dared—her hand went to her lightsaber.

Then the shadow was back, and suddenly something sleeted through the branches, shredding the leaves and vines around her. She snarled a war cry and ignited her weapon, swirling it up to send two thud bugs burning off through the jungle.

Above her, through the now open canopy, she saw a Yuuzhan Vong tsik vai, an atmospheric flier, huge and ray-shaped, and from it snaked long cables. To each cable clung a Yuuzhan Vong warrior. One passed less than two meters from her, and she braced for the fight, but he went on past, oblivious to her presence, striking the jungle floor and uncoiling his amphistaff in the same motion.

A terrible wail went up from her pursuers. She could see them now, all horribly disfigured, all Shamed Ones. They raised their short clubs and faced the warriors.

They didn't have a chance—she saw that immediately. For an instant, the tracker held her eye, and she thought he would give her away, but instead his expression went grim.

"Run!" he shouted. "We cannot win here!"

Tahiri hesitated only an instant longer, then made a series of steplike leaps to the ground. The first of the Shamed Ones had already fallen when her feet touched the spongy soil.

A warrior caught her motion from the corner of his eye and turned to meet her, snarling a war cry. His face transfigured in surprise when she answered it in his own language. He whirled his amphistaff toward her, a lateral strike aimed at her scapula. She caught the blade and cut toward his knuckles, but he parried with distance, pulled his weapon free of the bind, and lunged deep with the venomous tip. She caught it in a high sweep and stepped in, cut to his shoulder where the vonduun crab armor shed its fury in a shower of sparks, then dodged past, reversing the weapon and plunging its fiery point into the vulnerable spot in the armpit. The warrior gasped and sank to his knees, and she whipped the weapon around to decapitate him even as she launched herself at the next foe.

Combat was a blur, after that. Eight warriors had dropped from the flier. Seven were left, and fully half the Shamed Ones were bleeding on the ground. She had an image of the tracker, his arms knotted in a neck-breaking hold. She saw another Shamed One strike a warrior on the temple with his club only to be run through from behind. Mostly she saw the lightning-quick amphistaff strikes of the two warriors trying to flank her. She cut at a knee, smelled the scorch of flesh as the blade severed through armor. An amphistaff whipped toward her back and she had to roll beneath the blow. *Parry, thrust, and cut* became her entire existence.

Spattered with Yuuzhan Vong blood and bleeding from several cuts of her own, she suddenly found herself back to back with the tracker. He was all that remained of the six who had initially been following her, but there remained only three warriors.

For a moment, they stood like that. The warriors backed away a bit. The leader was massive. His ears were cut into fractal patterns; great trenchlike scars stood on his cheeks.

"I've heard of you, abomination," he snarled. "The one-who-was-shaped. Is it true what they say? These pathetic maw luur excretions worship you?"

"I don't know anything about that," Tahiri said. "But I know when I see a dishonorable fight. They were not only outnumbered, but poorly armed. How can you call yourselves warriors, to attack in such a way?"

"They are Shamed Ones," the warrior sneered back. "They are outside honor. They are worse than infidels; they are heretic traitors, not to be fought but to be exterminated."

"You fear us," the tracker rasped. "You fear us because we know the truth. You lap at Shimrra's feet, yet Shimrra is the true heretic. See how this *Jeedai* has laid you low. The gods favor her, not you."

"If the gods favor her, they do not favor you," the warrior snapped.

"They are delaying us," the tracker told Tahiri. She noticed he had blood on his lips. "They delay us while another tsik vai arrives."

"Quiet, heretic," the war leader bellowed, "and you may yet live to snivel a little longer. There are questions we would ask of you." His expression softened. "Renounce your heresy. This *Jeedai* is a great prize. Help us win her, and perhaps the gods will forgive you and grant you an honorable death."

"No death is more honorable than dying by the side of a *Jeedai*," the tracker answered. "Vua Rapuung proved that."

"Vua Rapuung," the warrior all but spat. "That story is a heretic's lie. Vua Rapuung died in disgrace."

For answer the Shamed One suddenly bolted forward, so quickly he took the leader by surprise, bowling into him before he could raise his weapon. The other two turned to help, but Tahiri danced forward, feinting at the knee and then cutting high through the warrior's throat when he dropped his guard to parry. She exchanged a flurry of blows with the second, though it ended the same, with the warrior flopping lifeless to the ground.

She turned to find the tracker impaling the leader with his

own amphistaff. For a moment they stared at each other, the Shamed One and she. Then the Yuuzhan Vong suddenly dropped to his knees.

"I prayed it was you!" he said.

Tahiri opened her mouth, but heard the stir of treetops that could only be another flier arriving.

"Come on," she said. "We can't stay here."

The warrior nodded and bounded to his feet. Together they ran from the clearing.

An hour or so later, Tahiri finally halted. The fliers seemed to have lost them for the time being, and the tracker had been gradually dropping behind. Now he staggered against a tree and slid to the ground.

"A little farther," she said. "Just over here."

"My legs will no longer bear me," the tracker said. "You must leave me for the time being."

"Just under this shelf of stone," she said. "Please. It may hide us from the fliers if they sweep here."

He nodded wearily. She saw he was clutching his side, and that blood covered his flank.

They scooted up beneath the overhang.

"Let me see that," she said.

He shook his head. "I must speak to you first," he said.

"What are you doing here? Did you follow me?"

His eyes widened. "No!" he said, so vehemently that blood sputtered from between his lips. Then, more quietly, "No. We thieved a ship from an intendant and came here to find the world of prophecy. We saw you land—is this the place, one-who-was-shaped? Is this the world the Prophet saw?"

"I'm sorry," Tahiri said. "I don't know what you mean. This is Dagobah. I came here for . . . personal reasons."

"But it cannot be coincidence," the tracker said. "It cannot."

"Please," Tahiri said. "Let me see your wound. I know a little about healing. Maybe I can—"

"I am dead already," the tracker gruffed. "I know this. But I must know if I have failed."

Tahiri shook her head helplessly.

The tracker straightened a bit, and his voice strengthened. "I am Hul Qat, once a hunter. Or I was, until the gods seemed to reject me. I was stripped of my title, my clan. I was Shamed. My implants festered and my scars opened like wounds. I gave up hope and waited for dishonorable death. But then I heard the word of the Prophet, and of the *Jeedai* Anakin—"

"Anakin," Tahiri whispered. The name twisted a blade in her.

"Yes, and you, whom Mezhan Kwaad shaped. And Vua Rapuung who fought—you were there, were you not?"

A deep chill ran through Tahiri. She had been Riina, then, and Tahiri, and she had nearly killed Anakin.

"I was there."

"Then you know. You know our redemption belongs with you. And now the Prophet has seen a world, a world where there are no Shamed Ones because it will redeem us, where the true way can be—" He coughed violently and slumped again, and for an instant Tahiri thought he was already dead. But then his eyes turned toward her.

"My companions and I wanted to find the planet for our Prophet. One of us, Kuhqo, had been a shaper. He used a genetic slicer to get access to an executor's qahsa and steal its secrets. He found intelligence gathered about the *Jeedai*, and evidence that there was some connection between you and this world. Some of your greatest came here, yes? And now you. And so please, tell me. Have I found it?"

He shuddered, and his eyes rolled. "Have I?" he begged again, so weakly this time it might have been no more than a breath.

Tahiri reached out and took his hand. "Yes," she lied, not even knowing exactly what lie she was telling. "Yes, you're right. You found it. Don't worry about anything now."

His eyes filled with tears. "You must help me," he said. "I cannot take the news myself. The Prophet must know where this world is."

"I will do it," Tahiri said.

This time she was not lying.

Hul Qat closed his eyes, and even without using the Force, Tahiri felt him leave.

Tahiri glanced at the opening of the cave, so near, and she knew that was not what she had come for at all. *This* was why she had come. The Force had brought her here, to meet this man, to make this promise.

She rose. The fliers would find her if she remained still for too long. She hoped they hadn't discovered her ship yet, but figured the odds were against it, since they hadn't been looking for her and she had concealed it pretty well. Even so, she might have a little trouble getting out of the system, depending on how many and what sort of ships were orbiting overhead.

It didn't matter, though. She had a promise to keep.

Even if she could figure out exactly what she had promised.

TWO

The port shields of *Mon Mothma* collapsed and plasma punched through the hull like a fist through flimsiplast. At the point of impact, matter became ions, and supersonic droplets of molten hull metal sleeted through the next four decks, arriving before the sound or vibration of impact, shredding the frail life-forms within before their nervous systems had time to register anything amiss. Behind that came a shock wave of superheated air expanding with such fury that blast shields bent and warped, and the wave-front swept the decks end to end, searing everything in its path. Two hundred sentient beings winked out in an instant, and a hundred more in marginal areas fell—perforated, burned, or both.

Then, like a giant taking back its breath, space sucked everything out through the gaping hole, leaving vacuum behind, and quiet.

At the helm of the Star Destroyer, it was far from quiet. Claxons blared and panicked young officers stuttered through emergency procedures. Simulated gravity vanished, and someone shrieked.

Wedge Antilles closed his eyes as the illusion of weight faded and reasserted itself.

I'm so tired of this, he thought.

He opened his eyes to a barrage of smaller plasma blasts aimed directly, it seemed, at his face as a squadron of Yuuzhan

Vong coralskippers made a run straight at the bridge. Turbo-lasers flared three of them into debris. The rest peeled away at the last instant to avoid impacting the still-functioning bridge shields.

Wedge didn't even blink. The skips weren't their problem right now. That would be the Yuuzhan Vong Dreadnaught analog that had just popped into existence and blasted a hole in their side.

"Twenty degrees starboard and twelve above horizon," Wedge commanded. "Now. Commence firing."

He swung on the lieutenant at tactical. "What else has joined our little party?" he demanded.

"Four frigate analogs, sir," the lieutenant told him. "Coralskippers—we're not sure how many flights, yet. And of course, the Dreadnaught. Sir, I'd say the Yuuzhan Vong reinforcements have arrived."

"Yes. We'll wait a bit to see if there are any more. Tell *Memory of Ithor* to watch our wounded flank. We'll have to slug this out."

His whole body itched at the prospect. In his heart and in the caves of his reflexes, Wedge was a starfighter pilot. Sure, capital ships had firepower, but they were so *slow* maneuvering. He'd feel a lot better in an X-wing.

He'd feel better without the weight of dead crew on his shoulders. Losing a wingmate was hard enough. Losing *two hundred* . . .

But he wasn't in an X-wing, and when he'd come out of retirement as a general, he'd known what he was getting himself into. So he watched, lips pursed, as the monstrous ovoid of a ship swung into view, as the *Mothma*'s turbo-lasers razoring toward yorik coral returned blossoms of plasma. Most of the lasers arrowed straight, then abruptly curved into sharp hooks and vanished as the tiny singularities the Yuuzhan Vong vessel projected pulled the light into them. About every third beam went through, however, scribbling glowing red lines in the coral hull.

"Sir, the *Memory* is unable to come to our aid. She's engaged with one of the frigates, and she's taking quite a beating."

"Well, get somebody there. We can't let them hit us in that flank again."

The controller looked up from his station. "Sir, Duro Squadron is requesting the honor of protecting our flank."

Wedge hesitated infinitesimally. Duro Squadron was a bit of a wild card, a collection of pilots—some with military experience, some without—dedicated to the liberation of their home system.

The fact that it was precisely that system they were fighting in right now could be a problem, for various reasons.

But it didn't look like he had any other choice.

"Tell them yes, without our thanks," Wedge said.

"Three more ships just reverted, sir," Lieutenant Cel informed him, a catch in her voice that might be the start of panic.

"That's it," Wedge said. "Or it had better be. Get me General Bel Iblis."

A moment later, a hologram of the aging general appeared.

"The reinforcements are here," Wedge told him. "Listening posts have them coming through the Corellian Trade Spine, so they're most likely our buddies."

"Is it too many to handle, General Antilles?" Bel Iblis asked.

"I hope not, sir. Is your force ready?"

"We're on our way. Good luck, General."

"And to you."

The image vanished. Wedge set his mouth grimly, watching the battle reports.

They had already spent a standard day in heavy fighting, driving through the outer defenses of the Duro system in a matter of hours. The inner system had put up more of a fight, but they'd been close to mopping up when Yuuzhan Vong reinforcements arrived.

Wedge had been expecting the reinforcements—counting on them, really—but they'd hit hard and fast. A reassessment of the situation put the odds marginally in favor of the Yuuzhan Vong, which again was no surprise.

It was also okay—they hadn't come here to win, but they couldn't leave yet, either.

"Prepare interdiction," Wedge said.

Four more Yuuzhan Vong frigates jumped into the Duro system, changing the odds yet again.

"Sir?"

"Interdict," he said.

The great ship's gravity-well generators came on-line, as did those of *Memory of Ithor* and *Olovin*.

Positioned as they were around the Yuuzhan Vong force, they would prevent the Vong from leaving the system, at least until the interdiction perimeter was reduced to dust.

Of course, none of the Galactic Alliance ships could leave, either.

"Break off the attack and form up in containment positions," Wedge said calmly. "I don't want any of those ships reaching hyperspace."

"What about Duro, sir?" Cel asked.

"Duro is no longer our concern, Lieutenant."

"Yes, sir," Cel said, clearly baffled.

Good. If his own people were confused, hopefully the Vong were more so.

The Alliance ships broke off their push toward the planet and retreated into a broad hemisphere, putting the Yuuzhan Vong fleet with the planet at its back, handing them back the defensive advantage that Wedge's earlier push had taken from them, but also trapping them more securely in the system.

"Hold the line," Wedge commanded. "We stick here."

Spreading the battle group so thinly gave the Yuuzhan Vong an obvious advantage, but the Vong ships seemed to hesitate, perhaps suspecting another of the traps they had been so often led into lately.

Still, caution was not natural to the Yuuzhan Vong, and they now clearly had the advantage in numbers. Several destroyers began forming up for an assault on the wall the Galactic Alliance had built.

"Do they have any interdictors of their own?" Wedge asked.

"No, sir."

"Good."

"Yes, sir. Sir, Commander Yurf Col is requesting communication."

Wedge repressed a sigh. "Put him on."

A moment later a holo of the Duros commander appeared. His flat face was unreadable in terms of human expression, but Wedge had enough experience with Duros to know he was radiating a cold fury.

"Commander," Wedge said, nodding.

The Duros came bluntly to the point.

"What in the space lanes are you up to, General Antilles? I've lost good pilots today, and now it appears you've given up our target."

"I'm sure you are as aware of the situation as I am, Commander," Wedge said. "The reinforcements make further assaults untenable."

"Then why are you interdicting? That makes no sense. I happen to know that we have twice as many ships in reserve. Summon them, and let's finish this."

Patience, Wedge thought.

"Perhaps you aren't aware that the Yuuzhan Vong have means of tapping our communications," he said mildly.

"Perhaps it hasn't occurred to you that you might have just passed on important intelligence to the enemy."

"If we obliterate that enemy, what they learn will be of little consequence. I don't know why you want to hold them here. They still don't have a decisive advantage—we can win this, if we attack instead of—whatever you're doing. And with a few reinforcements, we could certainly prevail."

"Commander, I understand this is your home system. I understand that for you, this fight is personal. That is, in fact, one of the many reasons I am in charge of this operation and you are not. You agreed to fight under my command, and you will do so. Do you understand?"

"I understand you have bungled this from the start. We could have won in the first few hours if you had followed my advice."

"That is your opinion," Wedge replied. "It is not mine, and mine is the one that counts right now."

The Duros's eyes narrowed. "When this is over, Antilles—"

"I suggest you worry about the present, Commander. The Vong are trying to punch through and open two fronts. If they succeed, this reduces our future options considerably."

"You are the one limiting our options. Two more frigates—"

Wedge cut him off. "Get used to this idea, Commander," he said, "and get used to it quickly—there *are* no reinforcements. Nor am I yet prepared to abandon this system. Do your part, Commander, and everything will go well."

Col remained unconvinced. "I warn you, General Antilles," he snapped, "if you don't explain this to me, I will force your hand."

"You will follow your orders, period," Wedge replied.

"General—" the Duros began, but Wedge waved the contact off and studied the reports. The attack looked like a feint to draw his net tight in one place while they hit it in another. But where?

The battle computers searched for the answer. By Wedge's reckoning, unless the Yuuzhan Vong pulled off something amazing, he would be able to hold them off for five or six hours without significant losses. That should be enough.

He studied the on-spec chart their sensors were building of the system—after all, the Yuuzhan Vong had occupied it for more than two standard years now, which meant his intelligence of it was probably a bit behind, to say the least. At this point, an unfortunate surprise was the last thing that interested him.

When the surprise came, it came not from some hidden Yuuzhan Vong trap, but from within his own ranks.

"Sir," control reported, "*Dpso*, *Redheart*, and *Coriolis* have broken formation, as has all of Duro Squadron."

"Have they." Wedge took a deep breath. "Get me Yurf Col again, immediately."

A few moments later, the Duros's hologram reappeared.

"Commander," Wedge said, trying to keep his tone even, "there must be a glitch in our communications. You seem to be forming an assault wedge when you were ordered to hold position."

"I have removed myself from your command, General Antilles," Col replied. "I will not have my people sit idle in their own system, not without a good explanation. You have refused to give me one. If you will not sustain the reconquest of Duro, I am forced to do it myself."

"You're committing suicide and placing this entire mission in jeopardy."

"Not if you join me."

"I won't."

"Then our deaths will be on your head."

"I'm *not* bluffing, Commander Col."

"You laid this course, Antilles."

"Commander—"

"You cut me off earlier. I return the favor. Join us or not."

The connection ended, and Wedge watched helplessly as the Duros ships dropped out of the perimeter, formed up, and drove straight for the largest concentration of enemy ships.

"Sir," Cel said, "the Duros ships are taking heavy fire."

"I can see that," Wedge told her.

"Sir, what are they doing?"

"They're trying to make me attack," Wedge said.

"Then it's a bluff, sir?"

A lightning storm was raging between the Duros ships and the Yuuzhan Vong vanguard. "No," he said, "it's not a bluff."

He turned to control. "No one else breaks formation," he said. "No one."

"Sir, they'll be slaughtered."

"Yes," Wedge said, gruffly, "they will."

One by one, over the course of the next few hours, the Duros ships vanished in bursts of plasma. Three hours after the last was gone, another message came over the comm board. Wedge gave the order to cease interdiction, and the Galactic Alliance ships jumped, leaving Duro once again to the Yuuzhan Vong.

THREE

A distorted grin sliced Onimi's crooked head in a sign of mock regard. "Sweet Nen Yim," he croaked. "How delightful your presence."

How disgusting yours, Nen Yim thought. She did not say it, and she did not need to. The tendrils of her headdress writhed and curled in revulsion, and her multifingered master's hand spasmed into a knot.

If the Supreme Overlord's jester noticed any of this, he made no sign, but stood there grinning at her as if they were close crèche-mates sharing a joke. They weren't; she was the most important of all shapers, and he was an appalling example of a Shamed One, a being upon whom the gods had placed a permanent stamp of unreserved disapproval. Why Shimrra, the chosen of the gods—the Supreme Overlord of her entire species—should choose him as emissary was utterly beyond her comprehension. It was more than an affront, it was a misery to even be in his presence, especially when she remembered—and she could hardly forget—that those fingers had once touched her, when he had disguised himself as a master shaper.

For that alone, he deserved the most ignominious death imaginable. She had plotted his murder even when she believed him to be her superior, and blessed by the gods. Now, when she had the means at her disposal and knew what he really was, she did not dare.

But she could still dream.

Onimi simpered and smiled. "Your thoughts croon toward me," he said. "Your tendrils ache for my touch. So much I can see of you, Nen Yim."

Well, he had noticed something, she reflected. He merely mistook her passion.

"Have you come on some errand, Onimi, or merely to waste my time in foolish conversation?"

"Conversation is not foolish that begs the fool," Onimi said, winking, as if that actually meant something.

"Yes, as you wish," she said, sighing. "Do you bring word from the Supreme Overlord?"

"I bring a dainty," Onimi said. "A glistering pustule from the gods, a gift for my sweet little—"

"Address me as master," Nen Yim said, stiffly. "I am no 'little' anything of yours. And come to the point. Whatever else the Supreme Overlord wants of me, I doubt he wants much of my time taken up, not with so much that needs doing."

From the corner of her eye she caught one of her assistants suppressing a smile, and reminded herself to reprimand her later.

Onimi's eyes went wide, and then he set a finger to his lips, leaned near, and whispered, "Fleeting time laps hours, devours days, months and years, passes them like gas."

She said nothing. What other response was there? But Onimi gestured, and with a great deal of reluctance she followed him down the mycoluminescent corridor of her central damutek, through the laboratories where she worked her heretical science to produce the miracles the Yuuzhan Vong needed to take their rightful place in a galaxy of infidels. When they passed into a corridor secured even from her, she began to grow intrigued, and more easily ignored the off-key singing of the jester, who was blasphemously describing in ancient octameter certain activities of the goddess Yun-Harla of which Nen Yim—thankfully—had never heard.

Of course that was spoiled now.

At last they arrived in a dim space. Something irregular and large bulked ahead. Light was in it, a faint shifting radiance so delicate it could almost be the colors of the dark behind her eyes.

She walked nearer, her shaping fingers outstretched to feel and taste the surface. It was smooth, almost slick. It tasted of long carbon chains, and water, and silicates. It tasted quick and familiar.

"This is alive," she whispered. "What is this?" She gestured impatiently. "I need more light."

"Eyes are the senses' gluttons," Onimi chortled. "They always want more, but they often tell us less."

But brighter lights came up, revealing the thing.

Sleek, that was the first impression. The glasslike surface curved into four long lozenges that sharpened almost to needles on one end and ended rounded on the other. The lobes were joined around a central axis, though she could not see how. She was reminded of the taaphur, a sea creature that existed now only as a genetic blueprint in the memory qahsa of the shapers and in its biotechnological derivatives.

Damaged, that was the second impression. The life that hummed beneath her fingers flickered in some places and was absent in others, where the hull—yes, hull—had gone dark.

"This is a ship," Nen Yim murmured, more to herself than to the useless Onimi. "A living ship, but not Yuuzhan Vong. This came from one of the infidel peoples?"

"Folds the mystery, and folds again to crumple, our chart is all torn."

"You mean you don't know?" Nen Yim asked, impatiently.

For answer, Onimi reached for her. Her tendrils prickled, bumps rose on her flesh, and her nostrils flared.

But he did not touch her. He handed her something instead—a small, portable qahsa.

"Secrets are like knives," he said softly. "Of your tongue a secret make, and your mouth is cut."

He left, then, and she watched him go with disdain. Idiotic, to warn her of secrets. She was a heretic, a heretic secretly kept by the Supreme Overlord. Everything she did was done in obscurity.

"Master Nen Yim?"

Nen Yim looked up from the qahsa. Her junior assistant Qelah Kwaad stood a few feet away, a look of great concern on her face.

"Adept," Nen Yim acknowledged softly.

"I hope it is not too impertinent, but my project—"

"I will examine your progress in due time," Nen Yim said. "My time."

Qelah Kwaad's tendrils retracted a bit. "Yes, Master Yim," she replied.

"And, Adept?"

"Yes, Master Yim?"

"I understand you are not used to the presence of Onimi and the effect he can have. But I will not have my subordinates laughing behind my back. Is that understood?"

The adept's eyes grew round with consternation.

"Master Yim, you cannot believe—"

"Do not use the word *can* in reference to me, Adept, in either the affirmative or negative form. What I can and cannot do is entirely beyond your control."

"Yes, Master."

Nen Yim sighed. "It is bad enough, Adept, that we have to bear the presence of such an abomination. It is worse to let him know he has caused amusement."

"I understand, Master Yim. But—why? Why must we

bear his presence at all? He is a Shamed One, cursed by the gods."

"He is Supreme Overlord Shimrra's jester, and, when it pleases him, his emissary."

"I don't understand. How can such a thing be? A jester, yes, but to entrust him with secret information—"

"What secret information might that be, Adept?" Nen Yim asked sharply.

"Your pardon, Master Yim, but the jester came, took you to the restricted area, and you returned with a portable qahsa. It seems obvious that he revealed something to you."

Nen Yim studied the adept appraisingly.

"Just so," she said. "You are correct. But perhaps you ought to concentrate more on your work and less on my activities."

Again, the adept looked abashed.

"You have great promise, Qelah Kwaad," Nen Yim said. "But in this place, we must all take care. We live outside the world of our people, and this place has rules of its own."

The adept straightened. "I am proud of my service here, Master. The Supreme Overlord has vindicated what the other shapers see as heresy."

"He has not," Nen Yim said. "Not publicly. Nor will he. Have you not noticed the guards?"

"Of course we are guarded. Our work is of great importance. If the infidels learn of us, they will surely try to destroy us."

"That is true," Nen Yim told her. "But a wall that keeps something out can also keep something in. No warrior, no priest, no outside shaper will ever learn what we do here. Shimrra values our heresy, yes—we produce new weapons and technology badly needed for the war effort. But he will never allow anyone beyond these to know *how* that technology comes into being."

"But why?"

"You are intelligent, Adept. Figure it out for yourself—and then never, never speak it aloud. Do you understand me?"

"I—I think so."

"Good. Now leave me."

Qelah Kwaad made the sign of obeisance and did as she was told. Nen Yim spared her a single glance.

Because, Adept, Shimrra must maintain the fiction that our inventions are gifts from the gods, and that he is the intermediary through whom these things flow. If the truth is discovered, and the Supreme Overlord shown to be a fraud . . .

Well, suffice to say, Adept, none of us will leave this service alive.

Which was fine with Nen Yim. It was her pride and her duty to serve the Yuuzhan Vong, and to die honorably for her people when the time came.

Putting the whole matter from her mind, she settled the qahsa before her and interfaced with it.

As she began to understand, her excitement grew—and her trepidation.

No wonder Shimrra had sent her his thing. It could change everything.

It could be their doom.

FOUR

"Can't say much for the atmosphere," Raf Othrem said, taking a sip of his Rylothan yurp and running his green-eyed gaze around the mostly bare metal walls of the place that called itself a tapcaf.

"What were you expecting, a casino from the Galsol strip?" Jaina Solo asked. "Yesterday this was just a piece of space junk the Yuuzhan Vong hadn't got around to pulverizing."

"And now they won't, thanks to us!" Raf said, raising his glass. "To Twin Suns Squadron, and our illustrious leader, Jaina Solo."

Jaina nodded wearily as they raised their drinks. Raf had all of the enthusiasm that came from having flown only one mission, and that a successful one. Not only had the battle been won, but her squadron hadn't lost a single pilot.

In time, Raf would lose that youthful exuberance.

She double-checked that thought and almost smiled when she remembered that Raf was actually a year her senior.

Let's not take our vast age and experience too seriously, Jaina thought.

She raised her own glass. "To the good fight," she toasted, and this time she did smile as her wingmates cheered.

Putting on a cheerful appearance was good for the team.

"A brilliant fight," Jag said. "We have the best flight commander in the galaxy."

Jaina actually felt a blush coming on—not from the words, but from the depths of Jag's blue-eyed gaze.

"No argument there," Raf said. "But I'd say one more toast is in order."

"Just one?" Mynor Dac said. "I can't imagine you shutting up for the rest of the night."

"No doubt," Alema Rar drily seconded.

Raf sent the Twi'lek a mock-glare, then raised his glass. "To General Wedge Antilles, and the plan that gave us back Fondor."

"I'll drink to that," Jaina said.

But before the glass reached her lips, something fell onto the table. A Rogue Squadron patch. She looked up into the round-eyed gaze of a young Duros. A very unhappy-looking Duros.

"Lensi?"

"Colonel," he acknowledged, his voice flat and clipped.

"Join the celebration, Lensi," Raf said. "Not that we normally mingle with disreputable Rogues, but—"

"I have nothing to celebrate," Lensi said, his gaze still focused on Jaina. "And I will no longer fly with Rogue Squadron. My people were betrayed today. Betrayed by General Antilles. Betrayed by Jaina Solo."

Jag came to his feet at that, followed closely by a growling, towering Lowbacca. Jag stared at Lensi with deadly calm. If Lensi was troubled by either Jag or the Wookiee, he didn't show it.

"Lowbacca, sit down," Jaina said. "Jag—please. Let him talk."

The Wookiee reluctantly followed orders, but Jag stood squared off with the Duros for several long seconds.

"Be careful what you say, Duros," he finally said. "Where I come from, there are penalties for slander."

"What's on your mind, Lensi?" Jaina asked.

"Many of my people died in the attack on Duro."

"They didn't have to," Jaina said. "The attack on Duro was a feint, designed to draw reinforcements from here. The Duros commander of the mission broke with the plan. He jeopardized both missions."

"He was not told the attack was a feint," Lensi said.

"No one was!" Raf exploded. "We were all in the dark."

"That's why it worked, Lensi," Jaina said. "Yuuzhan Vong intelligence is good. Wedge had to make the buildup look like it was aimed at Duro, and he had to make the attack there look convincing."

"Duro was the more lightly occupied," Lensi said. "We *could* have taken Duro. We were promised this." His face tightened into an even flatter mask. "We were used."

"Such is war," Jag said. "Fondor was considered the more strategic target. The liberation of Duro may come next, it may not." He nodded his head around the crowded room. "Many of the pilots here have lost a homeworld to the Vong. You think you're alone? You think every one of them wouldn't prioritize the liberation of their homeworld over every other, if they were given the choice? War isn't fought on the basis of sentiment and desire. Battles must accomplish tactical goals."

"Your 'tactical goals' see many of my people dead today."

"Because they disobeyed orders," Jag snapped. "They signed on under General Antilles. If they had paid attention to him, most if not all of them would still be alive. If you want to know who betrayed your people to death, look to the commander who broke ranks."

"We aren't children," Lensi persisted. "We should have been told."

Jag started to speak again, but Jaina cut in.

"Maybe," she said. "In hindsight, maybe. Or maybe we would all be dead now." She softened her voice. "You were a good wingmate at Sernpidal. I know you've done well with Rogue Squadron since I left. We're going to win this war. We're going to win back Duro. But only if enough of us keep fighting." She picked up the patch and tossed it to him. Reflexively, he caught it. "You have to do what your conscience dictates."

Lensi hesitated, looking at the patch. "Colonel Solo," he said, "I was there, after Sernpidal, when you slapped Kyp Durron for lying to us. You know what it feels like to be betrayed, to fight without knowing what you're really fighting for."

She raised her eyes and regarded him steadily. "I know what lots of things feel like," she said. "And you know what? I'm still fighting. I'm going to keep fighting until there isn't a single threat left in this galaxy. You think you're the only person who has lost something in this war? Grow up, Lensi."

The Duros regarded her for another long moment.

"Did *you* know?" he asked.

"No. But if I had, I wouldn't have told anyone. General Antilles did the right thing."

Lensi nodded curtly, turned, and left. He still had the insignia with him.

"General Antilles?"

Wedge stopped tapping his fingers on the Kashyyyk-wood conference table and acknowledged the heavy-jowled Sullustan.

"Yes, Admiral Sovv?" he said.

"What is your opinion on the matter?"

"We should have told Col," Wedge said, bluntly. "I should have broken orders and told him myself. He had a right to know exactly what he was getting his people into."

"Under perfect circumstances, yes," Admiral Kre'fey said. "But the circumstances were far from perfect. Bothan intelligence had—has—information that the Yuuzhan Vong have a spy placed high in the command structure of the Duros government-in-exile. Indeed, it was through that leak that the Yuuzhan Vong 'discovered' our plans to invade the Duro system—as we planned."

"Col might have been brought in," Wedge replied. "He was a hothead, but he could be trusted with a secret."

"Perhaps," the white-furred Bothan replied, "perhaps not. As it is, our plan was fulfilled."

"With more losses than necessary."

"Still fewer than projected," General Garm Bel Iblis said, from across the table. "The battle at Fondor was a total rout. We did them great damage, and now we have a secure position from which to strike at Coruscant."

"Gentlemen," Sien Sovv said, "I'm declaring the matter closed from a military point of view. Certainly General Antilles is not to blame. He followed the orders this council gave him. I refuse to allocate any resources for an internal investigation, not at this point in our war against the Yuuzhan Vong."

"That tables the matter of the Duros protest," Kre'fey said. "It's time we move on to what we do next."

Admiral Sovv nodded. "General Bel Iblis, how long before the shipyards at Fondor become productive again?"

"That will take some time," the aging general admitted. "Two, three months before any facility can go on-line. Ships—six months perhaps. Probably not sooner. But once construction actually begins, they will be quite productive. They should position us well for a push toward the Core."

"Good," Sien Sovv said. "In the meantime we should continue the process of isolating Coruscant from the rest of Yuuzhan Vong territory. Which brings me to this." He tapped the table, and a hologram of the galaxy appeared.

"Yag'Dhul and Thyferra are secure, finally, and Fondor is ours." Three stars near the dense, glowing center of the galaxy winked green, indicating the positions of the systems named.

"Coruscant, however, is still well supplied." Coruscant—or whatever it was the Yuuzhan Vong had renamed it—lit up, on the other side of the Core from the other three.

"It's time to threaten that."

A final star lit.

"Bilbringi," Wedge said.

"Yes. There is some evidence that the shipyards there are partially intact. More, it gives us a base from which to harry both the Hydian Way and the Perlemian Trade Route."

"It's too close to Coruscant," Bel Iblis said. "And too far from our own secure zone. We can never hold it." He shook his head. "We don't want another Borleias. No offense, General Antilles."

"None taken. Our actions at Borleias served their intended purpose. We never imagined we would keep it."

He turned to Sien Sovv. "But he's right, the Yuuzhan Vong can hardly ignore a threat that close to Coruscant. I don't think we have the ships to take it if they have advance warning. If they don't, I doubt we could hold it very long. Not and keep our own systems secure."

"They have the same problem," the Sullustan admiral pointed out. "As we've proven to them, they've taken more systems than they can hold. There's not much in the Bilbringi system, but there are no habitable planets. In any event, I have a tactical reason for choosing Bilbringi as a target."

Wedge raised an eyebrow and waited, as another sector of the galaxy lit up, this one Rimward.

"The Imperial Remnant," he murmured.

"Indeed," Sovv said. "Admiral Pellaeon has agreed to lend us his support in this enterprise, and Bilbringi lies within good striking distance of the Empire. Between us, we can carve a corridor through the Rim, eventually cutting Coruscant off completely."

Wedge bit back a protest. He'd spent most of his life fighting the Empire, and his opinion of Pellaeon was a mixed one, the recent alliance notwithstanding. But he decided to hear Sovv out.

"It's true Pellaeon can reach Bilbringi without passing through Yuuzhan Vong territory," Kre'fey said. "The same is not true for us."

"No. We will have to fight our way through several hyperspace jumps. Here is what I propose."

Lines began drawing themselves across the galaxy. "Our main fleet will launch from Mon Calamari, under Admiral Kre'fey," he said. "Part of the fleet at Fondor will move to meet them, under General Antilles. When they converge, they will be joined by a detachment from the Imperial fleet."

"The Vong will suspect a trick," Bel Iblis said, "after what we did to them at Fondor."

"Exactly," Sovv said. "But the only trick in this case is overwhelming force. I expect them to hold back reinforcements, fearing it is another feint, perhaps to draw defenses from Coruscant itself."

"Interesting," Wedge allowed. "Though there will be a trick in the coordination. The hyperspace routes are uncertain these days. If one of our fleets arrives too early, or too late—"

"The HoloNet is functioning at high efficiency in those areas. We should be able to coordinate down to the second."

"What's the Empire getting out of this?" Bel Iblis asked.

"Exactly what I was wondering," Wedge replied.

Sovv shrugged. "We long made efforts to convince Pellaeon that we must work together to free the galaxy from the Yuuzhan Vong threat. Our efforts have paid off, so far to our great benefit."

"I'm aware of our diplomatic efforts," Bel Iblis said. "As well as the Empire's recent aid to us—in return for help we gave them, I might add. I'm also aware that they want some of our planets in return."

Sovv's brows lowered. "They aren't 'our' planets anymore, General Bel Iblis. The planets in question belong to the Yuuzhan Vong now. Most are not even recognizable as the worlds they were a few years ago. I'm convinced we need the Empire's help to win this war. If that means showing them a little goodwill afterward, I don't see the harm. In any case, they aren't making any specific demands at this time—this is an effort to establish their good intentions, nothing more."

Good intentions that will place at least some of them as an occupation force spitting distance from Coruscant, Wedge thought.

Unfortunately, despite that, he agreed with Sovv.

"We can strike now," Wedge said, "press our advantage while we have one, or we can wait—wait for the Vong to grow more ships, breed more warriors, invent new bioweapons. Right now, they've bit off a little more of this galaxy than they can easily chew, as we've shown them in the last few months. We have to keep it that way."

He looked around. Everyone but Sovv was nodding.

"There *is* another solution," the commander said.

"You mean Alpha Red, the biological agent developed by the Chiss?" Wedge said. "Not as far as I'm concerned. Genocide is what the Emperor did. It's what the Yuuzhan Vong do. It's not what we do. If it is, I'm fighting for the wrong cause."

"Even if it's our only choice for survival?" Sovv asked.

"It's not," Wedge replied, flatly.

"The Yuuzhan Vong will not stop after one defeat, ten, a hundred. They will fight until every last warrior is dead.

Even if they win, the cost that will exact from our people will be tremendous—"

"That question is moot at present," Kre'fey broke in, "and would seem a waste of our valuable time to discuss it."

"Very well. I trust there are no other objections to pursuing the offensive against the Yuuzhan Vong at present?" the commander said.

There were not.

"Then let us discuss details."

FIVE

Kneeling in the presence of Supreme Overlord Shimrra, Nen Yim believed in the gods. It was impossible not to.

At other times, she had her doubts. Her late master, Mezhan Kwaad, had flatly denied their existence. In the clear light of logic, Nen Yim herself saw no particular reason to give them credence. Indeed, the fact that she herself created, with her own mind and shaping hands, things that all but a few of her people believed to be gifts from the gods suggested that all such evidence of their existence was similarly tainted.

But in the presence of Shimrra, her mind could not tolerate doubt. It was crushed from her by a presence so powerful it could not have mortal origin. It pressed away the years of her learning, of studied cynicism, of anything resembling logic, and left her an insignificant insect, a crècheling terrified by the shadows of her elders and the terrible mystery that was the world.

Afterward, she always wondered how he did it. Was it some modification of yammosk technology? Something erased from the protocols entirely? Or was it an invention of some heretical predecessor of herself?

He was shadow and dread, awesome and unreachable. She crouched at his feet and was nothing.

Onimi leered almost gently at her as she rose, shaking, to speak to her master.

"You have studied the thing?"

"I have, Dread One," Nen Yim replied. "Not exhaustively, as there hasn't been time, but—"

"There will be more time. Tell me what you have discovered thus far."

"It is a ship," Nen Yim replied. "Like our own ships, it is a living organism."

"Not at all," Shimrra interrupted. "It has no dovin basals. Its engines are like the infidel engines, dead metal."

"True," Nen Yim agreed. "And parts of its structure are not alive. But—"

"Then it is an infidel thing!" Shimrra thundered. "It is *nothing* like our ships."

Nen Yim actually reeled at the force of the statement, and for a moment she stood paralyzed, unable to think. To contradict Shimrra—

She drew her strength back to her core. "That is so, Dread One," she admitted. "As it is, it is an abomination. And yet, at its heart the biotechnology is similar to our own. The infidel engines, for instance, could be withdrawn and replaced with dovin basals. The living structure of one of our own vessels could have such a ship grown around it. This biotechnology is compatible with our own."

"Compatible?" Shimrra growled. "Are you saying that this is one of our ships, somehow transfigured by the infidels?"

"No," Nen Yim replied. "In outward form, this thing is very different from our vessels. The hull is not yorik coral. The architectures of our ships were derived from various creatures of the homeworld, and those structures can still be recognized in their design. The alien technology is different. It begins with relatively undifferentiated organisms that specialize as the ship grows. I suspect that some sort of manipulation is involved in the ontological process to guide the final outcome. That is why they used a rigid frame to grow the ship around—developmentally, it had no internal code to produce such a structure on its own."

"And yet you still maintain it is similar to our gods-given ships?"

"At the most basic level, yes. Cellularly. Molecularly. And that is the most *unlikely* level at which we should expect to find resemblance."

"Again. Could the infidels have stolen our technology and distorted it?"

"It's possible. But according to the qahsa, the planet of its origin is itself a living organism—"

"That is a lie," Shimrra said. "It is a lie because it is impossible. Ekh'm Val was deluded. He was duped by the infidels."

Nen Yim hesitated at that, but could not directly dispute it even if she wanted to.

Instead, she took another approach.

"I'm relieved to hear this," she said. "I thought the tale unlikely myself." She drew herself straighter. "Still, there is nothing in the protocols that could account for a ship like this, nor do I think this technology is a result of the manipulation of our technology. It is both alien and similar to our own."

Shimrra was silent for a moment. Then his voice came again, leashed terror.

"It is not superior."

"No, Dread Lord. Just different."

"Of course. And you can develop weapons against it?"

"I can. Indeed, Lord, there are already weapons in the protocols that would be most effective against technology of this sort. Oddly, they are weapons we have never built or had use for."

"As if the gods anticipated this necessity."

Nen Yim tried to keep her thoughts quiet.

"Yes," she replied.

"Excellent. You will assign a team to develop these weapons immediately. And you will continue to study the ship."

"It would be helpful, Great Lord, if I had other examples of the technology."

"No such exists. The planet was destroyed. You have all that remains."

Then why do you want weapons against . . . Nen Yim started to think, but savagely cut herself off.

"Yes, Supreme Overlord."

With a wave of his massive hand, Shimrra dismissed her.

A cycle later, Nen Yim settled onto a sitting hummock in her private hortium and regarded Ahsi Yim. The younger shaper was narrower in every dimension than Nen Yim, and her blue-gray flesh had an opalescent sheen about it. Her attentive eyes were a rare shade of bronze.

Her master's hand was very new, but they were peers.

"What brought you to the heresy, Ahsi Yim?" she asked softly.

The other master considered this quietly for a moment. The fine silver tendrils of lim trees groped feebly about the room in search of sustenance. Plants from the homeworld with no obvious use, Nen Yim had resurrected them from genetic patterns in the Qang qahsa. They pleased her.

"I worked on the changing of Duro," she said at last. "On the surface of things, on the record, we worked strictly by the protocols. And yet, often the protocols were not suitable. They were not sufficiently flexible for what needed to be done. Some of us—did what was necessary. Later I was assigned here, to Yuuzhan'tar, where so *much* went wrong. The strange itching plague—well. The masters there were very orthodox. I saw the shortcomings of that. At the same time, I saw evidence of the infidels' ability to adapt, to change their abominable technology not just in small ways, but in large ones. I determined that in time, because of this, they must ultimately triumph unless we did the same. So I practiced heresy."

"And were discovered. You would have been sacrificed to the gods if I had not had you brought here."

"I serve my people," Ahsi Yim said. "The protocols do not. I would die for that."

"So would I," Nen Yim said. "And so I risk both of our lives once more. Do you understand?"

Ahsi Yim did not blink. "Yes."

"You may have heard that the Supreme Overlord brought me something to examine."

"Yes." Eagerness showed in Ahsi Yim's eyes.

"It is a ship," Nen Yim said, "a ship based on a biotechnology much like ours. The phenotype is radically different, but the genotype is similar. More similar than anything in this galaxy thus far. And the protocols have in them certain weapons that seem designed peculiarly well to deal with it. Shimrra claims the gods must have anticipated our need. What do you think?"

Again, that long moment of consideration, but this time accompanied by an excited writhing of tendrils on her headdress.

"I think that is not true," Ahsi said softly. "The protocols have not changed in hundreds, perhaps thousands of years. They have not 'anticipated' anything else in this galaxy. Why should they anticipate this?"

"Perhaps nothing else here required the intervention of the gods."

Ahsi made a dismissive motion. "There is much here we could have used the help of the gods with. The *Jeedai*, for instance. And yet there is nothing in the protocols that even hints of them."

Nen Yim nodded. "I grant I believe as you do. Then what explanation do you offer?"

"Our ancestors met this technology in the past. We battled against it, and the weapons from that battle remain in the Qang qahsa."

"And yet no record of any such event exists."

Ahsi Yim smiled faintly. "Even the Qang qahsa can be made to forget. More recent events have been elided. Have you ever tried to learn of Shimrra's ascension to Supreme Overlord?"

"Yes," Nen Yim replied.

"The record of *that* seems implausibly thin."

Nen Yim shrugged. "I agree that records can be erased. But why erase knowledge of a threat?"

"You think this ship a threat?"

"Oh, yes. Shall I tell you a tale?"

"I would be honored."

"I have in my possession the personal qahsa of Ekh'm Val, the commander who brought this ship to Lord Shimrra. He was sent years ago to explore the galaxy. He came across a planet named Zonama Sekot."

Ahsi Yim's eyes narrowed.

"What? This means something to you?"

"No," she said. "But the name disturbs me."

Nen Yim nodded agreement. "Ekh'm Val said the planet itself was alive, its life-forms symbiotic, as if shaped to live together."

"They shape life as we do?"

"They shape life, yes. Not as we do. And the sentient race there is nothing like Yuuzhan Vong—indeed, from the records, I think they must be a race native to this galaxy—Ferroans."

"Then I retract my earlier statement. Our ancestors can hardly have met this world before."

"It seems unlikely. And yet, at the same time, it seems the only possible answer to the puzzle."

"What happened to Commander Val?"

"He was attacked and repelled, but he managed to capture the ship before leaving the system."

"And the planet?"

"Shimrra claims it has been destroyed."

"You do not believe him?"

"No. I've been asked to create weapons that might affect it. Why should I do that if the danger has passed?"

"Perhaps he fears there are more such worlds."

"Perhaps. Perhaps he merely fears."

"What?"

"If we *have* met this race before, and fought them— perhaps they remember it better than we. If we have the key to attacking their biotechnology, perhaps they have the key to ours as well. Ekh'm Val was defeated, after all."

"A few ships against a world."

Nen Yim smiled thinly. "Tell me—what sort of memory do you think our glorious ancestors are more likely to have purged from the Qang qahsa? A glorious victory or an ignominious defeat?"

Ahsi Yim pursed her lips. "Ah," she said. "And you think Shimrra knows something we do not."

"I think he knows many things we do not."

Ahsi Yim's tendrils curled in agreement. Then she leveled her liquid gaze directly at Nen Yim. "Why are you telling me this?"

"Because," Nen Yim replied, "I think you know things *I* do not. Have connections that I do not."

"What sort of things?" she asked, stiffly.

"For one, I think you have heard of Ekh'm Val before."

A long silence, this time. "Are you asking something of me?" she said at last.

"If this planet exists, I must see it for myself. The ship alone is not enough. I must know more."

"Why?"

"Because I think if I do not, our species is doomed."

Ahsi pursed her lips. Her tendrils knotted and waved. "I can promise nothing," she said, "but I will see what can be done."

SIX

From the bridge of *Yammka*, Nas Choka surveyed the ruins of the occupation forces from Fondor. They weren't much to look at.

He turned slowly to face Zhat Lah.

"How did this happen?" he asked. His voice was low, pitched only for the commander.

"Duro was attacked, Warmaster, as our intelligence suggested it would be. The executor there requested reinforcements. My men were hungry for battle, and I complied." His eyes narrowed. "Then they came. I recalled the ships when I understood the ploy, but they were prevented from leaving the Duro system by their interdictors. The infidels kept our forces pinned in the planet's gravity well and then *fled*. They are cowards!"

"Are you telling me cowards took the system you were entrusted with from you? You were beaten by cowards?"

"Warmaster, we were outnumbered. We fought until there was no hope."

"No hope?" Nas Choka asked, in scathing tones. "You were yet alive, and had ships, and say there was no hope? Are you Yuuzhan Vong?"

"I am Yuuzhan Vong," Zhat Lah growled.

"Then why did you not fight to the last? Might you not have taken a few more of their ships with you to the gods?"

"A few, Warmaster."

"Then why did you flee? Where is the honor in that?"

Zhat Lah's split lips twitched. "If the warmaster wishes my life, it is his to give to the gods."

"Of course. But I asked you for an explanation."

"I thought our remaining ships might serve better than to be cut to pieces in a battle we could not win."

"Did you?" Nas Choka asked. "You had no thought for your own life?"

"My life belongs to the gods. They may take it as they will. I do not flinch from death. If the warmaster wishes me to take my personal coralskipper back to Fondor, I will die in battle. But given the numbers, the rest of my ships would have been destroyed with relatively little damage done to the enemy. If this was wrong, the responsibility is mine. My men own none of it."

Nas Choka looked back out at the wreckage.

"Two frigates, all but undamaged. A battle cruiser with only minimal damage." He turned to Lah. "You did well," he said.

The commander's eyes widened fractionally with surprise.

"We have spread ourselves too much, over too many star systems," Nas Choka said. "We have lost too many ships because too many commanders have no more sense of strategy than to fight to the death."

He clasped his hand behind him and regarded Lah. "We have the late leader of your domain to thank for this situation."

"Warmaster Lah conquered most of this galaxy," Zhat Lah protested. "He gave us their capital, now our Yuuzhan'tar."

"Yes, and he spent warriors like so much vlekin doing so, and gave little thought as to how we would *hold* such vast territories." He waved his hand. "Things are changing, Zhat Lah. Things *must* change. The infidels have adapted. They have undermined many of our strengths, but we have undermined ourselves even more. The pride of our warriors weakens us."

"But the pride of our warriors is what we are," Zhat Lah protested. "Without our pride, without our honor, we are as the infidels."

"And yet you retreated because you thought it best."

"Yes, Warlord," he replied, his tone finally subdued. "But it was not . . . *easy*. I take the stain on myself, yet there is a stain."

"Listen to me," Nas Choka said. "We are the Yuuzhan Vong. We have been entrusted with the true way, the true knowledge of the gods. Our duty is to bring every infidel in this galaxy to heel and either send them screaming to the gods or bring them to the true path. There is no middle ground, there is no faltering. And there can be no failure. Our mission is more important than you or me, Commander, and it is more important than your honor or mine. Lord Shimrra himself has said it. And so, feel no stain. To win this war, we must set aside much we cherish. The gods ordain the sacrifice. We are blameless. We are those who do what must be done. And so I tell you again—you did the right thing."

Lah nodded, understanding lighting behind his eyes.

"Now," Choka went on, "these tactics—these feints and sudden withdrawals, these *strike-here-and-hide-there* maneuvers—what enables this? The infidels have no yammosk to coordinate their movements."

"They have communications, Warlord. Their HoloNet allows them to communicate instantaneously over the breadth of the galaxy."

"Precisely. But without their HoloNet, such precise coordination becomes much more difficult, yes?"

Lah shrugged. "Of course," he said. "But destroying the communications system is difficult," he said. "There are many relay stations, not always placed so as to be easily found. When one is destroyed, another may function, and the infidels have managed to repair or replace many we have destroyed."

"The destruction of the HoloNet has never been a priority before," Nas Choka said. "Now it is. And the gods have given the shapers a new weapon, one that should perfectly suit our needs."

"That is well, Warlord."

"It is." He paced a moment.

"I'm giving you a new battle group. You will remain here, at Yuuzhan'tar, on alert to strike quickly. The infidels are growing confident; they will attack again, soon. I can feel it. And when they do, we will have something new to show them. Something quite new."

SEVEN

Beneath the black sky of Yuuzhan'tar, Nen Yim moved invisibly. The guards at their posts did not blink as she passed; the singing ulubs stayed silent as she moved lightly across the grounds of the Supreme Overlord's compound. Damuteks glowed with faint luminescence, and ships coming and going were pale viridian or blood-colored mists of light in the sky.

Yuuzhan'tar had not always been dark at night. For millennia, it had been the brightest world in the galaxy, never knowing true darkness. Unliving metal had pulsed with unholy energies, hemorrhaging light and heat and noxious fumes to burn the womb of night.

Now that unnatural work had been undone, and any brightness came from the stars alone. Tonight, not even they troubled the closed eyelids of the gods, for a tarp of cloud had been drawn overhead, blotting even the fierce beauty of the Core. So long controlled by machines, the climate of Yuuzhan'tar was also finding its natural state.

To Nen Yim, it seemed paradoxically unnatural. She had been born and raised on a worldship, nurtured by an organism so large that she had been like a microbe in its belly, kept warm and secure. The vagaries of weather were only recently known to her, and though her mind rationally recognized that on some long-ago day the Yuuzhan Vong had lived on a world where seasons came and went, where rain fell when it wished or not at all—that this was, indeed, the natural course of things—her instincts rebelled at the capricious variability of it all. She was a shaper. She preferred shaping to being shaped.

And she despised being cold. She was cloaked in a creature of her own modification, a variant of the special ooglith cloakers that hunters wore. Its billion tiny sensory nodes gazed at the night, heard it, tasted it—and made her a part of it. For the first time in many, many months she was free of her guards, of her damutek. She did not fool herself that the freedom was real. If she did not emerge from her sanctum in a few hours, questions would be asked, and then a search would commence. Being invisible would not be enough, then. But the illusion was heady.

Though she had created the cloak for herself long before, there had never been any reason great enough to risk using it.

Now there was. A cryptic message, a meeting place, a possibility.

She passed from Shimrra's fortress compound easily enough. Even a hunter could not have managed that, but the cloak of Nuun she wore was better than the usual sort. It hid her very thoughts, it disguised her mass as a movement of air.

She moved on rougher ground now, down a slope and then up to the platform where a shrine to Yun-Harla, the Trickster goddess, overlooked a vast pit that had once been sky-reaching buildings. Dark waters filled it now, and the burring cries of p'hiili rose in shrill chorus with the bass cooing of large-wattled ngom. Like the lim tree in her hortium, they were re-created creatures from the homeworld.

A single figure awaited her in the shrine, beneath a statue of Yun-Yuuzhan that had been made from the skulls and long bones of the conquered. It, too, carried a message from Yuuzhan Vong history—like the creatures of the pool, it proclaimed, *This world is ours now.*

The one waiting was male, lean, his hair knotted in a patterned scarf. All but three fingers had been cut from each hand. Nen Yim stood watching him for long moments. His eyes held a contained and fierce intelligence.

Priest, she thought. *What could you want with me?*

She stood on the vua'sa's spine. Death seemed near. She wasn't sure what she had expected, but it wasn't a priest, alone, in the dark.

She moved out of his sight and removed the cloak, then walked back to the shrine.

This time his gaze found her instantly. His body remained still.

"You've come at a strange time to perform your ablutions," the priest said.

"I come when I am called," Nen Yim answered.

"So must we all," the priest answered. "I am Harrar."

Nen Yim's spine prickled. She knew that name. *So not just any priest. A very important one.*

"I am called Nen Yim, Honored One," she replied.

"You are a master. Our ranks are equivalent, so we may dispense with honorifics. My time is short, and I suspect yours is shorter still."

Nen Yim nodded.

"There are rumors of you, shaper," he said. "You labor alone, under heavy guard in the Supreme Overlord's compound. It is said you are most favored by the gods, and yet so few know you exist at all. Even a whisper is too loud a tone to speak of you in. It is said that some have died who could not keep that whisper in."

"And yet you know of me."

"I know when and whom to whisper to." He smiled thinly. "You, apparently, do not."

"I don't know what you mean."

"I mean your attempts to contact the Quorealist underground have been clumsy."

"I do not even know who or what the Quorealists are," Nen Yim asserted.

"Quoreal was the Supreme Overlord before Shimrra. Many do not think the gods chose Shimrra to take his place, they believe that Shimrra dishonorably murdered him. Quoreal's old followers are understandably a reticent group, but they still exist."

"These are new facts to me, if facts they are."

The priest shrugged one shoulder. "It does not matter who you thought you were trying to contact. The point is that if you persist, Shimrra will discover you, and I doubt that anyone is so favored by the gods as to survive that." He clasped his hands behind his back. "What I wish to know is this: Why is Lord Shimrra's most favored shaper trying to contact the pitiful remnants of his political enemies?"

"I know nothing of these politics," Nen Yim replied. "Shimrra is the Supreme Overlord. I owe allegiance to none other. I desire allegiance to none other."

Harrar cocked his head. "Come now. Why else contact us?"

"Us?"

Harrar's fierce grin expanded a bit. "Of course. Clumsy you may have been, but you have succeeded. Shimrra has enemies. You have found them. What do you want from us?"

"I've just told you, I seek no enemy of my Supreme Overlord."

"But you move in secret, without his knowledge. What do you want?"

Again, Nen Yim hesitated. "There is something I must see," she said. "Something I believe to be of vital importance to the Yuuzhan Vong."

"How intriguing. Shimrra will not let you see it?"

"I cannot ask him."

"More intriguing still. What is this thing?"

"It is very far from here," Nen Yim said. "I need help getting there. I need help finding it."

"You obfuscate."

"I am cautious. You tell me you are the enemy of my Lord Shimrra. In that case you are my enemy, ultimately, and I will not betray information into your hands." She paused.

"Suppose I merely lied to you, to test your loyalty?"

"Then I cannot trust anything you say," she said.

"In that case, our meeting would seem to be over." He paused again. "But I warn you, you are not likely to get another chance. You say this thing is of vital importance to our future. How important?"

"It could be our doom."

"And yet you fear Shimrra will not address it?"

"Yes."

"You think you know better what is best for the Yuuzhan Vong than our Supreme Overlord?"

Nen Yim drew her shoulders back. "In this case, I do."

"Very well. My pretense of disloyalty was meant to draw a confession of your own. I now believe you are loyal to the order of things. I swear by the very gods, I am also loyal to Lord Shimrra. May they devour me if I lie." He paused, and lowered his voice. "But like you, I do not think his judgment is infallible. Tell me of this thing you must see. Clearly you are willing to risk disgrace and death. This is not the time to balk."

Nen Yim clicked the nails of her master's hand together. Like her own master, Mezhan Kwaad, she had deadly weapons concealed in it. If she decided the priest could not be trusted, the p'hiili would feed well this night.

"It begins with a commander named Ekh'm Val," she said, softly.

His eyes widened at the name. "Ah," he said.

"You have heard of him?"

"Indeed. I begin to understand your caution. Please continue."

She told him, in brief, what she knew, but she left much out. She made no mention of her heresy, but couched her studies of the ship in orthodox terms. As she spoke, Harrar folded down into a cross-legged position and listened like a child does to the true-speaker in a crèche. When she was done, a moment of silence dragged a long tail.

"Astonishing," he said, at last.

"You understand the implications, then?"

"Some of them. Others will come clear. And perhaps I understand some you do not."

"I do not doubt that. The priesthood has its own knowledge, I'm sure."

Harrar drew his lips back from his teeth. "How kind of you to think so," he said.

"I meant no offense."

"Naturally not." He gestured. "Sit with me."

She complied, resting on a small polyp.

"You swear to me that all you have told me is true?"

"I swear it, by the gods," Nen Yim replied.

He nodded, then looked at her seriously. "Your master, Mezhan Kwaad, is said to have claimed there were no gods."

"She was, for all her virtues, perhaps insane," Nen Yim pointed out.

"Yes, my concern exactly."

"You fear for my sanity?"

"I might, save for one thing. Are you aware of the heresy?"

Her blood went cold and heavy. "Heresy?"

"Among the Shamed Ones. The obscene belief that the *Jeedai* are somehow the saviors of the Shamed."

"Yes," Nen Yim replied, hoping her composure hadn't slipped. "I was, after all, on Yavin Four when that heresy began."

"You were, weren't you? You're a part of the story, in

fact, at least in some versions. In a few, you died gloriously. In all, you vanished."

"I am not current on the folklore of the Shamed Ones, I fear," Nen Yim said, stiffly.

"No, I doubt that you are. This heresy now has a leader—a Prophet. Little is known of him, but he is gaining in power. Not long ago, he made a prophecy—of a new world, a home for the Shamed Ones, a promise of redemption. A living world." He placed his hands on his knees and leaned forward. "Does this not sound like your Zonama Sekot?"

"I know nothing of this Prophet or his babblings," Nen Yim said.

"Again, I do not doubt you." His eyes narrowed. "Do you know where this supposed world is?"

"No."

"So you would have me smuggle you from beneath Shimrra's nose, equip you with a ship—"

"I can supply my own ship," Nen Yim interrupted.

His eyes turned appraising, but he resumed. "Very well. So I need only smuggle you out, outfit you, and help you find this planet—which Shimrra claims is destroyed."

"That is what I desire, yes."

"I cannot do that," he said. "I am too highly placed. I will be noticed."

"Then I have come in vain," Nen Yim said, preparing the weapon in her finger.

"Perhaps not," the priest said. "Perhaps the Prophet of whom I spoke could aid you?"

Nen Yim relaxed, marginally. "You counsel me to collaborate with a heretic?"

"If you are correct about the threat this planet poses, then a temporary alliance with a heretic could certainly be forgiven. You were right, by the way, not to ask Shimrra to help you. Neither Ekh'm Val nor any of his crew remains alive. The Supreme Overlord fears this secret. That in itself tells me it is vitally important."

"On that we agree," Nen Yim allowed. "Still—what good could come of contacting this 'Prophet'? Even if he was so disposed, how could he help me?"

"How many Shamed Ones work within the Supreme Overlord's compound?"

"I do not know."

"How many of them can you name?"

She snorted. "One."

Harrar showed his teeth again at the thinly veiled reference.

"This heresy is widespread and well organized. It, as much as your Zonama Sekot, is a threat to the well-being of our people. I feel certain that if this 'Prophet' can be convinced you are with his cause, he will find a way to help you. Especially if, as you say, you have a ship."

"Yes," she said. "It's getting the ship off the surface of Yuuzhan'tar and out of this system that is the problem."

A new suspicion struck her. "You want to use me as bait."

"Indeed. But I will not pounce on the Prophet when he comes to free you. I will wait, until such time as you deem your mission complete. If done in exactly the right way, it might even be possible to convince Lord Shimrra that you were a hostage of the Shamed Ones, rather than the instigator of the expedition."

"You propose a trade in deceits."

"Consider. Two great threats to the Yuuzhan Vong— your mysterious planet, my Prophet. We can be rid of them both. If all goes well, you and I continue to serve our people. If not, we go to the gods, who know our motives were pure. Can you see a better path?"

"No," Nen Yim said. "I cannot. But I know little of this Prophet. I have no way of contacting him."

"I cannot contact him directly, of course," Harrar said.

"But there are ways of bringing things to his ears. I can arrange this. Are we agreed?"

"We are," Nen Yim said.

And though she felt she had sealed her doom, she made the trip back through the darkness with lighter feet, and the air felt almost warm.

Harrar watched the shaper move out of sight, wondering again how she had managed to meet him without an entourage of guards. Did she have some sort of concealing cloaker, like the cloak of Nuun the hunters wore?

Probably. She was a master shaper, after all. That didn't matter.

What mattered was that he had committed himself to the proposition that she did not represent a trap laid for him by Shimrra or someone in the Supreme Overlord's hierarchy who disliked him. Every natural instinct warned him away, but something very deep—perhaps something from the gods themselves—told him he should trust the strange shaper. Rumors of the planet Zonama Sekot had circulated very quietly among the Quorealists and some priestly sects for many cycles, and he knew for a fact that Ekh'm Val was not the first Yuuzhan Vong to encounter the planet. Nor, indeed, had Ekh'm Val been sent by Shimrra, though the commander himself hadn't known that.

If Zonama Sekot existed—and especially if the shaper was right about there being some hidden history between it and the Yuuzhan Vong—then it could be very important. In any event, the priesthood was being kept in the dark about something that it clearly should know about.

He had lately begun to have his suspicions about Shimrra. Not voiced ones, certainly, but suspicions nonetheless. And today—which had already brought so many interesting new thoughts—brought another.

Nen Yim did not know, perhaps, how much Harrar knew

about shapers and their protocols. He was the first to admit that he did not know everything. But one thing was clear—Nen Yim operated outside the realm of normal shaping, and the heresy of the Shamed Ones was not the only heresy around. Mezhan Kwaad, Nen Yim's late master, had been a heretic, and had died for it.

And here was Nen Yim, alive, favored by the Supreme Overlord, and perhaps practicing her own heresy in guarded secrecy.

If true, it could mean only one thing: Shimrra himself was a heretic. And that—like everything else in this situation—had the potential to change everything.

If things went as planned, he might manage to kill three targets with a single thud bug.

He rose, and smelled the air, and felt destiny in his veins.

EIGHT

Nom Anor turned the message this way and that in his mind, and saw it sharp in every angle. It was hard to wrap his thoughts around it without feeling the cut, so pregnant with the possibility of betrayal it seemed.

"Who sent you, Loiin Sool?" he asked the messenger, softly. The messenger was a Shamed One, his shoulders and face a mass of poorly healed scar tissue. His eyes were concealed by a constricted uruun cloth, placed there before he'd begun his descent into the dark, dank places of Nom Anor's domain. The domain of the Prophet.

A wave of his hand, and Loiin Sool would never see anything again.

"I come on behalf of the shaper Nen Yim," Sool answered. "I know little more than that. I was taken from my work detail, given the message, and sent to find you."

Nom Anor nodded. Sool had been checked for implants, of course, though no test short of thorough dissection was certain. Was someone looking at him now, from some hidden pore in the messenger's skin?

If so, they saw not Nom Anor but the Prophet Yu'shaa, his face hidden behind a grotesque ooglith masquer that showed only one spectacularly Shamed, eyes festering with inflammation and lesions rendering the visage almost unrecognizable as Yuuzhan Vong in origin.

His surroundings would tell them little more. Yuu-zhan'tar was a warren of rusting holes like this one.

"Why does the shaper not come to me herself?"

"She may not leave Lord Shimrra's compound, I am told. She takes great risk even in sending this message."

That was undoubtedly true. What little Nom Anor knew of Nen Yim suggested that her role was one that Shimrra was not eager to have widely known. He had lent her for a time to Tsavong Lah, but since her return from that liaison, she had been little seen or heard from. Indeed, Nom Anor had wondered if she had been quietly disposed of.

And perhaps she had. There was no knowing whether this message actually came from her. Since he'd lost Ngaaluh, his spy in Shimrra's court, much was uncertain.

"Why does she seek me out?" Nom Anor asked.

"She heard of your prophecy of the new world. Her studies lead her to believe it is a true one. She desires to see this world for herself."

"So you have already said. Why does she seek my aid?"

"Who else could give it? Shimrra and his minions are corrupt. They have done everything they can to deny the existence of our redeemer. He and the elite will do much more, because they know that if the truth is known, they will be seen as the false leaders they are. And you, my lord, will be seen as the true Prophet."

"What does a shaper care for that?" Nom Anor wondered aloud.

"Nen Yim seeks only truth," Sool said.

"You've already told me you do not know her," Nom Anor pointed out. "How can you speak for her or pretend to understand her motivations?"

"This is the message, Prophet," Sool answered. "I only repeat it."

A vague chanting had gone up among Nom Anor's

acolytes. He began to wish he had received Sool in private rather than in front of thirty or so followers.

A firm voice cut above the rest: "Praised be the Prophet. He has indeed prophesied truly. The planet of our salvation, our deliverance, is now in our very grasp. And Lord Shimrra's own shaper knows it is true! Our destiny has become a force stronger than gravity."

"Do not be hasty, Kunra," another voice said. "This may be nothing more than a trap, a deception to lure the Prophet into their grasp."

"If so, they must fail," Kunra said. He turned to Nom Anor. "You are the Prophet, are you not? Did you not see this, as well? Did you not see yourself walking through the forests of the new world, preparing it for us?"

"I saw it," Nom Anor agreed. He had little choice. He had added that little embellishment a few days before. But what was Kunra up to? Kunra had been with him since the beginning of this whole farce. He knew who Nom Anor really was—that the "prophet" and his planet were equally fabulous.

"Then the time has come to rise against Shimrra."

"No," Nom Anor slipped out. "Do not presume to interpret my prophecy when I still sit here among you. The time is not yet come."

"But we have found the planet," Kunra said. "Let me go, Great One. I will liberate the shaper from Shimrra. I will quest with her for the new world. If there is betrayal, our cause will suffer little. If this is truth—"

"Truth must be practical," Nom Anor said. "We would have to flow rivers of Shamed blood to liberate this shaper, and still she does not know the location of the planet."

"I don't understand," Kunra said. "Do you fear your own prophecy?"

"Quiet," Nom Anor said, his mind whirling furiously. Zonama Sekot was, indeed, important—if only because

Shimrra feared it so much. He knew, too, that the shaper had been given what remained of the Sekotan ship to study, and it would seem she had discovered something quite important. This message suggested one of two possibilities. Either she was telling the truth, and she needed help from outside the system to escape Shimrra and find the planet, or—more likely—they thought Nom Anor knew where the planet was. They couldn't know that he had learned of the planet by eavesdropping on Shimrra and Ekh'm Val, that what he had learned there was all he knew.

Well, not quite all. He had heard rumors that the Jedi had found the world.

Which struck him suddenly as a very fortuitous piece of information.

"The prophecy is indeed nearing fulfillment," Nom Anor told his followers. "But something remains. A piece is missing. When I set foot upon the new world, I shall not be alone. *Jeedai* will be with me."

A collective gasp went up at that. Even Kunra seemed disconcerted.

"Great One—"

"The time has come," Nom Anor said, solemnly. "As Vua Rapuung fought with Anakin Solo, so shall I and the *Jeedai* free this shaper and find our world."

Cheers, of course.

Let the Jedi do the work and take the risk of freeing Nen Yim. If they failed, they would be blamed, rather than him. If they succeeded—then perhaps he would indeed bring his own prophecy to fruition. At the moment, he had little to lose.

NINE

Han Solo scowled and shook a crooked finger at Tahiri. "Kid," he drawled, "I hope you aren't counting on another lucky break your whole life, because you've just used up whatever you may have had coming."

"Easy, Han," Leia interposed. "Anyway, look who's talking. They don't call it Solo luck for nothing."

" 'They' don't know what they're talking about," Han replied. "I've never needed luck—I've always depended on skill."

"Of course you have, dear," Leia said, raising her eyebrows.

"Yeah, well, I—anyway, that's not the issue," Han grumbled. "The issue is you, young lady, flying off against good advice to a planet that's *always* been trouble for this family, alone, running past a Yuuzhan Vong frigate in an X-wing—"

"I didn't have a choice," Tahiri pointed out. "The frigate was sort of between me and escape."

"Sure you had a choice. From what you say, they probably didn't even know you were there—they were after their own runaways. You had a whole planet to hide on. You could have picked a better opportunity to leave—like after *they* did. It's a real miracle that you got out of the system, jumping on a half-fried engine—it's amazing you didn't end up on Tatooine. *And* Ylesia. *And* Bonadan. What was your blazing hurry?"

"I made a promise," Tahiri said.

"A promise? To what, a marsh spider?"

"No. To a Shamed One."

"A Yuuzhan Vong?" His tone was incredulous, but then his face registered his mistake. Everyone was still getting used to exactly who she was now.

That didn't mean she was going to let him off the hook. "I made a promise to a *person*," she said. "Because it was the right thing to do."

Han closed his eyes and looked momentarily very, very tired. "If I could name the times I've heard that *right thing to do* line . . . Tahiri, you're too young for this. You've been through a lot. Can't you just—just—take a rest?"

"Good advice," Leia interposed, taking Tahiri by the shoulders. "Can't you see how tired she is? Why don't we talk about this after she's been to the 'fresher and caught a nap? It can wait that long, can't it, Tahiri?"

"Yes," Tahiri said.

"But—" Han began, but Leia cut him off.

"My husband is just trying to tell you he was worried about you and he's glad you're home."

"I know," Tahiri said. "And I appreciate it."

Han's face softened, and then set into lines of reluctant acceptance. "Well, yeah. But I still think—"

"Why don't you get cleaned up, Tahiri, and we'll have a bit of dinner. We can talk more then."

"It *is* good to have you back, Mistress Tahiri," the golden droid assured her as she made her way toward the refresher.

"Thanks, Threepio," she said. "It's good to be back."

She meant it. She'd grown up on Tatooine and in a Yuuzhan Vong creèche, she'd studied the ways of the Jedi on Yavin 4, but more and more the *Millennium Falcon* felt like home. It was a feeling both comfortable and unsettling, but from what she'd gathered, that was a large part of what *home* was all about.

"I hope you weren't injured in your travels," C-3PO went on.

"No, I'm just a little banged up. And tired."

"Well, now you can rest. And, I must say, *Onih k'leth mof'qey.*"

That sent a little shock through her. *"Don't—"* she began, but cut herself off. This was *not* an abomination—it was 3PO.

C-3PO caught the sudden anger in her tone, however. "I'm dreadfully sorry, Mistress Tahiri. I only wanted to—"

"Make me feel welcome," she guessed, "both as a human and a Yuuzhan Vong."

"Yes, mistress."

"It's okay, Threepio. I'm still working the bugs out of this. It's just, hearing a droid speak that language—"

"Oh, yes. I understand how the Yuuzhan Vong feel about droids. In the future I shan't—"

"No. Like I said, it's okay. These are exactly the things I have to face." *And hope I can.*

"Very well," C-3PO said, with extravagant relief. "But, if I may ask, is the integration of your former personalities . . . complete?"

Tahiri smiled. "It's complete. But it's like—like being raised by parents who taught you one set of values, and then learning a different set of values in school. Which is right? There are conflicts in what most people feel and believe. I'm no different in that respect, maybe just a little more extreme. Do you understand?"

"I believe so."

"Part of me was raised to believe that machines— especially thinking machines—are abominations. But that's just something I learned. It's not part of who I am. It's not part of the Yuuzhan Vong on any intrinsic level, either—it's just what the leaders and priests teach us as crèchelings. It's something that can be unlearned, that must be unlearned, because it's wrong. You're my friend, Threepio, or at least I hope you are. And if, now and then, I have an unthinking reaction to you, I truly hope you can understand and forgive me."

"Oh, very easily," C-3PO said. "Thank you for explaining it to me." His voice shifted back to consternation. "Oh, heavens, I'm holding you up when you should be resting. I'll go now."

"Wait, Threepio."

"Is there something else?"

"Just this." And she threw her arms around him and gave him a hug.

"Oh, my," C-3PO said. But he sounded pleased.

She woke, not knowing exactly where she was. She lay still in the darkness, letting the world return to her, solidify about her, fearing something but not knowing what.

The Millennium Falcon, she thought. *Right. That's where I am.*

She glanced at the table chrono and realized she'd been asleep for almost a standard day. Shaking off the dream-shroud, she pulled on her Jedi robes, visited the 'fresher, and then went looking for Han and Leia.

She found them in the lounge, discussing something in low and somewhat heated tones. She coughed softly, not wanting to eavesdrop.

The two turned toward her.

"Finally up, I see," Leia said. Her voice sounded a bit odd.

"Yeah," Tahiri replied. "I guess I was more exhausted than I thought."

"You ought to be," Han grunted.

"I'm ready to talk now, if that's okay."

"Why not?" Han muttered. "Have a seat."

She slid in next to Leia and clasped her hands together in front of her, trying to think how to start.

"You said something about a promise," Leia prompted.

"Right." Briefly, Tahiri laid out the events on Dagobah. "The Shamed Ones were looking for a planet," she said, when she was done with the narrative. "A planet their Prophet thinks may bring them redemption."

"Dagobah? Why Dagobah?"

"These Shamed Ones sort of worship the Jedi. They found out somehow that Anakin and Luke had been there—that it had something to do with their training."

Han raised an eyebrow. "That's interesting. How exactly would they know that?"

"That's not hard," Leia said. "The Yuuzhan Vong have been obsessed with the Jedi from the very beginning. We know they have good intelligence. Anyway, the story about Luke meeting Yoda there isn't exactly a well-kept secret."

"But they were mistaken," Tahiri said. "Dagobah isn't the world the Shamed Ones are looking for."

Han had the same expression on his face he usually wore playing sabacc. "Oh? And what world do you think they *are* looking for?"

"The same one Master Skywalker was looking for. And found. Zonama Sekot."

Han's eyes widened slightly. Then he puffed and raised his hands in a gesture of frustration.

"Leia," he said. "You tell her."

"Tell me what?"

Leia pursed her lips. "Kenth Hamner contacted us while you were asleep, on a heavily coded channel. He wants to talk to you."

Kenth Hamner. "The liaison between the Jedi and military?" She couldn't quite picture his face. She seemed to remember it was long.

"Right."

"Did he say what it was about?"

"Not exactly," Leia said cautiously. "But it involves

Zonama Sekot—and a dissident movement within the Yuu-zhan Vong."

Han looked at her earnestly. "Tahiri, whatever it is, you don't have to do it."

"Of course I do," Tahiri said. "I promised the Shamed One—"

"You promised him you would tell his Prophet about Dagobah," Han interrupted. "You made no promises concerning Zonama Sekot."

Tahiri smiled slightly. "My promise was one of *izai*, not one of strict legality."

"What?"

"*Izai* is the essence of a promise. The Shamed One thought he had found the planet foretold. I promised him that I would take this news back to his Prophet. But Dagobah *isn't* the planet foretold. Therefore, the *izai*—the essence of my promise—requires me to carry the news that the planet of prophecy has been found."

Han pushed his palms into his face. "This is making my head hurt," he said.

"I think I need to speak to Kenth Hamner," Tahiri said firmly.

"We're already on the way there," Han grunted. "But I hope you know what you're doing."

"I do."

"No," Han said, a little angrily, "you *think* you know what you're doing. It's a conceit born out of being young. Jaina thinks she knows what she's doing. Anakin thought he knew what he was doing."

"Anakin *did* know what he was doing," Tahiri said, softly. "If he hadn't done it, there might not be a single Jedi alive today. I know I wouldn't be here. Didn't you know what you were doing when you came back to save Master Skywalker at the Death Star all those years ago?"

"I was older than you," Han said, rising from the table.

He got up and went toward the cockpit. But he stopped and turned, with one hand on the hatch.

"And, to answer your question," he said, "no, I didn't have the faintest idea what I was doing." He chuckled briefly, shook his head, and vanished into the corridor.

Kenth Hamner did indeed have a long face. He also had a firm handshake, and an office so spare it might have been a storeroom. The view was interesting, though. His window looked down upon a landscape of bloodred and black swirled together, laced over with silver coils and meanders of tide creeks and pools. Beyond that, jagged black mountains sawed at a sky the same metallic color as the water.

Land was scarce on Mon Calamari, but often dramatic.

"Salts," Hamner said, noticing her interest. "When this island was forming, there was a lot of volcanic activity—and geysers the size of volcanoes. Those deposits are millions of years old."

Tahiri nodded, preoccupied. What would the old Tahiri have thought of this view? Or Riina? She found it beautiful, but where did beauty come from? Not from the Force, because the Yuuzhan Vong didn't know the Force, and yet had concepts of beautiful and ugly.

It occurred to Tahiri that she had seen many things she thought of as beautiful since her integration, but nothing she considered truly ugly. Was that strange? Probably. But maybe ugly was a smaller concept than beautiful, and the overlapping tastes of her dual origin had virtually canceled it out.

Kenth had turned his attention to Han and Leia, so she continued her regard of the landscape.

"It's going to be a big push," Kenth was saying. "Exactly how big I'm not at liberty to say."

"So soon after Fondor?" Han asked.

"The Yuuzhan Vong are off balance. It's a good time."

"Yeah," Han said doubtfully, "they're trying to defend too many worlds with too few forces. I hope the Alliance isn't about to make the same mistake."

"Don't worry. This goal is doable."

"It's not an attack on Coruscant itself?" Leia asked.

"Nothing so ambitious," Kenth said.

Tahiri felt Leia's relief in the Force, and Han's, too. An attack on Yuuzhan'tar would exact a horrific cost in ships and personnel, and whatever was going on at the moment, Twin Suns—and Jaina—were sure to be in the thick of it. After her "vacation" from the military, Jaina had insisted on rejoining the fight. Tahiri had heard from her only once since she left, right after the Battle of Fondor.

She missed Jaina. Han and Leia's relief was her own.

"Well, looks like the rest of the gang is here," a new voice interposed.

Tahiri spun from the window. A shortish, neatly goateed man stood there.

"Corran!"

"In the aging flesh," he said. "It's nice to meet you, Tahiri."

The surge of joy she'd felt at seeing the former CorSec officer faded a little at the odd turn of phrase. So he knew she had changed, of course—and he had that guarded look in his eyes. That was Corran—suspicion was as natural a part of him as it was her. Still, it felt bad.

He's wondering if I'm friend or foe, she realized. That felt worse.

"I *do* remember you, Corran," she said, trying not to let the hurt and anger show in her voice. "I'm just happy you're still talking to me after the mess I got you into at Eriadu." She hoped the shared reference would set him more at ease.

"There was plenty of blame to go around," Corran said.

"Anyway, I turned out okay. The Givin have written a po-
etic theorem about you, did you know that?"

"I shudder to think what that even means," Tahiri said.

Hamner cleared his throat. "I hate to break up the reunion, but—"

"Yeah," Han said. "What's this about, exactly?"

Hamner set something on the desk.

Tahiri recognized it immediately. "A Yuuzhan Vong
qahsa," she said.

Hamner nodded, and stroked the cilia-covered knobs in
the back. A face suddenly extruded from the front, a Yuuzhan Vong visage in miniature. Though the detail wasn't
that of a holograph, it was still clear that the face was horribly disfigured—and not in the way the Yuuzhan Vong
preferred.

"A Shamed One," she murmured.

"We got this from a Yuuzhan Vong courier two days
ago," he said.

"Intercepted?" Corran asked.

"No," Hamner replied. "It was sent to us."

"Sent?" Han echoed. "What's the story? Another
ultimatum?"

"No. It's not from the official command structure. For
some time now we've known that there is an underground
movement within the Yuuzhan Vong."

"It's from the Prophet," Tahiri said.

Kenth raised an eyebrow. "Yes. We've heard of him, of
course, but it's been unclear exactly what his goals are. While
any division within the Yuuzhan Vong weakens them, we've
never known what the rebel attitude toward the Galactic
Alliance is. We know the Jedi figure into their creed, but
little more than that."

"Anakin started it," Tahiri said. "Or, in a way he did. He
and Vua Rapuung, when they rescued me on Yavin."

Hamner nodded. "There were inchoate movements after

that, yes, but it's more recently—with the rise of this prophet, 'Yu'shaa'—that the resistance has really taken on substance. He seems to have unified the malcontents. There are even reports of sabotage and assassination, especially on Coruscant." He folded his hands. "It's not the origin of the cult that concerns us right now, but rather the motives of the Prophet himself. Until this"—he nodded at the qahsa—"we haven't had much to go on."

"And now you do?" Leia asked.

"I'll let you decide for yourself." He touched the qahsa again, and the face animated, speaking in accented Basic.

"I greet you," the face said. "I am known as Yu'shaa, the Prophet. It may be that you have heard of me, that I am the leader of the Shamed Ones, those accursed by the gods. That is true, so far as it goes. We are treated as Shamed by our brethren—or by many of them. But we are not accursed. Many of us were once honored and commended by our people. Many of us made great sacrifices for Supreme Overlord Shimrra. Yet we are treated with contempt because our bodies reject the modifications and implants the Yuuzhan Vong have chosen as symbols of rank and pride.

"Before coming to this galaxy, we had little to hope for except dishonorable death. We believed the lies our leaders told us. But now the membranes have been torn from our eyes. We see that we may be redeemed by redeeming our people.

"The Jedi taught us that. The Jedi show us the way. They fight not to show their strength, but to help the weak. You may know that Anakin Solo fought beside one of our own, Vua Rapuung, and restored his honor. Thanks to the Jedi, *we* are not Shamed. Rather, it is Shimrra and the others who lead who are accursed, who have set our people—and the people of this galaxy—on a course that can bring only Shame to us all.

"The Jedi have helped us in the past. They have shown us

a glimpse of the true path. I have seen in dreams and visions where that path leads. It leads to a planet, a planet that can heal and redeem us, that can bring the mighty down and raise up the humble and end the terror we all find ourselves enmeshed in. It is the planet of prophecy. It is Zonama Sekot.

"I have seen this planet, but the gods have not granted me the ability to find it. I do not despair, because I believe the Jedi know where it is.

"Here is what I beg of you: that you take me, and me alone, to the planet of prophecy, so that I may see it for myself, so I can know that my vision was true. I wish also to speak with the Jedi, and seek their counsel and wisdom.

"Unfortunately, I do not have the means to come and go as I please. I live within the clenched fist of Shimrra's hand, and shall need help escaping. On the planet you once called Coruscant, I await your judgment. This qahsa contains a schedule of times I might meet you in a secluded place. It also contains what I have been able to gather about the planetary defenses of Yuuzhan'tar. I give this as a gesture of good faith, but be wary—I am unsure how complete the information is.

"I look to the stars, Jedi. I look to you. All our worlds can be better, I am certain. I have information that can be of benefit—which might end the war—but I cannot use it unless I reach Zonama Sekot. I may not speak of it here—if this falls into the wrong hands, the danger will be great, and I will not betray others. Heed my humble call, I beg you."

With that the figure seemed to lean forward, as if bowing, and then the image froze.

"It's a trick," Han blurted into the following silence. "You all see that, right?"

"It could be," Hamner said. "But the Prophet is real. His opposition to Shimrra is real. This could be a genuine offer."

"He's not offering anything," Han replied. "He's just asking. He's asking us to fly right to the heart of the Yuu-zhan Vong empire and try to attempt some kind of crazy rescue. It's a setup. Couldn't be clearer."

"It's not a setup," Tahiri said.

All eyes turned toward her.

"Tahiri—" Leia began.

Tahiri pushed ahead. "His followers are already looking for Zonama Sekot. I met some of them on Dagobah."

"Means nothing," Han replied. "How do we even know this guy on that thing is actually this 'Prophet'? Shimrra has a pretty good spy network with us. How much better do you think it must be among his own people? He figures this Prophet guy would intrigue us, and now he's baited the trap with him."

"I don't think so," Tahiri said. "I think that was the real thing."

"Based on what?"

"A feeling."

"A feeling." Han rolled his eyes. "A feeling."

"Kenth," Leia said, "what about the information on the qahsa? The data about planetary defenses. Can we check it out?"

"I have, to a certain extent. It looks good. We were able to get a drone in and out through some of the weak spots he described. And we have a secret weapon of our own—a captured Yuuzhan Vong ship."

"You're really thinking about biting at this?" Han asked, incredulously.

"We think the right team would have a shot."

"What team?" Leia asked.

"He means Corran and me," Tahiri said.

"Correct."

"Wait one vaping minute," Corran said, before even Han

could object. "I thought we'd agreed she would only advise beforehand."

Leia turned to the Corellian. "You were already briefed on this, Corran?"

"Yes," the pilot admitted. "Admiral Sorr reassigned me to the mission, but we didn't discuss *this*."

"I'm laying it on the table now so we can talk about it," Kenth said. "Tahiri speaks their language and knows their ways. She's flown ships like this before. I doubt very much this mission could succeed without her."

"Well, it's blinking well going to," Corran replied. "Or I'm out."

"I'll do it," Tahiri said.

"No, you *won't*," Han exploded.

Tahiri sighed. "You mean a lot to me, Captain Solo. Both of you do. I've never really had parents—not human ones, anyway—and I respect you. But this is something I have to do. Jaina and Jacen do their part. Anakin did his part."

"And look how that turned out." Han was trying to sound flip, but she felt the stab of Han's pain at the mention of his youngest son.

"That's the chance we take," she said softly. "It's the chance you've been taking all your life. I know you don't want to lose anyone else. I know you worry about Jaina and Jacen, and you don't want to add worry for me to that. But this war has gone on far too long. If things keep going like they're going, it will only end when one side is exterminated. We have to find another way. That's why Luke and Jacen went to find Zonama Sekot."

"Yes, about that," Leia said. "Hasn't it occurred to anyone that this might be more than a trap for a Jedi or two? That it might be a prelude to another attack on Zonama Sekot?"

"That's why I'm here," Corran said. "If I figure this

'Prophet' isn't operating in good faith, I'll do what's necessary to fix things."

"Luke should have something to say about this."

"I tried to contact him," Kenth said. "But there is some problem with the HoloNet in that sector."

"We just finished *saving* that relay," Han said. "It should be working."

"But it isn't," Kenth said. "We've sent a team to check it out. In any case, we can't talk to Luke."

"We'll have to use our own common sense, then," Han said. "You're walking into this playing by Yuuzhan Vong rules, Corran."

"Maybe. That's why I want to do it alone."

"Maybe you don't trust me," Tahiri said.

Corran smiled. "I didn't trust you even when I knew who you were. Your impulsive actions nearly cost me my life on a couple of occasions, remember? I know you mean well—"

So much for there being plenty of blame to go around, Tahiri thought.

"I've helped betray the Yuuzhan Vong once already," she pointed out.

"You helped betray a military commander to save yourself and your friends. Tell me—if we discovered the only way to win this war was to kill every Yuuzhan Vong, would you do it?"

"No. Neither would Luke or Jacen."

Corran nodded and stroked his beard. "Don't dodge. What if it really came down to them or us?"

"There *is* no them or us, Corran. Do you really think the Shamed Ones want this war? Do you really think that malice is built into the Yuuzhan Vong at the hereditary level?"

"It's built into their culture."

"Exactly. And culture can change."

"Sometimes," he said. "If people want it to, and work at it."

"And that's what this mission is all about, right? If we let this door close, we may never see another one open."

"Now wait," Han said. "We've gotten a little off track here. We never settled that Tahiri can *do* this."

"Yes, we did," Leia said. Her voice was equal parts pride and sadness, and it sent a chill up Tahiri's spine. For an instant, looking at Han in his frustration and Leia in her acceptance, she felt a love for them so powerful it nearly made her cry.

"Thank you," she said.

Han crossed his arms and puffed out a breath of air. "Well, fine—then we're going, too."

"We'd rather have you here, in reserve, when we start the new action," Kenth said.

Han's brow wrinkled in consternation and Tahiri felt a sudden new ambivalence. Whatever was coming up, Jaina would probably be involved. Would Han want to be away, in unfamiliar territory, protecting her, when his own daughter might need him?

But he was Han, and he'd already started. "Hey," he said to Kenth. "Don't start thinking I'm regular military. If Corran won't go—"

"Oh, space it," Corran said. "I'll go. Now, let's see this ship we're going to use."

PART TWO

PASSAGE

TEN

"I've got blips on the horizon," Corran muttered.

"I see them," Tahiri said, her heart sinking slightly. Everything had gone fine, up until now. The holes in Yuuzhan'tar's planetary defenses had been where they were supposed to be. They had come through the upper atmosphere fine. Corran hadn't even complained about her flying. But now, just when they were almost there, trouble came hunting like a qhal.

"They haven't seen us yet," she told him. "They're atmospheric fliers—they don't have the legs we do."

"Doesn't matter," Corran said. "The minute they figure out something is bogus, this mission is over. And you're coming in *way* too steep."

"I know," Tahiri said. She could feel the yorik coral hull of the ship beginning to blister. She straightened out infinitesimally, but that sent them bouncing violently across a thermal boundary.

"I thought you knew how to fly these things," Corran grunted.

"I do," she said, feeling her irritation grow. "You want to avoid our blip friends, don't you? That means coming to ground *fast*, before they come in range to scent us out."

"They're going to *see* us," Corran said. "Because we're going to burn like a meteor if you don't slow up."

"All the better," Tahiri said. "You saw the system chart. There must have been half a billion satellites in orbit around

83

Coruscant. Without anyone to maintain them, they must fall by the dozens every day."

"Good point," Corran conceded. "They won't notice us as we disintegrate."

"Right."

"We're only ten klicks from the ground now."

Tahiri nodded. "Hang on, and hope the dovin basals in this thing are healthy."

She nosed up ever so slightly, and now her goal came in sight—Coruscant's single sea. It didn't look like the holos she'd seen. There, it had been a sapphire in a silver setting, an artificial bathing pool on a planetary scale. Now it was a vast jade bezeled in a landscape of rust and verdigris.

The fliers were almost in range.

"This is going to be really, really close," she told Corran.

"Great," Corran said, teeth gritted.

"From what I've heard, you've done crazier things than this," Tahiri said.

"Yes. Me. I'm a highly trained pilot. You've flown, what, three times?"

"The controls are yours if you want them."

The controls, of course, consisted of a cognition hood that fit on Tahiri's head. She guided the ship by becoming a part of it. A non–Yuuzhan Vong could fly one—Jaina had proven that—but it helped to have the language and the instincts.

And her instincts told her she couldn't wait any longer or Corran really was going to have cause for complaint. She cut in the dovin basals, pushing them away from the planet, killing their velocity. She nudged the applied force up quickly, so quickly that the living gravitic drives couldn't also fully compensate for the g's they were pulling. She felt her weight double, then triple, and the blood in her brain started looking for a way out of her toes.

Hang on, she thought. *Hang on.*

Blotches of darkness filled her vision, and her chest felt like a bantha was sitting on it. She saw the blips coming into range, entering—

Then the lozenge-shaped craft hit the water and skipped like a stone. Everything went crazy for a moment. She didn't quite black out, but the ship's pain jammed through her own thoroughly confused senses. She growled, then howled.

When it all made sense again she saw green.

They were sinking.

"Well," Corran said. "That was—interesting. Are you okay?"

"Yeah. Now let's see if it was worth it."

The blips—or, rather, the projected symbols that represented the approaching craft—continued to get closer.

Something in the ship creaked as they continued to sink.

"I wonder how deep it is here," Corran mused.

"Not too deep, I hope," Tahiri said. "If I use the drive with them this close, they'll notice. The hull should be able to take a good bit of pressure."

The blips were right overhead, now, and they suddenly broke their pattern.

"Not good," Corran said.

"*Khapet,*" Tahiri snarled. She'd screwed up. Now they would have to fight, run, and hope to make it to a safe place to jump to hyperspace before they were overwhelmed. *Nice going, Tahiri. Prove to Corran you really are the stupid little girl he remembers.*

"They're going," Corran breathed. "They must have just been investigating the splash. Or the burn trail." He nodded. "Good call. I don't want to do it again anytime soon, but . . ."

"That's two of us," Tahiri said, sighing and watching the fliers continue on their patrol.

Somewhere, something cracked. It sounded like ceramic breaking.

"Okay," she said. "Let's just ease us up a little."

"Do that," Corran said, "but don't surface—wait, how well can this thing work underwater?"

"Well enough. Unless I have to use voids."

"Yes, let's not do that," Corran said. "Can you disable the function?"

"Sure. But why?"

Corran tapped his datapad and pulled up a chart.

"The Western Sea is like any sea—it's fed by rivers. But because Coruscant is Coruscant, the rivers are artificial. Big pipes, to be exact. If we take this one"—he indicated a spot on the chart—"it will get us pretty close to where we're going."

"Assuming the tubes are still there," Tahiri said. "Yuuzhan' tar isn't Coruscant."

"It's worth a look," Corran said. "Anything that will keep us below the level of detection—and between what Jacen and our best intelligence tells us, they don't have very secure control of a lot of the old underground. That's why our Prophet is there, presumably."

"It's not the way he told us to come."

"No, it isn't," Corran said. "Which gives it another mark, as far as I'm concerned."

Tahiri nodded and changed her heading. "I hope we don't bump into anything," she said. "I can only see ten meters or so."

"Just go slowly. We're not in a hurry anymore—the rendezvous is hours away."

They found the river, a mammoth tube whose diameter the ship's radar analog suggested was a hundred meters or so. Tahiri kept them centered in it, and worked her way slowly up its length.

"That's funny," she said, after a few minutes.

"Funny *ha-ha* or funny *we're about to die*?"

"Odd. What were these tubes made of?"

"Duracrete, mostly. Why?"

"That's what the sensor signature was like when we started in. But it's changed, now."

"Changed how?"

"It's irregular."

"Maybe it's decomposing," Corran suggested.

"And not metal," she added.

"Let me guess. It's alive."

"Probably."

Corran scratched his beard. "The Yuuzhan Vong must be replacing the abiotic drainage systems with biotic ones. That would be typical."

"Yes."

"How far back was the boundary? How long have we been in this new part?"

"We just passed it. We're only a few tens of meters in."

"Right," Corran said. "Back up. I want to think about this for a moment."

Tahiri shrugged. "You're in charge."

"Yes, I am. I was wondering if you knew that."

It didn't quite sound like he was kidding.

Tahiri reversed direction until they were back in the old tunnel.

"What would they be using in place of the old pipe?" Corran asked. "Were we about to swim up the gut of a giant worm?"

Tahiri considered. "I'm not really sure," she said. "The shaper damuteks have succession pools in their centers. Waste goes into them to be purified, and they have roots that go down into the planet to draw up water and minerals."

Corran nodded. "I remember hearing that Anakin crawled down through one of those 'roots' so he could hide in subterranean caves long enough to build a new lightsaber."

"Yes, he did."

"And you think the Yuuzhan Vong are converting the Western Sea into a huge succession pool?"

"Maybe. Or it might be more like a ship's maw luur. It's the same idea—a combination nutrient bank and sewage treatment plant—but the technology is a little different because a ship's maw luur is a closed system. Here, I'm not sure which they would use—but in a lot of ways, Coruscant was more like a worldship than a normal planet, right? No natural ecosystem?"

"Yes. In fact, the Western Sea served something of the purpose you describe anyway."

"Sure. So while they're still deconstructing the place, maybe their interim design is based more on worldship than planet."

"Makes sense. So if this is a big maw luur, we're—" His eyes widened. "Get us out, *now*."

Tahiri gave the command, and the dovin basals quivered to life. They began moving back toward the entrance.

"New plan," Corran said. "I've no intention of going up a world-sized digestive tract."

"I hate to say this," Tahiri said, "but that revelation—"

Something slammed into the ship, hard.

"—may have come a little late."

"What is it?" Corran said.

"Something big," Tahiri said. "We're inside it."

"Well get us *outside* it!"

"I'm trying, but it must have ten times our mass."

Her skin suddenly began burning. "Uh-oh," she muttered. "It can digest yorik coral, whatever it is."

"Part of the maw luur?"

"There are symbiotic organisms in a maw luur that help break down larger things. Nothing this big, though."

"But this is a really *big* maw luur," Corran said. "Digesting really big things."

"True," Tahiri replied. "Anyway, if you've got any suggestions on what to do here—"

"Fire the plasma cannon."

"In an enclosed space?" Was Corran crazy? "That could be bad."

"So could being digested."

"Right."

She bit back a shriek as plasma ejected into the water and brought it instantly to boiling, scalding and compressing her hull. The pressure and heat mounted, peaked—and then they were tumbling free. When they finally stabilized, the water in the eyelamps had gone dark blackish red, and nasty chunks of pulverized meat floated all around them.

"Well, that was disgusting," Corran said.

"Yes," Tahiri informed him. "And this tube is sucking."

"I agree. So let's get out of it."

"No," she said, trying to remain calm. "I mean it's sucking us up it—capillary action, probably, like the roots of a succession pool."

"Surely not too hard to counteract with the dovin basals?"

"Not at all," Tahiri replied. "If, that is, the dovin basals were working."

ELEVEN

"The dovin basal is dead?" Corran asked.

"Not dead," Tahiri said. "But it's badly damaged. I'm trying to coax something out of it, but it's sort of in shock right now." *Of course, it could also be dying,* but she kept that thought to herself.

"We're going faster," she said, instead. "Whatever's pulling at the other end of this tube is increasing its draw."

"How fast?" Corran asked. His voice was maddeningly calm now. Did he think this was *her* fault?

"Only about sixty klicks a minute," she said.

"That's *fast*, when you don't have anything to damp inertia, which I'm guessing we don't right now. If we hit something at this speed . . ."

"Like another predator?"

"I'm thinking more along the lines of a *full* stop," Corran said, punching at the datapad. "This tunnel is going to split eventually, and again, and again—little rivers flowing into the big one, streams into the rivers, sewers into the streams—eventually we're going to hit tubes too small to go through."

"That was going to happen anyway," she pointed out. "You must have had some plan for us to exit this thing in the first place."

"That sort of assumed we were going to be under power," Corran said wryly.

"We may have some power. I'm starting to feel something in the dovin basal."

"It's coming back on-line?"

"It's a living thing. It can't go on- and off-line."

"Fine. It's coming around?"

"Somewhat. I might be able to nudge it into responding, but it won't be able to keep it up for long, so I'll need to pick my moment. Or moments—I think short bursts of power would be okay."

Corran frowned down at his chart. "Originally, there was a nexus up here where six smaller tubes branch off. It's probably coming up fast. If you can take the third from your left, do it."

Almost as he said it, they burst into a flattened sphere full of water. Something black with a lot of tentacles went whipping by them, furiously fighting the current. Tahiri bit her lip, trying to interpret the ship's failing senses through the murk.

"One, two, three—it might be four," she muttered. "There's not time for a better count."

She sent a gentle command to the dovin basal, which quivered and then reached out. It didn't take much—just enough to divert them into the right stream.

"I think I did it," she said.

"Good," Corran said, "now—"

"No!" Tahiri yelped. The rim of the tube loomed.

A sudden shock nearly tore them from their crash couches, and an unholy shriek of impact filled the cabin. A series of lesser shocks followed as the ship rattled down the smaller tube, turning end over end.

Tahiri's stomach churned, and her last meal made a good try at escaping its intended fate.

"Sorry about that," she managed.

"Can you get this tumble under control?" Corran asked.

"I could," she said, "but I really like tumbling." Didn't he think she was trying? "What's our next turn?" she asked.

"The next node, we take the second from the right."

The dovin basal was starting to come out of its funk, though Tahiri could tell it was very weak. They couldn't fight the current, but her control of their forward motion improved. They made the next turn without clipping anything, and the next. The tube had narrowed so much that they had only a few meters' clearance.

"This is almost it," Corran said. "The next intersection used to be a cooling tower. We should be able to go up into the water jacket. We can park the ship there and go the rest of the way on foot."

"Let's just hope they haven't replaced the cooling tower with, I don't know, a lorqh membrane," Tahiri said.

"Don't tell me what that is, okay?" Corran said.

A few moments later, the ship bobbed to the surface in a large, open area. Tahiri made out a flat, sturdy-looking surface a tier above, and gently coaxed the ship up to it.

"Well done," Corran said.

"Thank you. Are we where you thought we were?"

Corran studied the chart. "Yep. From here, we can find access tunnels to the place we were supposed to meet this Prophet. All we have to do now is find him, bring him back here, and do all that in reverse."

Tahiri sighed. "And find another ship. I don't think we can even make orbit in this one, much less a hyperspace jump."

Corran's jaw clamped, then he shrugged. "Well, we've stolen ships before. We can do it again."

But she could tell he was worried. The quipping was to set *her* at ease, because he still thought she was a kid.

"Fight what's in front of you," she said. "Let's go find out more about this Prophet."

*   *   *

"Can't say the Vong have improved much on this," Corran remarked, as they wound their way through the dark caverns that had once been Coruscant's underworld. Now it was a mass of corroding metal, strange, pale growths, and luminescent lichen. It looked as if it had been abandoned for centuries rather than months. Despite the setbacks Jacen had engineered with the dhuryam—the World Brain—the Yuuzhan Vong shapers seemed to be making headway.

"Of course, it was never exactly homey down here," he added.

"*Yuuzhan* Vong," Tahiri corrected. "Did people live here back in the old days?"

"Lots," Corran said. "The vast majority of people who lived on Coruscant weren't what you would exactly call comfortable."

Tahiri shivered. "I can't imagine living like this, below-ground, surrounded by metal, no sky, no stars."

"Is that Tahiri or Riina talking?"

There was something subtly testing in his voice. "Neither one of them would have liked this," she said. "Tahiri grew up in the desert and in the jungles of Yavin Four. Riina grew up in a worldship. Both were surrounded by life."

"Riina didn't grow up anywhere," Corran said. "Riina was created in a laboratory."

"You think that makes a difference?" she asked, stung. "How do you know all your memories are real? If you found out your memories of Mirax were implanted, that there was no such person, would she be any less real to you?"

"Unh-unh," Corran said. "Not buying the sophomoric philosophy. Part of you was once a real person. Part of you was created, like a computer program."

"You think Threepio isn't real?"

"You know what I mean."

"I know what you mean," Tahiri said. She'd pretty much had enough of this, because she didn't know whether to cry or hit him. "And I'll bet I've thought about it a lot more than you have. What I *don't* know is why you're pushing this, here, now. I thought we covered this before leaving Mon Calamari."

Corran stopped, regarded her in the light of their lamps.

"No, we didn't. Or, rather, none of my worries were really resolved. You asked if I trusted you. It's not that I don't trust you, Tahiri—I don't know who you *are*. I don't know what might be sleeping in you, waiting to wake up when the right stimulus comes along. And I can't believe that you can be sure about that either."

That was a *tu'q*, a solid hit. "No, of course I can't," she finally managed. "But I'm not part Tahiri and part Riina. There aren't two voices in my head. Those two fought, and joined, and I was born. They were sort of like my parents. Nothing about either one of them is perfect in me. Even if I inherited something nasty from Riina, it will be flawed. I'll be able to fight it."

"Unless you don't want to. Unless it's something that would have appealed to both Tahiri and Riina."

She conceded that with a nod. "You've already taken the risk, Corran. Why didn't we have this conversation days ago?"

"Because I wanted to see something of who you've become."

"And who have I become?"

"You're bright and talented and far too confident. I'm not sure you're afraid of anything, and that's bad."

"I'm afraid," she said.

"Of what?"

"Fear. Anger."

"The dark side."

"Anakin saw me as a Dark Jedi with Yuuzhan Vong markings. He was strong in the Force." She shook her head. "It's not some hidden Yuuzhan Vong part of me that should worry you, Corran. It's the Jedi part. Tahiri was trained as a Jedi from childhood. I—the person I've become—was not."

His eyebrows beetled up. "That's an interesting thing to say. I hadn't thought of it that way."

"Most people haven't."

"Okay," Corran said. "We'll take this up later, when we aren't skulking."

"Are we skulking now?"

"Yes, because we're almost at our destination. If there's anyone waiting for us, I'd rather they didn't interrupt an interesting conversation."

A few moments later they passed an immense shaft of some sort. Faint daylight illuminated it, so she could guess that it was perhaps two kilometers in diameter. Looking up, she could see a faint circle of rose-colored light.

"How deep is this shaft?" she wondered aloud.

"About three klicks."

"What in the galaxy *was* this?"

"A garbage pit," he said. "They used to shoot dangerous garbage into orbit from here, with magnetic accelerators."

"That's a lot of garbage," Tahiri said. "This is where we're meeting him?"

"Yes. In about fifteen minutes, if he's on time."

While they waited, Tahiri looked around a bit. A lot of Yuuzhan Vong life had crept into the pit.

"What are those called?" Corran asked her. He was pointing at a plant with thick, reedlike stalks that glowed a vivid blue color.

"I've no idea," she admitted. "I've never seen one before. There are a lot of things like that down here—things from the homeworld that weren't needed or wanted on the worldships. Or maybe they're new, engineered to live on metal."

She touched the glowing cylinders. They were cool, and the fine hairs on the back of her hand stood up.

Ten minutes later, they heard the faint echoes of foot-steps. Tahiri put her hand on the grip of her lightsaber. It might be the Prophet, but it might be anything.

A faint green luminescence appeared, carried by a tall, well-formed warrior.

"It's a trick!" Tahiri whispered. She ignited her light-saber. Corran's blazed on an instant later.

The warrior stopped, now fully illuminated.

"Jeedai!"

"Look at him," Tahiri said. "He's not malformed. He's not Shamed!"

But the warrior had dropped to his knees. *"Jeedai,"* he said in Basic. "Welcome. But you are not correct. I am in-deed Shamed."

After the initial shock, Tahiri had begun to notice other details—like the fact that the warrior wore no armor, and that some of his scars and tattoos were incomplete.

"You speak Basic," Corran noticed.

"For your convenience I am equipped with a tizowyrm."

"Are you the Prophet?" Corran asked.

"I am not. I arrive before him, to make certain all is safe. My name is Kunra."

"And is it?" Corran asked. "Safe?"

"You are *Jeedai.* I have no choice but to trust you. My fear was that our communications had somehow been in-tercepted, and that I would find warriors here."

Tahiri switched to Yuuzhan Vong. "Why were you Shamed?" she asked.

The warrior's eyes widened. "One-who-was-shaped!" Then his eyes switched back to Corran, and he returned to Basic. "The slayer of Shedao Shai! We expected *Jeedai,* but not the most august of them."

"Ah, there are still a few higher on the ladder than us," Corran said. "Luke Skywalker, for instance."

"But he does not figure in our sacred tales!"

Tahiri was in no mood to let the warrior become distracted. "I asked you a question," she snapped.

The warrior bowed his head. "I was a coward," he said.

A cowardly warrior? Tahiri thought. *No wonder.*

"You seem to have some courage," Corran said. "You came down here, not knowing if you would find us or an ambush."

"I serve the Truth now. It gives me courage, though I am still unworthy."

"And yet the most worthy of my disciples," a new voice said.

Tahiri glanced up. A tall figure had just come into the chamber. His face was a mass of unhealed scars and festering sores, his right ear missing. The sacks below his eyes were distended, yellow, and—

No, something was wrong. She looked more closely.

It's not real, she realized. *He's wearing a masquer.*

"You're Yu'shaa?" Corran asked.

"I am. It is my honor to meet the great Tahiri Veila and Corran Horn."

Tahiri acknowledged that greeting with a curt nod.

The Prophet bowed. "This is truly a blessed day," he said.

"Right," Corran said. "Though for a blessed day, we've had some fairly unblessed setbacks. Including the fact that our ship was destroyed in coming here."

"You were discovered?" the Prophet asked, a bit sharply.

"No. At least I don't think so." Tahiri watched him carefully while Corran described what had happened.

The Prophet nodded when he finished. "You are correct, Blessed One—it is unlikely that you were discovered. I suspect your firing of the plasma weapon caused some sort of malfunction in the maw luur's reflexes. There are hundreds, if not thousands of such malfunctions every day, and I doubt this one will be closely scrutinized. As to the other, once more we see that the universe favors our cause. The final member of our party claims to have a ship at her disposal."

"*Final* member of the party?" Corran made it sound like, *You want me to kiss a gundark?*

"Yes. A shaper who holds the secret to our redemption."

"I thought *you*—"

"I am the Prophet. I speak the truth and foretell what is to come. I am not myself the key to redemption—I merely *see* it."

Corran glanced at Tahiri. "That's interesting," he said, "but our mission, as I understood it, was to come here and get you and take you to Zonama Sekot. Now you want us to change the mission to include someone else. In my experience, changes in the mission can lead to unpleasant results."

"I *am* sorry," the Prophet said. "But as you said, your mission has changed already—now we must have a ship. As to the shaper—I could not speak of her on the qahsa. She is placed very close to Shimrra—it is how she discovered Zonama Sekot in the first place."

Corran sighed. "Explain."

"A commander named Ekh'm Val went to Zonama Sekot," Yu'shaa said. "He fought there and was defeated. But he returned with something of the planet, which this shaper has studied. She discovered a certain inexplicable kinship between the biology of Sekot and our own biotechnology."

"Again, interesting, but—"

"We are from another galaxy, Jedi Horn. We crossed the starless night for age upon age. Our legends go deep, and yet nowhere is such a thing hinted at, at least not in anything I ever heard. And yet here, in this time of darkness, two things are given us. To me, a vision of Zonama Sekot as a sign of our redemption. To the shaper, the revelation that we have some prior relationship to this planet—a relationship that Shimrra fears. I do not know what these things mean, but they can hardly be coincidence. But like me, this shaper must *see* the world of salvation with her own eyes, to know the truth—to know exactly what it all means."

"And how do you know she isn't betraying you?" Corran asked. "You say she's part of Shimrra's inner circle? I'm sure he would like to get his hands on you at least as much as on the two of us."

"No doubt. But I believe her. Ekh'm Val was murdered upon his return from Zonama Sekot, along with all his surviving warriors. Shimrra fears even the rumor of this planet. The shaper is already as good as dead, merely for knowing what she knows. Shimrra would never allow her to leave his compound, much less travel freely to the very planet he fears."

"So you're saying we have to break her out of Shimrra's compound?" Tahiri blurted, incredulous.

"Yes. I'm afraid it's the only way."

"Yu'shaa," Tahiri said, "why are you wearing a masquer?"

She felt Corran's reaction in the Force—a sudden heightening of suspicion. But he didn't say anything, and she was watching the Prophet for his reaction.

But the Prophet showed no surprise, nor should he have—any Yuuzhan Vong would see the masquer for what it was: an organism that presented a false face to the world. "You know our ways," he said. "I wear this masquer for my people. I have sworn not to remove it until our redemption has come. For you, I might take it off, but I have adhered it with dhur qirit. The removal process is very lengthy."

So it was basically sutured to his face. That made sense, sort of—several Yuuzhan Vong sects in the past had habitually worn masquers as a matter of daily ritual. They had, in fact, originally been developed for that rather than as a means of disguise.

But here, in this context, Tahiri didn't like it.

Corran obviously didn't, either. "No offense, Yu'shaa," he said, "but Tahiri and I need a moment to discuss this alone."

"Of course."

They walked a comfortable distance.

"How does this smell to you?" Corran asked.

"I don't really like it," Tahiri said. "But part of that might be a reflexive dislike of Shamed Ones."

"You think that affects your read of the situation?"

"I hope not. I'm trying to fight it. But there's something about him I don't like, that's for sure."

"Well, that makes two of us. But the question isn't whether we like him, or even whether we trust him. The question is, *Is he telling us the truth at this moment, as he knows it?*"

"I can't say for sure," Tahiri said. "But this all seems pretty elaborate for a trap."

"My thought exactly. It doesn't make any sense—if they were going to do something, why not here? No, this has the feel of a real plan, albeit a pretty shoddy one. In fact, it's sort of reassuring." He smiled. "Are you still game?"

"Of course. I thought you would be the one to object."

"We're in pretty deep already. You've shown me you can handle yourself. And Kenth was right to send you along—I couldn't have made the call about the masquer. Let's at least see what the plan is."

"There are hidden ways into Shimrra's palace," Yu'shaa told them. "Some have been discovered, but there is one I am still certain of. I have been reluctant to use it, for once I do so I cannot do so again. Once within, we must make our way to the shaper compound."

"If she has a ship, why can't she just fly it out?" Tahiri asked.

"I don't know," the Prophet replied. "I know only that she requires defense of a substantial sort, or the escape will be impossible."

"That's not all there is to it," Corran grunted. "She

wants it to look like a kidnapping, doesn't she? So she can have deniability later."

"That seems possible," Yu'shaa agreed.

"Hmm. Do you have a diagram of this compound?"

"Yes."

"How many warriors will we have to face?"

"My followers will help, of course," Yu'shaa said. "They will create a nearby disturbance, which should draw warriors to another part of the palace compound. And you have friends inside the damutek, of course."

"That's all well and good," Corran said, "but how many warriors will we have to face?"

"My guess is all I can give you, but I suspect no less than ten."

"And as many as?"

"If things go wrong? A few hundred."

"Ah," Corran said. "Then your people, the ones creating the distraction—"

"Will likely be killed, yes. But they are willing to die."

"But *I'm* not willing to let them die," Corran said. "Not for me."

"They die for their own redemption, Jedi Horn, not for you. It is only if our mission fails that they will have died in vain."

"Still, I—hang on."

Tahiri felt something in the Force, then, a flash of insight from Corran. He was staring at the glowing plants they'd been discussing a moment ago.

"I think I have an idea," he said. Tahiri thought he sounded reluctant. "It might buy us the edge we need, and get fewer of your people hurt in the process."

"The Jedi shall lead the way," the Prophet said. "Tell me your plan."

"I wish you wouldn't keep saying things like that," Corran said, "but here's what I'm thinking . . ."

TWELVE

When they emerged from the darkened tunnels and into the light of Supreme Overlord Shimrra's palace, Tahiri's knees went momentarily weak at the sight. His command ship, an enormous winged sphere, was nested at the top of it, as if the whole palace were a scepter, a symbol of might.

"Pretty impressive," even Corran admitted. "Now what?"

Yu'shaa pointed a finger toward a much more modest, star-shaped complex. "That is the shaper damutek," he said. "Wait here for a few moments. When our ruse begins, it will be there." He pointed to a large, hexagonal building rather low to the ground, with a roof of gabled mica. "It is an amphistaff breeding gla. The guards will think my people are raiding for weapons."

Corran counted at least fifty warriors patrolling the vast plaza.

"Your people will be slaughtered."

"They will not fight for long. They will flee, and your brilliant plan will make certain that most of them are not followed."

Corran sighed. "I'm not so sure it's brilliant."

"They *may* escape," Yu'shaa said. "You have given them a better chance than they had. If they do not, they will die with honor, something more than Shimrra would ever allow them. They will die knowing they have blazed the trail to redemption."

Corran looked back at the damutek. "And we just go in the front door?"

Tahiri was staring at the damutek as well. The momentary reflex to worship she'd had at the sight of Shimrra's palace was gone, replaced by a cold feeling that lay on the borderlands of anger and fear. Bad things had happened to her in such a place.

"Yes," she said. "We just go in through the front door."

"And where will we meet you?" Corran asked the Prophet.

"There is a shrine to Yun-Harla nearby. The shaper will know where it is. If I survive, I will see you there."

"You haven't seen whether you survive or not?" Corran asked.

The Prophet smiled. "I am confident that I will."

"Well, good luck anyway," Corran said.

"Yes. May the Force be with you."

As the sounds of the Prophet's footsteps faded, Corran opened his mouth to say something, and then stopped. He looked at Tahiri.

"Yes," Tahiri assured him. "That was weird for me, too."

Nom Anor continued grinning as he left the two Jedi. While nothing was certain, he did expect to survive the coming battle, because he did not intend to be in it. His followers would fight, and they would die, and he would leave by the way he had come in and make his way to the shrine. If the Jedi and the shaper died as well, then he would vanish back underground and try to think of something new.

He wasn't particularly happy that Corran Horn had been chosen to come. While it looked good to his followers, for him it would be a continual danger. Horn was not the sort to be lulled easily out of suspicion. If he discovered the "Prophet's" true identity, Nom Anor suspected that the appearance of present good intentions would not overshadow his actions against the Jedi in the past.

Of course, Tahiri was a problem, too. Her knowledge of Yuuzhan Vong ways made her another potential threat. She'd seemed less than entirely convinced by his explanation for the masquer.

He paused in the darkened tunnel, considering. Perhaps he shouldn't go through with this, after all.

But, no, he had to. Since Ngaaluh's death, Nom Anor's influence had begun to wane. Shimrra was now extremely vigilant against spies at his court, even at the highest levels. Sweeps of the lower levels had increased, and Shamed Ones removed farther from where they might do harm. Worse, while his following hadn't dropped off, it hadn't grown, either, partly because too many of them were getting killed without any apparent movement toward the ultimate goal of "redemption." The potential for an uprising that might catapult Nom Anor to power was farther away than it had ever been. He needed a new catalyst, a new source of strength. He needed, in short, new allies.

Still . . . He patted the pouch-creature fastened to the flesh beneath his arm. It contained the one piece of his past as a respected executor. He wasn't even sure why he'd risked bringing it, but . . . if he were to deliver two Jedi, a rogue shaper, and the planet Zonama Sekot into Shimrra's hands, it might be enough to . . .

No it wouldn't. Not if even a suspicion of his role as Yu'shaa were to enter Shimrra's mind.

No, he would have to work with what he had. It was far too late to flinch. Nor could he panic at the prospect of the trip he faced.

He did not, like his superstitious followers, believe in an ordained destiny—destiny was something created by sheer force of will, and that was something he had in abundance. So he would play the role of compassionate holy man for the Jedi. He would win them or they would die.

For Nom Anor, there could only be forward and upward, never back or down.

One moment nothing was happening; the next a yellow-green explosion blossomed from the side of the building across the square and the outer wall collapsed in sticky shards, as if it had melted. Warriors all across the square raced for the source of the explosion, but before they could reach it, a mob of Shamed Ones sprang from a pit near the buildings and fell upon the warriors with coufees, amphistaffs, batons, even pipes and rocks.

The fighting was confused by distance, but Tahiri could tell they weren't faring very well, though they fought with absolute conviction, some impaling themselves on the amphistaffs of the warriors, immobilizing the weapons long enough for their companions to drag their foes down by sheer weight of numbers. This distraction wouldn't last long. She tensed to run.

"Hang on," Corran said. "Wait until—"

Even as he spoke, new actors appeared, four figures in brown cloaks bearing long glowing tubes of light.

And everywhere went up the cry of *"Jeedai,"* from warriors and Shamed Ones at once. But their tones were quite different. The Shamed Ones were exulting, while the warriors were crying out in challenge and fury—and perhaps a little fear. There were few things that could bring a warrior greater honor than bringing down a Jedi in combat—the warriors didn't worship them as the Shamed Ones did, but they had learned respect.

The *"Jeedai"* suddenly turned and ran, and guards went after them, howling. Indeed, guards who had not already left their posts now did so. Corran had called that one pretty well. If there was anything that could make a warrior forget every duty he had, this was it.

Of course, when it came to their superiors' attention that

they had abandoned their posts to chase Shamed Ones bearing the light-plants that grew below their feet, things would not go well for any of them.

"Now," Corran said.

Tahiri was already springing forward, now utterly focused on the single guard who still remained at the front closure of the damutek.

To the guard's credit, he wasn't too distracted by the fighting to see them coming. Unfortunately, his attention did not do him much good against two Jedi.

At the door, Tahiri put her hand against the membrane.

"*Veka, Kwaad.*"

The opening dilated.

"That was easy," Corran said.

"It should be," Tahiri answered. "This damutek belongs to my domain."

"Master Yim," someone asked from the doorway.

She looked up from the series of kul embryos she'd been vivisecting. It was Qelah Kwaad. "What is it?"

"There's some sort of disturbance in the outer compound. They say it is Shamed Ones."

"Disturbance? What are they doing?"

"They've attacked the amphistaff nursery."

"Trying to arm themselves, I suppose," Nen Yim replied. "Go, secure the laboratories."

"Yes, Master Yim." The adept hurried off.

Well, she considered. *This must be it.* She straightened from her task and moved to the wall. From a pouch adhered to her belly, she withdrew a thorn-shaped creature with a thin, hard shell, located a nerve cluster in the wall, and thrust it in. It hissed softly as it began injecting toxin into the damutek. It would paralyze the living structure's defenses, allowing whoever was coming after her to do so without having to deal with corridor-sealing membranes and debilitating gas. Of course, those defenses had not stopped the Jedi on Yavin, but this needed to move quickly. The thorn tapiq would soon dissolve and leave no trace of itself or its effect.

She grabbed an enveloping cloth surrounding a set of selected shaper bioware and a qahsa and hurried up the corridor toward the Sekotan ship. She was amazed at how calm she felt. Of course, she still hadn't taken any irrevocable steps. She could counteract the effects of the tapiq, and she probably had the means at her disposal to stop the Jedi.

But no. Zonama Sekot was a mystery she could not let lie. The planet called to her. She would go, if she survived the next few moments.

The ship was as she had seen it the day before, shimmering gently, waiting for her. Excitement grew in her. She was stepping forward, touching it with her master's hand, when several figures burst through the doorway into the room.

Two humans, and, by their whipping, burning unlife brands, certainly Jedi. They were engaged with eight warriors. Both of the humans already bore several bloody gashes, but as she watched, two more Yuuzhan Vong warriors fell from sizzling, cauterized wounds.

One of the remaining guards turned to face her.

"Master Yim, flee. There is danger here."

She knew him—Bhasu Ruuq, quiet for a warrior. She thought she'd caught him giving her admiring glances before.

"My apologies," she said. She extended her master's hand, and a long, whiplike sting no thicker than a straw snaked out and impaled him through the eye. He died without a sound. She curled her hand, and the sting wrapped around the neck of another warrior and bit through the arteries of his neck. She released it, recalled it, and shot it back out to kill a third.

The Jedi cut down the last of their stunned opponents and stood panting over corpses, staring at her.

The gaze of the yellow-haired one struck Nen Yim like a thud bug, and a jolt of recognition ran through her. Everything changed, suddenly, and she realized her only triumph was death.

"You," she said. "You've come to kill me."

Tahiri gave Nen Yim a cold grin.

"You think so?" she said. "Why would I do that? Merely because you tortured me, turned my brain inside out, tried to turn me against everything I had ever known?"

"You two know each other, then," Corran speculated.

Tahiri nodded grimly. "She's one of the shapers who experimented on me. Her name is Nen Yim." She looked at the fallen warriors. "I see you've got a new hand. Like Mezhan Kwaad's."

"Mezhan Kwaad was a master. Now I am."

"I should have known it was you," Tahiri said. Rage was suddenly a whirlwind in her. "Watch her hand, Corran. She has—"

"I saw what she did to the warriors," Corran said. "If she thinks it will work on me, she's welcome to try."

"She's mine, Corran," Tahiri growled. She stepped forward, raising her weapon to guard between them. Turning to the shaper, she continued, "You have no idea what you've put me through, Nen Yim. I nearly died. I nearly went mad."

"But you did not."

"I did not. Nor did I become what you were trying to make of me."

"That was fairly clear when you decapitated Mezhan Kwaad," the shaper replied.

"Yes," Tahiri said. "That was a quick end for her. My torture lasted a lot longer."

The rage was blackening in her, a vua'sa nearing a rival's den. She watched for the slightest twitch of the shaper's hand, the smallest excuse to—

To what? Kill her?

She took a deep, slow breath, and lowered her weapon. Her hand was trembling and her belly was tight. She willed the muscles to relax.

"We've come a long way through a lot of trouble for you," she said. "I don't intend to kill you, not now. You're the reason we're here, aren't you?"

"I wish to see Zonama Sekot," the shaper said. "If you have come to take me there, then yes."

"We should talk about this later," Corran said.

"We will," Tahiri said. "We certainly will. After we've gotten out of here but long before we reach Zonama Sekot. Do you understand me?"

"I understand you," Nen Yim replied. "But for now, if we're to escape, you must do as I say."

"Time's wasting," Corran said. "What do we do?"

"The warriors I killed. Use your weapons on them."

Corran grinned wryly. "I thought so." He did as instructed, cutting through the wounds that were already there, erasing any sign that they had been killed by a shaper's hand. Tahiri watched in disgust. A Yuuzhan Vong ought to own the violence she did.

"Next?"

"I need an opening in that wall, large enough for this ship to pass through. I'm certain your infi—your weapons can accomplish it."

Tahiri nodded at Corran, and together they moved to the coral wall indicated and began carving chunks from it. While they were still less than half done, shouts went up behind them.

Before Corran could react, Tahiri spun and charged the new attackers. There were three of them.

"Finish!" she cried. "I'll take these."

All three bore amphistaffs. She hurled herself at them as if committed to a full-on charge, but at the last instant stopped short. As a result, the counterattack from the lead warrior was also short. She picked up the rigid end of his staff in a high bind and cut down through the juncture of neck and shoulder, sweeping her blade around to catch a second attacker in a high parry. Then she dropped, instinctively ducking the slash from the third. Even so, the second warrior recovered quickly and wrapped his suddenly flexible staff around her ankle. Tahiri used the Force to leap away, and the warrior yanked her back, which was what she'd been planning. She went with the pull, and both of her feet hit him in the face. He grunted and fell back, but didn't release the staff. As she fell, she reversed her weapon and let the third warrior impale himself through the armpit. Black vapor exploded from the wound and the scent of burning blood sang in her nostrils.

She rolled to get back to her feet, but the remaining warrior kicked her in the side of the head. The blow rang in her skull, and white lights threatened to blot out her vision. She swung wildly, but failed to connect with anything. Then everything went strange as something hard and sharp went through her shoulder.

"Oh," she said. "Oh." Her arms were suddenly rubber.

The warrior grinned in triumph.

"No," she told him. "No, absolutely not."

She grabbed the amphistaff that had impaled her, but she barely felt it. She tried to focus beyond the pain, use the Force to throw herself back, but all she saw was the snarling face of the warrior who was about to kill her, and all she felt was her body husking out, going light, fading . . .

She saw the warrior look away, and then suddenly he was headless. His body dropped away almost gently.

Corran stood above her. "Come on," he said.

"Poison," Tahiri mumbled. She tried to stand, but her legs were already beyond answering her demands.

She was vaguely aware that Corran got her up on his

shoulder and was taking her toward the strange ship. After that, time condensed. She remembered yelling, and concussions, and the ship shivering. New voices, then nothing.

Nen Yim settled in the pilot's couch and placed the cognition hood on her head. The ship hadn't come with one, but it had been an easy matter to implant a Yuuzhan Vong matrix ganglia to the alien but relatively straightforward neural web. It ought to respond like any Yuuzhan Vong ship.

She hadn't been able to regenerate all the ship's systems, and had replaced them with specially bioengineered equivalents. She had installed dovin basals in place of the abominable machine drive; she wouldn't have known how to repair that even if she had wanted to. The frame she could do nothing about, and she'd left many of the other bits of infidel technology in place because she either wasn't sure what they did or because it was unclear whether the ship would function properly without them.

A flutter of tension moved through her as she melded with the ship's senses. The ship felt confused, uncertain, as if it was wondering—as she was—whether the repairs and modifications would work. Her experiments suggested they would, but of course she had never flown it.

We'll try this together, yes? she thought to the ship, and received a tentative affirmation.

Where were the Jedi?

She could not see them from the transparent cockpit, so she activated the ship's exterior optical sensors and quickly located them. They seemed to have gotten into another fight, and the yellow-haired one was down, wounded.

That wasn't entirely bad, Nen Yim considered. Things might go more smoothly if the girl died.

A few moments later, the two were on board and Nen Yim dilated the inner and outer locks.

"Tahiri's hurt," the male Jedi called. "It's an amphistaff wound."

"Do what you can for her," she told him. "I can't help at the moment. We have to leave."

Hoping once again that the inelegant mixture of Sekotan and Yuuzhan Vong technology wouldn't fail her, she willed the ship to fly.

In a blur they were through the opening, though she felt it scrape along her skin on one side. No damage, though—the hull could shed starstuff for a time, so yorik coral was no real problem. She might even have been able to break through the wall with the nose of the ship, but the Jedi had been there with their swords, so why not use them?

"We're meeting the Prophet at the shrine of Yun-Harla," the Jedi told her. She didn't like his tone of voice. It sounded as if he imagined she was under his orders.

"I'm aware of that," she said, trying to remain calm when all her instincts told her that she was far too high above the ground, that she was going to fall.

There was the shrine, the same one she'd met Harrar at what seemed like a very long time ago. The skies were still eerily quiet, as if Yuuzhan'tar were asleep, as if they hadn't just fled from the compound of the Dread Overlord himself. Oddly, the quiet brought a sense of doom that she hadn't felt up until now.

She settled the ship down next to the shrine and opened the hatch. Outside, a breeze was blowing, thick with the astringent scent of blister flowers. She was glad they'd bloomed before she left—she'd wondered what they would smell like.

She noticed a movement from behind the shrine, and saw the grotesque figure of a Shamed One coming toward her.

"This, then, must be the Prophet," she murmured. He was tall, and his body looked well formed enough, save for a lump beneath his left arm that was probably a limpin implant gone bad. He wore a masquer that bore every mark of the Shamed she could imagine, as if he had cataloged every possible disfigurement before having it made, as if he was determined to carry the burden of all the Shamed on his own neck.

It was both revolting and oddly intriguing. What sort of Yuuzhan Vong would do such a thing? And why?

"I am Yu'shaa," he said as he boarded. His gaze fastened on her, intense, nearly animal. This was no simpering Shamed One, no. This was an altogether different breed of the creature. He carried his marks with impossible dignity.

"I am Nen Yim."

"I am honored, Master," the Prophet replied. "You undertake a great task. All went well?"

"Could have gone a bit more smoothly," Corran muttered.

"According to plan," Nen Yim said.

"Tahiri being stabbed was not in the plan," Corran said.

"The one-who-was-shaped is injured!" the Prophet exclaimed.

"A risk we all take," Nen Yim pointed out.

"She's dying!" Corran said. "Isn't there anything you can do?"

"I will heal her," Nen Yim said, "when I have the chance."

"You'll heal her—"

He stopped when someone else stepped into the ship. He yanked out his infidel weapon and ignited it.

"No!" Nen Yim shouted. "This is Harrar, a priest. He's going with us."

The male Jedi crouched into a fighting stance. "No, I—"

A blast of plasma slammed into the ship—the skies were no longer quiet. Cursing, Nen Yim realized she had disengaged from the long-range sensors. As she reengaged now, she saw a flier above them and ten more within range. She closed the hatch and jolted the dovin basals to life. The ship jumped straight up, slamming into the atmospheric flier.

The flier flipped over and smashed into the shrine, then slid into the water below, food for the p'hiili.

The other fliers quickly dwindled, but faster ships were coming, from everywhere. She turned toward what she perceived to be the most open space. Far above, the rainbow bridge was a faint band in the sky, another legacy of their conquest of Yuuzhan'tar. They had shattered a moon to make it.

She saw with some relief that she was faster than the pursuing ships, if only marginally so. Most Yuuzhan Vong spacecraft had been designed primarily for space, and were clumsy in atmospheres. The Sekotan ship was sleeker, streamlined.

Once they were in vacuum, it might be a different matter.

"Prepare for a darkspace jump," she called back.

"Bloody—" the male Jedi sputtered. "*No!* Not this close to the planet. We're still in the atmosphere!"

"That's bad?" Nen Yim asked.

"*Yes,* that's bad. Have you even laid in a jump?"

"I'm not sure what you mean."

"You've never flown?"

"No."

"Watch her," Corran told the Prophet, casting a glance at the priest as he did so. This thing was going sourer every second. He moved quickly to stand next to the shaper.

"Okay," he said, "let's—look, we'll make a short jump first—Borleias. Do you have a star chart in there, anything like that?"

She shook her head. "No," she said. "Or maybe. I'm not attuned enough to see it if there is one. But there are ships approaching."

"Any way to show me the ships?"

"Yes."

A nearby wall panel coruscated, revealing a surface that raised icons to represent ships and their movements.

"I can't tell how close they are, because I don't know the

scale here," Corran said. "But I think you ought to bear aught-six-two-aught-aught-one."

"I don't know what that means."

"That way!" Corran pointed, feeling an entirely appropriate déjà vu.

"Do not order me."

"Look, I'm a pilot. You certainly aren't. Anyone knows a hyperspace jump this near a singularity is suicide."

She ignored the comment. "There are ships that way, too," she reported.

"Yeah, I see them. Does this thing have any guns?"

"Not that I'm aware of."

"Well—fly fast. And figure out how to plot a jump."

A coralskipper came up on their tail and started to fire. The first few shots missed, but the next connected, and the ship shuddered slightly. It almost seemed to cry faintly, as if remembering its earlier trauma from such weapons. That shook Corran a bit—was the ship sentient? And if so, why did *he* hear it when Nen Yim was the one under the cognition hood?

But then he understood. The ship existed in the Force.

He'd assumed from its obvious organic nature that this was a new model of Yuuzhan Vong ship. Now he didn't know *what* it was.

The coralskipper unloaded again.

"Jink!" Corran said. "Jink!"

"I've no idea what you mean by that," Nen Yim said.

Corran felt like strangling something—possibly himself, for letting such a relatively simple mission get so far out of control. "Why can't any of these stinking ships have normal controls?" he muttered.

"You mean controls of metal and plasteel?" the shaper asked.

"Yes. Yes!"

"It does," she replied. "This ship is a grafting of machine

and biotechnology. The original controls were—I could not understand them."

A grafting of machine and bio— later. "You took them out?"

"No, they're beneath that screen, covered by a lamina. The sight of them offended me."

"Oh, I see," Corran said, as he staggered toward the place she had indicated. "You're completely insane. You've appointed yourself pilot, you've no idea what you're doing, and you don't mention to the only *qualified* pilot that there are controls—" He ripped off the lamina, revealing an entirely familiar set of instruments.

"I can fly this," Corran grunted. "I can fly this! Get back there and help Tahiri!"

"I don't—"

"—know what you're doing," he repeated. "We'll all be killed, here, now, and you'll never see your mystery planet."

"Very well," Nen Yim said. She removed the cognition hood and started back toward Tahiri.

"If she doesn't live," Corran called back to her, "the whole deal is off."

"Then she will live," Nen Yim shot back.

Corran threw the ship into a scissor-roll, dodging a fresh barrage of plasma bursts. One scorched along the hull, and he felt the ship's cry of pain.

Then he felt the wound close, itch, and heal.

Interesting.

The controls were on the old-fashioned side, but the ship itself handled like nothing he'd ever flown. And despite what Nen Yim had said, he found controls for lasers and—something else.

Well, let's see if they work. He veered hard port and up, making the turn in half the time a ship this size ought to, and came in above one of the pursuing skips. Hopefully, he squeezed off a few shots.

The console said he had four forward lasers. Only one fired. The beam scorched out—and was swallowed by the skip's void.

Corran wisped by the skip, feeling rather than seeing the other two on his tail, and then pulled up, hard, and grinned when the fire from the two pursuing skips struck the one he'd just shot at.

"I guess they don't have their war coordinator on-line yet," he said.

"It's being jammed," Nen Yim's voice floated up from the back. "I've seen to it."

Useful, this shaper. Annoying and incredibly dangerous, but useful. "How is Tahiri?"

"I told you. She will live."

A wave of relief swept through him, and he turned his full attention back to the problem at hand.

Ships were everywhere now, and not just in the direction he was leaving, and not all just skips. He began working out a jump, but not knowing the engine capabilities made that tricky—he'd have to get it right, not almost right. There wasn't going to be time . . .

"Hello," Corran murmured to himself. "What's that?"

The silhouette looked familiar, but he couldn't be sure. It might not even still be functioning, but at the moment it was his only hope. He changed course toward the object.

A skip whirled in from below starboard, and from sheer curiosity, he tried the other weapon the ship seemed to have, but nothing happened. The skip, on a wrong vector to keep up with him, missed its own shot and went on, banking to come after him but losing kilometers in the process.

"Fine," he muttered. Obviously, whatever the weapon was, it didn't work.

Six or seven skips were going to have a shot at him in about a minute, but the satellite he'd seen at long range was pretty close now. Basically a five-meter-diameter sphere bristling with knoblike protrusions, it hung quietly in its orbit.

As Tahiri had said earlier, there must have been millions or billions of satellites around Coruscant when the Yuuzhan Vong took it. The new tenants had been working to clear them out, but that was a huge job. Some had fallen of their own accord, but some . . .

He fired his single laser at the sphere, and whooped when the blue sheen of a shield went up.

Laser light was suddenly everywhere as the sphere began to whirl in complex maneuvers, firing at every ship it saw. Corran ignored those shots directed at him and just punched the drive as hard as it would go, which was *hard*. The skips went wild, spinning around the satellite, firing at it. Only one or two recovered from the surprise quickly enough to follow his new vector, and by the time they were even thinking about catching him he'd laid in his calculations and was watching the stars sleet away.

"Whew," he said, finally able to relax.

"What was that, some sort of war machine?"

With a start, Corran realized the Prophet was standing just next to him.

"No," he said. "It's a training device for star pilots. Once fired on, it goes into offensive mode. Of course, the lasers are so weak they can't do any damage, so most of the power goes to its shields. But with their voids gobbling the first few shots, the Yuuzhan Vong pilots would take a while to figure that out."

"Clever," the Prophet said.

"Thank you," Corran said. "Now I want to see Tahiri."

Tahiri came to with Nen Yim bending over her.

"She will be weak," she was telling someone. "Perhaps for some time. The arm might be useless. It is too soon to say."

"Corran?" Tahiri mumbled. She turned to see him.

But Nen Yim wasn't talking to Corran. She was talking to a Yuuzhan Vong, a thin man with a headwrap. A priest!

Tahiri reached for her lightsaber, but didn't find it there. "Corran!" she shouted.

"I'm here," the familiar voice said. "Calm down. We seem to be among friends." He didn't sound convinced.

"Who are you?" Tahiri asked the priest.

"I am Harrar."

"Another of our merry band of pilgrims," Corran grunted.

"The shapers and the Shamed are not the only ones with curiosity about this new world," the priest explained. "I arranged to meet Nen Yim at the same place as the Prophet."

"Then you embrace our heresy?" the Prophet asked.

"I embrace nothing," Harrar replied. "I reject nothing. But Shimrra has gone to great lengths to keep this planet from our knowledge. I want to know why."

"Where are we?" Tahiri asked.

"Hyperspace," Corran replied. "You missed our exciting exit. This really is some ship."

Tahiri was taking in the rest of their surroundings, now. Like a Yuuzhan Vong vessel, Nen Yim's vessel looked grown, organic. In no other way did it resemble a yorik coral craft.

"What sort of ship is this?" she asked.

"The ship is from Zonama Sekot," the Prophet replied. "It was badly damaged. The shaper healed it. It is good—we arrive at Zonama Sekot returning one of its own."

Tahiri was about to ask more, but Corran spoke up.

"Oh, yes, that," he said. "We're not going to Zonama Sekot."

THIRTEEN

All eyes turned to Corran.

Yu'shaa was the first to speak. "Blessed One, what can you mean? After all we've done? My followers died so that we might make this voyage. They put their faith in you."

"And I put my faith in your words, Yu'shaa—your promise that this voyage would include you and you alone. Now we have a shaper and a priest, and I don't know anything about either of them."

"I explained about the shaper," the prophet said. "I knew nothing about the priest."

"Consider," Harrar interposed. "Nen Yim and I risk far more than this—Prophet. He is already hunted, already condemned. He has little to risk on this journey and everything to gain. I, on the other hand, am a powerful and honored priest. Not only have I consorted with *Jeedai*, but I also seek Zonama Sekot, a planet absolutely taboo to us. If Shimrra learns of this, I will be dispatched without honor."

Corran nodded. "Probably. Unless Shimrra himself planned this whole fiasco."

"I assure you, he would never do such a thing," Harrar replied.

"But I've only your word for that, and we are, you know, on opposite sides of a war." *Not too diplomatic, Corran.* He started again. "Look, you three aren't the only ones who think Zonama Sekot is important. There are already

Jedi there, negotiating with it. Your people have attacked the planet at least once. Bringing one of you there—especially one seeking peace—that was one thing. Bringing three of you is another matter."

"Contact these other *Jeedai*," the Prophet urged. "Discuss it with them. Surely they will agree that if peace is to be achieved, the initiative must come from both the *Jeedai* and the Yuuzhan Vong."

"He's right," Tahiri said.

Corran shot her a hard look. "I'd like to speak to Tahiri alone," he told the others.

"Of course," Harrar said. The others didn't say anything, but they stayed where they were as Corran escorted Tahiri to what was appeared to be some sort of common area.

"Corran—" she began, but he cut her off.

"No," he snapped. "Listen. We're outnumbered here. I can't have you disagreeing with me in front of them."

"Then maybe you should stop making decisions without consulting me. We're a team, remember?"

"And I'm by far the senior member of the team. If you want to disagree with me, fine. But do it in private. We can't have them thinking you and I are divided. And in the end, I certainly hold the power of veto, because I'm the only one who knows where Zonama Sekot is."

"Contact Kenth. See what he thinks. Or better yet, talk to Master Skywalker."

"Well, it seems Sekotan ships don't come equipped with HoloNet transceivers," Corran replied. "If they did, I would do just that."

"We could go to Mon Calamari, get a decision from the council."

Corran lowered his voice. "That's where I'm going to tell them we're going."

"But we aren't? Where are we actually going?"

"Zonama Sekot."

"What? But you said—"

"I lied. I wanted to see what their reaction would be."

"And?"

"I can't tell yet. Let's give it a few days, see what shakes out."

"That's dangerous," she said. "I'm pretty weak. If it comes to a fight . . ."

"If it comes to that, I'll deal with it," Corran said, grimly.

"What does that mean?"

"Sorry. The old man has to have some secrets. But if this goes sour, none of us will make it to Zonama Sekot. Orders from headquarters. Do you understand what I'm saying?"

"Yes," Tahiri replied. "I understand you perfectly."

"Good. Now, did you notice anything a minute ago? Any reaction I might have missed?"

"I doubt it. But I don't like the priest."

"Why?"

"Nen Yim and the Prophet are both heretics. I can't imagine a high-ranking priest cooperating with either of them."

"If a high-ranking shaper can be a heretic, why not a priest?"

"I suppose it's possible," she said. She sounded dubious.

"If you suspect him, why did you think we ought to continue the mission?"

"Because it's important. I think Nen Yim and the Prophet are on the level. We have the priest outnumbered, and I don't think he'll try anything until we reach the planet— whatever else he has planned, he wants to reach Zonama Sekot as much as the rest of us."

"Could he have some sort of tracer on him?"

"Maybe. That would be bad."

Corran considered that for a moment.

"Rest," he said. "Keep your eyes and ears open. We've got time to think about this. It's a long trip."

*   *   *

Tahiri found Nen Yim at the helm of the ship gazing out at the stars. She stood there for a moment, trying to control her feelings.

But she needed to talk to the shaper.

"Jeedai," the shaper said, without turning.

"Master Yim." She said it in Yuuzhan Vong.

"So some of our implants *did* take."

Anger flared again, but Tahiri fought it down. "Yes," she said. "I am no longer human and I am not Yuuzhan Vong. Congratulations."

"Congratulate my late master, not me."

"So you take no blame for me?"

"Blame? What blame is there? Mezhan Kwaad was a shaper. She shaped you. Had I been in charge of the project, I would feel no remorse for what you've become."

"Right," Tahiri said. "No remorse. No pain. No passion. There's nothing in you, is there, Nen Yim? Except maybe curiosity and duty."

"Duty?" Nen Yim murmured, still staring out at space. "Do you know when the last time I gazed on stars like this was?"

"Should I care?"

"It was on the worldship *Baanu Miir*, one of the older ones. Its brain was failing, and an involuntary muscle spasm ripped one of the arms open. I stood in the vacuum staring at the naked stars, and I swore that no matter what, I would save that worldship and the people on it. I practiced heresy to do so, and still I failed. Even yet, the people might have lived, if your infidel friends hadn't obliterated the new worldship we were meant to move to."

Now she did turn to Tahiri, and despite her calm tones, her eyes blazed. "I have risked my life, and I have taken life and shaped terrible things for my people so that we never have to live in the abyss between galaxies again. I have risked even more to see the secrets encoded in this universe around us and solve their riddles. Perhaps you do not call this passion. But hatred, I think, might fairly be called that. You, *Jeedai,* slew my mentor. *Jeedai* destroyed the new worldship and doomed thousands to miserable, honorless deaths. I have hated *Jeedai.*"

"And you hate them still?"

"I have stepped back from my hate. My heresy requires that I see things as they are, not as I wish them to be, not as I fear them to be. The riddle of Zonama Sekot may well be the central question of Yuuzhan Vong existence, and the *Jeedai* seem to be involved. Since I must place the good of my people before my own whimsy, I must remain open to all possibilities, even the possibility that the creed of this ridiculous Prophet has salience."

"And what about me personally?"

"You?" She shrugged. "Mezhan Kwaad sealed her own doom. She practiced her heresy too openly, almost flaunted it. Worse, she ruined a noble warrior merely because she feared he would disclose their illicit affair. That brought about her downfall. You were the instrument of her death, and that again was rooted in her failure—had her shaping of you been competent, you could never have turned on her. I hated you for a time. I find now I do not. You hardly knew what you were doing."

"Oh, yes I did," Tahiri said, recalling the crystallized fury of that moment. "I remember it very well. I could have disabled her instead of killing her. But after the pain she put me through, that you helped put me through—"

"And so you hate me?"

That's a good question, Tahiri mused. "In the Jedi view," she told the shaper, "hate is to be avoided. If there is hatred in me for you—and there may be yet—I do not want it. The Yuuzhan Vong have taken much from me—my childhood, my identity, someone I loved. But I am as much a part of you now as I am native to this galaxy. I have reconciled my different natures. Now I want to help see that reconciliation between my parent peoples."

"You seek an end to the war?"

"Of course."

Nen Yim nodded. "I do not see the same honor in pointless slaughter the warriors do, I must admit. Pursuit of it has bred stupidity. We have taken far more worlds than we need, and probably more than we can defend. Shimrra, I sometimes think, is mad." She cocked her head, and the tendrils of her headdress did an odd, squirming dance and settled in a new arrangement. "How are your wounds?"

"Better, thanks to you," Tahiri admitted.

"It was simple enough. You responded well to the antitoxin." Nen Yim shifted her gaze back to the stars. "You must convince the other *Jeedai* to go to Zonama Sekot. If what you said about your goals is true, you must help me."

"I can't," Tahiri said. "I agree with him. Even if I could trust you, and the Prophet, there is also the priest to consider. Why did he come?"

"I think his reasons are compound. He is a highly placed member of his caste. Heresy is a great danger to that caste, and here he has the opportunity to study not merely two heretics of two varieties, but also the leaders of their respective movements. He would understand his enemy. Yet he is also jealous of the secret of Zonama Sekot, and perhaps truly angry at Shimrra for concealing the knowledge of it. When we know Zonama Sekot's secrets, however, I cannot say what he will do. Turn on us as well as Shimrra, probably, and reinforce the power of his priesthood. If Zonama Sekot is truly of consequence to our future, castes will battle for control of it, both ideologically and in fact."

"All that to say you don't trust him."

"I think that no matter the outcome of this expedition, he plans our deaths."

"Then why did you bring him along?" Tahiri exploded.

"To learn what I can from him. There are other factions among our people, you know. Shimrra has detractors in other quarters—the Quorealists, for instance, who supported the predecessor he slew to attain power. It may be Harrar is one. Certainly he knows about them. Also, I want to keep him where I can see him. He is less dangerous to me that way."

"Well, we agree on that," Tahiri said. "I don't trust him, either."

"We'll keep an eye on him together, then."

It was a transparent ploy, but Tahiri felt a sudden, involuntary affinity for the shaper.

That's stupid. It's what she wants me to feel.

But they were of the same domain, and domain loyalties ran deep, far deeper than simple like or dislike. Was this why Corran didn't trust her?

Move on to something else. "Is there any way of knowing if Harrar has a tracer or villip implanted in him?"

"It would have to be a very unusual one to be a danger to us," Nen Yim replied.

"Why?"

"Because I have released a virus that attacks and swiftly kills all known variants of such organisms. If anyone on this vessel has such an implant, we can expect them to be briefly ill as the waste products flush through their system."

"I'll watch for that, then," Tahiri said, and left the helm, confused. Anger brought certainty, and with it gone, she didn't know what she felt.

Nen Yim turned her eyes back toward the stars.

Perhaps that will persuade her, she thought. *Perhaps now she can convince the older* Jeedai *to resume the voyage to Zonama Sekot.*

After all, it was true. She did not want Shimrra's minions

following her to Zonama Sekot, and she had taken measures to prevent it.

But the older Jedi was suspicious of her, of all of them. Well he should be. The Prophet's simple belief that Zonama Sekot was the salvation of the Shamed Ones and thus the Yuuzhan Vong was not her own. Zonama Sekot was the greatest single threat her people had ever faced, she was sure of it. If her investigations bore that out, she would take matters into her own hands.

Despite its organic origins, the Sekotan ship was laid out along lines more similar to the metal-and-plasteel ships Tahiri had known than to Yuuzhan Vong vessels. Behind the cockpit was a crew cabin comfortably large enough for six or seven people, and six somewhat more cramped sleeping cells. Behind that was a spacious storage area that looked more Yuuzhan Vong in design—Nen Yim had had room to spare when she took out the old hyperdrive. It was filled with things that Tahiri remembered from the shaper laboratory on Yavin 4. She looked in only once.

Whatever the original crew of the ship had eaten had been replaced by muur, a Yuuzhan Vong yeast-based staple. She and Corran settled down to a meal of it around a table that extruded from the floor, sprouting like a mushroom when a discolored place on the wall was stroked.

None of the Yuuzhan Vong seemed to be in earshot—the Prophet was nowhere to be seen, and Nen Yim was back in her makeshift laboratory, as was Harrar.

"Four days, and no one has shown any symptoms," Corran said. "Of course, that could mean several things. Either no one had implants, or the implants weren't affected by the virus, or there never was any virus."

"Well, that's what everything boils down to when you don't trust anyone," Tahiri pointed out. "We just don't know."

"You like this stuff?" Corran grunted, reluctantly taking another mouthful.

"No one likes it," Tahiri said. "Yuuzhan Vong don't eat for enjoyment. Unless it's to make a statement, you know, eating the flesh of the vua'sa you killed in ritual combat or whatever."

"Still not exactly pleasure. Relish maybe."

"Right," she said, taking another bite. She knew he was trying to make a joke, but she didn't feel like laughing. Corran was hard to read these days, as if he was making an effort not to let her see too much of him in the Force.

They both turned at a soft sound in the doorway. Harrar stood there.

"I hope I'm not intruding," the priest said.

"Not at all," Corran said. "Can I help you?"

The priest nodded. "It's been four days. May I ask when we reach Mon Calamari?"

Tahiri shot Corran a glance. *Four days,* she sent in the Force. *No sign of betrayal.*

He didn't answer in the same way, but pursed his lips and nodded. "Where's the Prophet?" he asked.

"Locked in his cabin—praying, presumably," the priest replied.

"Okay," Corran said. "Let's get everyone together. I—"

And then the ship screamed.

FOURTEEN

Qelah Kwaad abased herself before the polyp throne as the rumble of Shimrra's voice washed over her. She cringed and was ashamed.

"Rise, Adept Kwaad," Shimrra said.

Knees shaking, she did so. "Dread Lord," she said. "How can I please you?"

"You already have. The mabugat kan were of your shaping, were they not?"

"They were, Lord Shimrra," she said.

"Master Yim brought them to my attention. She said you were the brightest of her pupils."

"She did?" Qelah was surprised. She had always thought Master Yim was jealous of her.

"We have used them with great success. The infidels are now largely without long-range communications. It has been an invaluable aid to our war effort."

"Thank you, Lord. I am pleased to have been of service."

"Of course you are," Shimrra growled reproachfully, and his Shamed jester capered gleefully.

She felt like cowering back into a crouch, but the Dread Lord had bid her stand, so she stood her ground.

"The loss of Master Yim was a great blow," Shimrra went on. "But her work must continue. You will be elevated to master."

Qelah hoped her fierce exultation did not show.

"I am not worthy of the honor, Great Lord, but I will do my best to excel." She knew she was babbling, but she couldn't stop. "I have developed a new sort of ship, one that should counter many of the new strategies of the infidels. And as for the *Jeedai*—"

"What of the *Jeedai*?" The words came out with such force that her tendrils felt as if they were being swept back, but this time she was not dismayed.

"I believe I have an answer to them," she said.

"Besides the mabugat kan, I have for some time been developing a powerful new suite of bioforms designed specifically to counter the threat of the *Jeedai*. I am not far from completion."

"That has been promised before," Shimrra said. "But the promise has never been fulfilled. Those who fail me do not find favor."

She understood that lack of favor also meant lack of breath, but she plunged on. "I am certain you will be pleased, Dread Lord," she told him.

"Very well. You will ascend to master tomorrow. You will work directly beneath Ahsi Yim."

Qelah took a deep breath. She had a chance at more. Could she flinch from taking it?

No.

"Yes, Lord," she said. "A member of Nen Yim's domain."

Shimrra's mqaaq'it eyes flared a brighter red. "What could you mean by that, Qelah Kwaad? Do you imply something?"

"Nothing, Lord," she said. "I spoke out of turn."

"I hear something in your words, Qelah Kwaad," Shimrra said, dangerously. "Shall I rip open your mind and see what I find there?"

"It is only that things have been strange," she said, in a rush. "Master Yim stayed apart from us, working alone. She was totally absorbed in some new project none of the rest of us knew about. And then the *Jeedai* came, and took her away, and whatever it was, I know not what, but Ahsi Yim—" She broke off.

"Go on," Shimrra breathed.

"Ahsi Yim—did not seem surprised. And I heard her tell someone, *They took the ship.*"

In fact, Ahsi Yim had seemed as surprised as anyone, and she had said no such thing. It was actually a warrior who had told her he'd seen a strange ship fly out from the damutek. By now, everyone knew it.

"You think Ahsi Yim had some part in Nen Yim's kidnapping."

She lifted her head and spoke more boldly. "If it *was* a kidnapping, Lord Shimrra. The damutek's defenses failed. I do not see how infidels could accomplish this."

"The Shamed heretics were also involved," the Supreme Overlord pointed out.

"With respect, Lord—would they know how to disable a damutek's defenses and leave no trace of how it was done? I could not do so. Was some shaper greater than Nen Yim Shamed, that this knowledge would reside with the rabble?"

Shimrra somehow seemed to tower even higher, filling the room, the world, the universe.

"What do you know?" he thundered, and she suddenly realized she had somehow misstepped. "What do you know of the *ship*?"

A great invisible claw seemed to clamp about her head, its grip growing swiftly tighter. She felt the joints of her body twitching strangely. Her nerves turned to fire, and she sought something, anything to say, and anything that would turn his gaze away from her. If he had asked her at that moment if she was lying, she would have admitted it, admitted that her words were nothing more than thud bugs cast toward Ahsi Yim, so that Qelah Kwaad might be master shaper.

But he hadn't asked that. He'd asked about the ship.

"Nothing more than that it exists!" she moaned.

"Nen Yim told you nothing of its origins or nature?"

"Nothing, Dread Lord," she gasped, swaying. "She stayed to herself! She did not speak of it!"

The pressure suddenly dropped away. The pain recoiled itself back into her brain.

"Your ambition is clear," Shimrra murmured. "But you raise interesting points. They bear investigation." He glanced at Onimi. Then he looked off at some unseen thing above her.

"Go," he commanded. "Return tomorrow and learn your fate."

She left. When she returned the next day, she was again directed to take up her master's hand, and she never saw Ahsi Yim again.

FIFTEEN

The ship's scream was a distant thing somewhere in the back of Corran's mind. The thudding jolt of sudden hyperdrive decantation was more immediately tactile.

"What the—" He leapt up and stumbled toward the helm.

"Are we under attack?" Harrar asked.

By that time, Corran could see stars through the transparent canopy. "I don't know," he said. "But given my luck so far on this trip, I wouldn't doubt it."

"This region isn't charted," Tahiri said. "Maybe we hit a gravitic anomaly."

Corran bit back a reprimand for telling that much, but decided to take his own advice and not dress the young woman down in front of the Yuuzhan Vong. "We're in charted space," he said, instead. Which was true, barely.

"Then what could it be?"

"Dovin basal interdictor mine, maybe. The Yuuzhan Vong have them set up all along the major routes to pull ships out of hyperspace."

"Right. *Millennium Falcon* got pulled out by one on the Corellian Trade Spine."

"Yep. Let's hope we have an easier time of—oh, Sith spawn." He'd been rolling the ship to try to discover the cause of their sudden reversion. Now he saw it.

It wasn't what he was expecting.

He was staring down the pointy end of a white wedge

133

larger than many planetbound cities, and he suddenly felt much younger, not in a good way.

"That's an interdictor, all right," he said. "An Imperial interdictor."

"I suppose there's something to be said for not jumping to hasty conclusions," Harrar put in, a bit sarcastically.

"No apologies," Corran said. "It was still a good bet. This, on the other hand . . ."

"But aren't they our friends now?" Tahiri asked.

Corran snorted. "Friends? No. Allies, yes." He pushed the engines and went into a series of extemporaneous maneuvers as salvos of coherent green light flashed around them.

"Either way, should they be firing at us?"

"No, and maybe they wouldn't be if we weren't in something much more like a Yuuzhan Vong ship than anything else they've seen. Or if we could hail them and tell them who we are, but I don't see a comm in this thing, unless our shaper friend has hidden it like she did the rest of the controls. As it is, we'd better put a little distance between us and that thing."

"What's it doing way out here?"

"I'm not even sure where 'here' is," Corran grumbled, "but I've got a good idea why *they're* here."

"Why?"

"Can't say. Top secret."

Kenth might have told me a bit more about the war plans. I should have figured the push would be in this sector. Bilbringi, maybe? That Interdictor must be part of the Imperial force. But why is it alone? Watching the back door?

Didn't matter. They couldn't talk to it and they sure couldn't fight it, so their only choice was to run like crazy.

"What is wrong?" Nen Yim appeared from aft.

"We've just been yanked out of hyperspace by the Imperials." *Such a familiar thing to say,* he reflected. *Almost comfortable.*

What a ridiculous thought. Was he actually nostalgic for the war against the Empire?

"The Imperials?" Nen Yim said. "I'm no tactician, but aren't they—ah. They think this is a Yuuzhan Vong ship."

"The lady takes the hand," Corran said. A laser seared along the vessel's side, and he fought for control.

"Jump to hyperspace," Nen Yim said. "I see no nearby planets."

"I can't. It's an interdictor—it'll pull us right out again and probably fry the engines as well."

"Not necessarily," Nen Yim said.

"No, interdictors work just fine on Yuuzhan Vong hyperdrives. It's simple physics."

"Yes, but—" She suddenly stopped.

"What?" Corran shouted back over his shoulder. "I seem to remember you were going to jump from the bottom of a gravity well. But if you've got something, let me know."

"You must give me your promise of secrecy," the shaper said, her spooky hair doing particularly spooky things.

"I can't do that." Corran sighed. "Not if you've got something that can be used against us."

"I certainly cannot divulge war secrets to you without your vow of secrecy," Nen Yim said.

"Why not? Aren't we trying to end this war? Isn't that what this mission is about?"

The ship shuddered and bucked as laser fire hammered its hull.

"The war isn't over yet," the shaper reminded him.

"Master Yim," Harrar interjected. "If we die, and our mission fails—"

"What mission?" Nen Yim snapped. "He won't take us to Zonama Sekot. He's taking us to Mon Calamari, probably to be imprisoned. I would rather die here, especially if it prevents placing yet another weapon against us in their hands."

"We *are* going to Zonama Sekot," Corran shouted. "We're

on our way there right now. But it's going to be a mighty short trip if something doesn't change soon."

Nen Yim's brows lowered dangerously. "Is this true?"

Harrar gripped the shaper's arm. "I do not fear death any more than you do, Nen Yim. But if you would see this planet—"

"It is untested," she said. "A variant of a shaping one of my apprentices developed. I created it to use against any Yuuzhan Vong ships that might follow us, but now I see it might be used against one of your interdictors."

"Well, let's find out!" Corran said. "Because in about ten seconds . . ."

Nen Yim nodded and slipped on her cognition hood.

A moment later Corran felt something pass through the ship and then—release.

"What did we just do?"

Nen Yim actually smiled. "If this works, the artificial gravitic anomaly should vanish in a moment. I suggest when the moment arrives, you take us into hyperspace."

"Tahiri, lay in a microjump," Corran said.

The young woman nodded and bent to the task.

A laser tore through the cabin behind them, a direct hit that pierced both hulls. Air screamed away into vacuum, and Corran felt as if he had a hot wire through his gut. He could only imagine what a pilot truly attuned to the ship would feel.

Then the wound healed, and the air stopped getting thinner. Neat trick, that. But he wondered what the ship's healing limits were.

And got an answer, of sorts, from the ship itself. Another hit like that would be too much.

"We're no longer being held," Tahiri said.

"Life is good," Corran replied, and punched them to where the stars didn't shine.

*   *   *

"I don't suppose you're going to tell me what that thing was?" Corran asked, as his pulse began to slow to something approaching normal.

"I don't suppose so, no," Nen Yim replied. "But its field test seems to have gone quite well."

"Yes, congratulations," Corran said. *How long before you use it against us?* Well, at least he knew it existed, whatever it was, and unless she was lying it was a prototype, not likely being used at this very moment against the Galactic Alliance.

"This is making my head spin," he muttered.

"What?" Nen Yim inquired.

"Nothing."

"Not to interrupt," Harrar said, "but I'm wondering if what you said about our destination is true?"

Corran turned and noticed that the Prophet had joined them.

"Yes," he said. "It's been our destination from the very first."

"You deceived us," Nen Yim accused. "Why?"

The Prophet drew himself to his full height and crossed his arms. "To see how we would react," he said. "If we had tried to force the location of the planet from him, then he would have known we were not to be trusted, and we would never have finished the trip." He looked pointedly at Corran. "Isn't that correct, *Jeedai* Horn?"

"That about sums it up," Corran replied. "That's a pretty savvy analysis for a holy man."

"Understanding is the essence of enlightenment."

And also the basis of espionage, Corran added to himself. *I wonder what your job used to be before you were a Prophet.*

Maybe Tahiri could tell from—something. He made a mental note to ask her later.

"How far, then, are we from our destination?" Harrar asked.

"I'm not certain, because we have to proceed in small jumps for a time. Probably a few days."

The next jump brought them to the fringes of an unnamed star system. The primary appeared as a tiny blue sphere, but around it sparkled a vast ring that shone as if it were made of a few hundred trillion corusca gems. Tahiri watched in fascination. Sometimes it seemed cloudlike, sometimes almost liquid.

"You must have seen many such wonders," Nen Yim said.

Tahiri had heard the shaper's approach, but hadn't turned. "Doesn't matter," she said. "Every star system is unique. Every star system has its own beauty."

"This one certainly has. Is that ice?"

"I would imagine," Tahiri said. "I wasn't trying to figure it out—I was just enjoying the sight of it."

"Perhaps the system is poor in heavy elements. The original torus of matter condensed into ice balls, which were then torn apart by tidal forces."

"Maybe a wandering giant made it as a wedding gift for a nebula," Tahiri said.

"Why should you assert such a ridiculous explanation?" The shaper seemed truly puzzled.

"Why must you pick everything apart?" Tahiri asked. "Besides, if you believe Yun-Yuuzhan made the universe from his severed body parts, you ought to be able to believe anything."

Nen Yim was silent for a moment and Tahiri thought the conversation was probably over.

"Belief is a strange thing," the shaper said at last. "It has immense inertia. My master did not believe in the gods at all."

"And you?"

The shaper's headdress tendrils knotted thoughtfully. "Religion, I think, is metaphor, a way of relating to the universe that does not require reason. It's not very different from your appreciation of this star system for its mere appearance. My joy comes in *understanding*. You're right—if I could take the universe apart and put it back together, I would."

"And thus rob yourself of half the wonder," Tahiri said.

Nen Yim snorted disdainfully. "Wonder is you making up stories about giants and wedding gifts," she said. "Wonder is my people attributing the creation of the universe to an act of dismemberment. It is avoiding true mystery through fantasy. And if the universe refuses to conform to your fantasy, does it cease to be wonderful? That is a conceit of the highest order."

"Your own explanation was no better than a guess."

"True. But it is a guess that can be investigated and tested. It is a guess I will gladly relinquish if proven wrong. It is a guess that will serve as a tool to help me find the truth. For me, that is a far greater wonder than anything taken on faith."

"So you don't believe in the gods?" Tahiri asked.

"I think there must be something behind them that is real. I do not think they are real in the orthodox sense."

"That's interesting. What do you think they are?"

"I've no idea. I don't have even a guess to use as a starting point."

"How about this?" Tahiri mused. "Here's a guess for you. Your gods are actually a misunderstanding of the Force."

"The energy field you *Jeedai* claim informs your powers?" She sounded dubious.

"You don't believe in the Force?"

"In the sense that it's clear you draw on some sort of energy to perform your tricks, as your machines draw on a power source, yes. That does not mean it is some all-pervasive mystical energy with a will of its own, as you *Jeedai* seem to believe. Indeed, if it is, how can you explain the fact that the Yuuzhan Vong do not exist in the Force?"

"Well, that's a mystery," Tahiri said. "But the Force isn't like a battery. It's a lot bigger than that."

"So you believe. If so, perhaps your Force and our gods are *both* misunderstandings of something that somehow encompasses us all."

Tahiri felt a little chill. That was what Anakin had believed, or very near.

"You believe that?" she asked.

"Certainly not," the shaper replied. "But ... thank you."

"For what?"

"At least I have a guess to proceed from, for now." She glanced about. "Where is Corran Horn?"

"He's taking a break before the next jump to hyperspace. What did you need to see him about?"

"I don't want to raise any undue alarm, but I think something is wrong with the ship."

"Wrong?"

"Yes. The space-folding function of the dovin basals seemed erratic in the last jump. I checked them, and there may be a problem."

"What sort of problem?"

"I think they are dying."

SIXTEEN

"Bilbringi system in ten minutes," Commander Raech of *Mon Mothma* announced. "Prepare for iminent combat."

Wedge clasped his hands behind his back, didn't like the feel of it, and crossed his arms in front of him instead, staring into the nothing of hyperspace, wondering what would greet them when they decanted.

"You fought at Bilbringi before, didn't you sir?" Lieutenant Cel asked. "Against Thrawn?"

Wedge gave her a tight grin with little real humor behind it. "Are you a student of ancient history, Lieutenant?"

"No, sir—I was ten during the blockade of Coruscant. I remember it very well."

"Well, yes, Lieutenant, I did fight here at Bilbringi—as an X-wing pilot. I don't think I ever got anywhere near Thrawn."

"No, sir. You divided Thrawn's fleet by attacking the shipyards, didn't you?"

Wedge looked at her, puzzled. "Now you're just sucking up," he said. "Who would remember that?" he asked.

"They made a big deal of it on the vids," she said, a little abashed. "It was a great victory."

"It was nearly a terrible defeat," Wedge said. "We got decanted early by Imperial interdictors, too far from the shipyards. Thrawn wasn't even supposed to be there at all—we'd set it up ten different ways to make it look like we were going to hit Tangrene. But Thrawn was spooky that way. Absolutely brilliant. If he hadn't been assassinated by his own bodyguard during the battle, there's no way we would have won."

"You sound as if you admired him, sir."

"Admired him? Sure I did. He was a different sort of enemy."

"Different from the Yuuzhan Vong, you mean, sir?"

"Different from the Vong, the Emperor, any other Grand Admiral—from anyone," Wedge replied.

Cel nodded as if she knew what he meant. "What do you suppose Thrawn would make of the Yuuzhan Vong, sir?"

"Ground Vong, probably—if he had a few examples of their art."

"Yes, sir," Cel said. She paused. "I've heard good things about Admiral Pellaeon."

Wedge nodded briefly. "He was here, too. Of course, he was with Thrawn, fighting for the Empire. I'll have to ask him how he remembers that whole thing, once this is over." *It's like some weird reunion,* he thought. *Pash was here then, as well, a starfighter pilot like me.*

Now he was the general in charge of the flight group, Pash Cracken was the commander of *Memory of Ithor*, and Pellaeon was on their side.

"The best thing about Pellaeon was that he knew his limitations," Wedge said. "Don't get me wrong, he's a very good tactician and excellent at command—but when Thrawn died, he didn't kid himself that he could salvage the battle. That alone set him apart from most Imperial commanders, who more usually had inflated opinions of themselves. It's why we were able to beat them early on. The Vong are a little like that."

He said that last more to reassure the obviously nervous lieutenant than because it was the absolute truth. True, a lot of Yuuzhan Vong commanders fought on when they ought to retreat, but it was from a very different sensibility than what had motivated, say, Grand Moff Tarkin. A more dangerous sensibility.

"Yes, sir," the lieutenant said. "Let's just hope *we* don't get surprised at Bilbringi."

"Lieutenant," he said, as the reversion alarm began belling, "I can promise you that if we are, I'm absolutely never coming to this system again."

But realspace brought no surprises. They decanted exactly as planned, and in a few moments tactical displays began explaining, in their mechanical way, the situation.

Which was also pretty much what they had expected. Below them, toward Bilbringi's primary, were what had once been the Bilbringi shipyards. Some of the shipyard structures were still there, though the Golan II Battle Stations that had guarded them were conspicuously absent.

And in the asteroid belt near the shipyards, the Yuuzhan Vong had set up their own shipyards. Of course, the Yuuzhan Vong *grew* their ships, feeding them the raw materials of the asteroids.

Finally, there was a sizable flotilla assembled. He counted two interdictor cruisers—made obvious by their spicular configuration—and twelve additional capital ships ranging in size from about half to nearly twice the size of *Mon Mothma*.

His battle group was less than a third as large, but then again, he was less than a third of what was really in store for the Yuuzhan Vong at Bilbringi.

"Orders, General?" Commander Raech asked.

"Start bringing us in," Wedge said. "Pellaeon and Kre'fey are under orders not to rendezvous here until we've assessed the situation and given the clear, and pinpointed their most strategic positions. Let's do our job and make sure we don't lead them into a trap."

"Very good, sir."

The battle group began to move in.

"Sir," the officer at control informed him, "message coming in from *Memory of Ithor*. For you, sir."

"Thank you, Lieutenant, I'll take it."

A moment later, Pash Cracken's voice came over the comm. "Well, General," Pash said, "seems like old times."

"Yes, I was just thinking that, too," Wedge replied. "At least things are starting smoother this time."

"You can say that again. Boy, they've really redecorated, haven't they?"

"Yep. Maybe I'll hire them to do my place on Chandrila," Wedge quipped.

"Right. Early Vong deco. Whoops—looks like they're moving," Pash said. "I'll let you get back to the general thing. Don't forget I'm back here, okay?"

"That's not likely. Good to have you on my wing, Pash."

"Thanks, Wedge."

Wedge turned his attention back to the coming battle. The Yuuzhan Vong ships were in motion, all right, forming quickly into two groups. One was about the size of his own, and included one of the interdictors. The other, more massive group began moving away from the shipyards.

"Steady," he said. "They're still a long way away. Let's see if they do what I'm hoping—hah."

The smaller battle group vanished from sight and screen.

"Microjump, sir," Cel reported excitedly. "They're behind us now."

"Sure. They're putting us between the two interdictors so we can't leave. They've got all they need to crush us, and they know it." He studied the chart. "So we'll have Pellaeon drop in here in sector six, and Kre'fey in twelve." He looked it over one more time. Was he missing anything?

"Control," he ordered, "send those coordinates to the respective fleets." He turned to the commander. "Battle stations, but no hurry. We'll engage the smaller fleet, try to make it look like we've bitten off more than we can chew and are trying to take out the interdictor so we can run along home. Our reinforcements will be here long before the second group catches us—they won't be microjumping with those interdictors going."

The voice of control came back. "General, we seem to have a problem."

"Yes?"

"We can't seem to contact either Beta or Gamma."

"Can't seem to or can't?" Wedge asked.

"Can't, sir."

"Contact central control and have them relay the coordinates, then."

"Sir, we can't reach Mon Cal, either. Or anyplace else. It's like the entire comm network has gone down."

Wedge looked back at the shaping battle. If he didn't call the other commanders, they wouldn't show up. The battle plan was absolutely clear on that point—better to lose one battle group to some unexpected Vong tactic or invention than three. Without the other two flotillas, this could get pretty nasty, and not for the Yuuzhan Vong.

"Yes, Lieutenant," he murmured. "I think I've just about had it with Bilbringi."

SEVENTEEN

Han Solo gazed unhappily at one of the most beautiful sunsets he had ever seen.

And he had seen a *lot* of sunsets on a lot of different worlds, but as Mon Calamari's primary hit the ocean horizon and threw its shadow across the waves, the sky went as subtle and iridescent as mother-of-pearl.

Gaudy sunsets were easy to come by, especially on worlds with dense or dusty atmospheres—understated beauty was more difficult, not only because it was rare, but also because it sometimes took a lifetime to learn to appreciate it.

Which was why it was too bad he couldn't really enjoy it. The problem wasn't with the sunset—it was that he was on Mon Calamari to see it.

"We can't fight every battle in this war," Leia pointed out.

"What?" Han grumped. "*I* didn't say anything."

"You didn't have to. You've been brooding ever since Twin Suns pulled out. In fact, since Tahiri left."

"We should've gone with her," he opined.

"Which one? Jaina or Tahiri?"

"Take your pick."

Leia shook her head. "Jaina's a starfighter pilot. It's what she wants to be. It's where she sees her duty. She's been flying with the Galactic Alliance forces for months now. If we tried to horn our way into the Bilbringi push somehow, she'd—well, she wouldn't like it, to say the least. And

Tahiri—Corran can take care of her. I know he can." She crossed her arms. "But that's not it, is it?"

"Whaddya mean?"

"You're bored. Two weeks without someone trying to kill us, and you're bored out of your mind."

"I'm not *bored*," Han replied. "I just—there must be *something* we can be doing besides sitting around looking at *sunsets*."

Leia sighed and settled into one of the divans. She gave him one of *those* looks. "Nothing's happened in, oh, days that *needs* you, Han. Sure, things are happening, but they're things almost any competent pilot could deal with. But when something comes along only Han Solo can handle—"

"All right, that's enough sarcasm for one night," Han said.

It was a mistake. A glimmer of hurt appeared in her eyes. "I'm only being *slightly* sarcastic, Han," Leia said. "Maybe not at all. In war, sometimes the most important thing—and the hardest—is to just sit still."

He made a face. "You really know how to—"

She reached out and took his hand. "Stop right there," she said, "and I may show you something else I know how to . . ." She trailed off suggestively.

"I dunno," Han said. "It's an awfully nice sunset."

Leia gestured to the place next to her on the divan and raised her eyebrows.

Han shrugged. "You've seen one sunset, you've seen 'em all."

Something pinging interrupted his sleep. Han sat up and muzzily looked around for the source, finally identifying it as the comm unit in their room. Easing out of bed, he stumbled toward it and opened the channel.

"Yeah?" he mumbled. "This *has* to be good."

"I'm not sure *good* is the right word, Solo," a distorted voice said.

Han snorted. He wasn't falling for *that* again.

"Cut it out, Droma, and tell me what's up. What's the Ryn network into now?"

"I've no idea what you mean, Solo," the voice replied. "But something is definitely up."

"Look, it's late—no, it's early," Han said, rubbing his eyes with palm of his hand. "What is it?"

"The Vong have deployed something new," maybe-Droma said. "They launched them a few days ago. Some kind of unpiloted drones, we think, unless they've developed some really small pilots."

Han was wide awake now. "What kind of drones?"

"We don't know what they *do*, if that's what you mean. But it can't be good. Figured I'd give you a heads-up. You might mention it to the military, too."

"Yeah, I might," Han said. "Is that all you can tell me?"

"At this time, yes. We're trying to track one of them, but they're slippery."

"Some kind of weapon?"

"If I knew that I would tell you. But the Vong are excited about them."

"Thanks," Han said. Then more heavily: "And Droma, if this *is* you—I don't appreciate the subterfuge. I mean, security is security, but I thought the two of us—"

But he was talking to a dead comm.

"Who was that?" Leia asked, from behind him. He hadn't heard her approach, but he wasn't surprised, either.

"One of our pals in the Ryn network, I think. Maybe Droma. You heard?"

"Yes."

He reached for the comm. "I'd better pass this on."

But when he tried to call control, he got put on hold.

ALL CIRCUITS RESERVED FOR MILITARY PURPOSES.

He frowned at the device, and then started for where he'd left his trousers.

"I'm going down there," he said.

"I'm right with you."

They arrived to a tense but relatively quiet situation room. They were greeted briefly by Sien Sovv.

"The first wave is about to go in," the Sullustan said. "Under Antilles. He should be coming out of hyperspace in five minutes."

"Mind if we stay?" Han asked. "When you've got a spare minute I have something to brief you on."

"Of course you may stay. Your daughter is with Antilles, isn't she?"

"Last I heard. But that's not why I came down."

"Can it wait, then?"

"I think so," Han said.

He watched Sovv return to control, feeling itchy. He hadn't spent much time in situation rooms—he'd always been on the other end of things, mostly ignoring everything he heard from control. Sure, battle computers were great, but they didn't feel anything. They didn't have instinct to help them out.

"General Sovv!" someone shouted.

"What is it?"

"Admiral Pellaeon hasn't reported in, sir. He was supposed to alert us when he had reached position for the Bilbringi jump."

"What's the problem?"

"The HoloNet relay in that area seems to be down."

"Can you boost the signal from the next nearest?"

"I can try." The comm technician frowned and fiddled with something. "Sir, transmission coming through from HoloNet relay Delta-aught-six!"

"Put it on."

An excited voice crackled over the comm. ". . . some kind of ships, very small. They look Vong, but don't fit any of our profiles. We can't get them all. Six of them have—" Loud static replaced the voice.

Small ships? The drones his unknown caller had warned him about?

"We've just lost touch with Gamma," another communications officer reported. He punched wildly at his controls and then looked up, his face very pale. "Sir, the HoloNet's down. I can't find a live relay anywhere."

"General," Han said, "I think my news just became a lot more important."

"The HoloNet is down," General Sovv confirmed twenty standard minutes later, in a hastily convened meeting of the war council. "The cause is undetermined, though there is some evidence that it's due to a new Yuuzhan Vong weapon—some sort of drone."

"*Some* evidence?" Han interrupted. "You heard the report from Tantiss Station."

Sovv conceded that with a nod. "We assume the other stations were destroyed in the same way," he said. "Whatever the details, it seems clear that this was an extremely well-coordinated strike at the heart of our communications network. The timing is . . . suspicious."

"But not conclusive," Bel Iblis said. "They may have known we were planning to strike—they *probably* did—but not where. By taking down the entire HoloNet, they jeopardize our success whatever our target."

"I tend to agree," Sovv said. "An examination of when the relays went off-line indicates that the first to go were not those nearest Bilbringi. In fact, the process seems to have started some time ago, albeit in sectors we aren't for the most part in communication with anyway. Still, your whole point remains valid. Without the HoloNet to coordinate the other two fleets, General Antilles is very much on his own."

Jaina, Leia thought. But her daughter was still alive. She could feel that much.

"Then all that fighting we did at Esfandia was for nothing?" she said.

"We don't know if Esfandia is still up or not—all the relays linking it Coreward are gone, though. We're as cut off as the fleets."

"General Antilles is no fool," Bel Iblis said. "The other fleets have orders not to make the jump to Bilbringi without his go-ahead. When he realizes he's lost his lines of communication, he'll retreat, as per his orders."

"If he *can*," Han said. "But if they *were* expecting the attack—or even if they weren't, and they have interdictors—he'll have to fight his way out."

"Can he do that?" Leia asked.

"No," Sovv replied. "Our intelligence tells us that the Vong fleet at Bilbringi is too strong for Antilles to defeat without backup."

"And the Vong haven't lost *their* communications," Bel Iblis pointed out. "They can call for backup anytime."

"What will Pellaeon and Kre'fey do when they don't hear from Wedge?" Leia asked.

"They will hold their positions for a time, but when they're sure no communication is forthcoming—"

"Oh, it's forthcoming," Han said. "Which force is larger?"

"Beta—the Imperials."

"Where is it?" Han demanded.

"That's classified, Captain Solo," Sovv said.

"Classified?" Han sputtered. "This whole thing has already gone south, General. I say we need to salvage what we can."

"What do you propose, Solo?" Bel Iblis asked.

"We don't have the HoloNet. Hyperwave's not good enough for those distances. The only thing we have faster than light is ships, and the *Millennium Falcon* is the fastest ship there is."

"He's right," Leia said. "We need to set up a courier service, and fast. It's not just this battle, either—the Yuuzhan Vong will certainly take advantage of this blackout to strike. We could lose whole star systems without knowing about it."

"Yeah, but they are already too thin to keep the systems they have," Han said. "But our main concern right now—"

"—is the fleet," Sovv replied. "Quite right. General Solo, if you're willing, I'm putting you in charge of a courier service to the fleet. Find four other ships, military or otherwise, but people you trust. Reestablish the lines of communication between Antilles, Pellaeon, and Kre'fey. I'll also take suggestions on someone to head up a more widespread emergency information service. As it stands now, we are in a vacuum, and everything we have won is in jeopardy."

EIGHTEEN

"Well?" Corran asked Nen Yim. "What can you tell me?"

They had made four more jumps since Nen Yim had given them the assessment of the ship's living engines, and each had been rougher than the last. The vessel's pain had gone from a pinprick to an aching throb, and Corran was happy that most of the ships he flew hadn't had feelings. Sure, it handled well—when it wasn't sick.

"The deterioration is marked," Nen Yim said. "The dovin basals were damaged by the Imperial ship, and the gravitic strains of repeated jumps have worsened their condition."

"Why didn't you tell me this before the repeated jumps?" Corran asked.

"It took a few passes through darkspace before I could be certain. Also . . ." She paused, and her tendrils writhed like snakes. "Also, I think my coupling of a Yuuzhan Vong drive with a ship designed for an unliving drive may have been imperfect and contributed to the deterioration. The wound only hastened this. Each time we jump, micro gravitic anomalies appear inside or very near the dovin basals."

"Eating them from within," Corran said. "Wonderful. Can this be repaired?"

For the first time since Corran had met her, Nen Yim actually seemed apologetic. "No," she said. "Not with the resources available here. Also, it is clear that my understanding of Sekotan biology is flawed, or this would not be happening. I need more samples."

"I don't think it's biology," Tahiri said. "I think it's the Force."

They both turned to her. "Explain," Corran said.

"This ship exists in the Force," Tahiri explained. "You can feel it, can't you, Corran? And the nearer we get to Sekot—"

"The stronger the connection becomes," he agreed. "Yeah, I've felt that." It was as if the ship was eagerly returning to a long-lost family.

"So maybe this ship is rejecting the engines, because they *don't* exist in the Force, and the closer we get to Zonama Sekot, the stronger that rejection becomes."

"That seems unlikely," Nen Yim said. "The Force, whatever it may be, should not govern simple biological reactions. The links between the Sekotan ship and our engines *should* work."

"Yet they don't, and you don't know why," Tahiri said, a little too smugly for Corran's tastes. Still, he was impressed with her reasoning.

"Granted," Nen Yim reluctantly acquiesced.

Tahiri leaned against the bulkhead and crossed her arms. "Look, you said it yourself—you need a guess to start from. You've been asking why Yuuzhan Vong and Sekotan technology are so similar. Turn that around—how are they *different*? Because if Sekotan life-forms exist in the Force and Yuuzhan Vong life-forms *don't*, somewhere, somehow, there must be a *big* difference."

Nen Yim's tentacles contracted, writhed briefly, and settled against her head.

"It's a place to start," she admitted.

"That still doesn't help us now," Corran pointed out. "If we're stranded in space without any means of communication, that's going to remain speculation." He folded his arms across his chest. "Oh, and plus, we'll die."

"The engines can stand another jump, maybe two or three, if we do it soon," Nen Yim offered.

Corran sighed, looking at his charts, which were easily as speculative as the topic they were discussing. He suddenly, powerfully, missed Mirax, Valin, and Jysella, and even that nasty father-in-law of his. In fact, it was actually kind of handy, having a father-in-law who might drop in with his big red Star Destroyer to save the day.

Wasn't likely to happen this time, though.

"It's risky," he said, coming back to the moment, "but I believe I could get us to the system in one more jump, assuming there's not an uncharted black hole in our path. But if Tahiri is right, as soon as we arrive, the engines will fail, if they don't fail during the jump."

"But we'll *be* there," Tahiri said. "And even if we can't land, Master Skywalker, Jacen, and Mara can help us."

"The alternative is to stay here and wait for the dovin basals to die—or to attempt another destination," Nen Yim said.

"Well, maybe if we're going *away* from Zonama Sekot . . ." Corran began.

Nen Yim shook her head, a very human gesture. Corran wondered if she had learned the negative from being around Tahiri and him. "Even," she said, "if we accept the young *Jeedai*'s idea as a working hypothesis, it would only predict the rate of deterioration to slow if we go elsewhere. The damage already done will not heal."

"Three jumps, then, best-case scenario?"

"I don't understand that phrase, but I would expect no more than three jumps. Fewer would be better."

"Fine," Corran said. "We go ahead, then. Everybody to crash couches. This could get rough."

It got rough.

Even before reversion, something felt wrong, and the

instant they hit normal space the stars went out again as the ship somehow made an extra microjump of its own. In the jolting, Corran was reminded of a stone skipping on water, and hoped it was a poor analogy and they didn't keep on jumping.

Existence rushed back, but there were no stars—instead, enormous bands of roiling red and yellow filled their tumbling view.

Tumbling . . . and falling down a gravity well, Corran realized. They were caught in the pull of a titanic planet, at least the size of Yavin 4, probably larger. The controls and the ship's feelings told him that one of the dovin basals was completely off-line—or in shock, or dead, or whatever—which meant they weren't going to be doing any starhopping anytime soon. The other two were working, though one was fading fast.

"Come on, baby," Corran grunted, trying to get the wild spin under control and establish a stable orbit. But something was throwing everything off, and the pull was so strong . . .

There was another pull, too. The ship felt it, felt Zonama Sekot, and it wanted to go *home*.

He managed to kill the tumble and roll, which made it at least possible to get their bearings. His sensors were showing another planet, this one roughly the size of Corellia, about a hundred thousand klicks away. And there was something else, too, something in orbit around it. A moon? They were too far away to tell.

"We've got a chance," he said. "If we can get close enough to Zonama Sekot, its gravity well will have a stronger pull on us than the big planet. If the engines quit now—well, we're all going to gain some weight."

He pulled the drive levers back, and the ship throbbed in protest. The air suddenly smelled foul, like burning hair and fish oil.

"Not much more," he whispered to the ship. "But more."

The second dovin basal suddenly hummed awake—he could feel it like a heart near breaking, sending pulses of agony through everything else, but the ship suddenly surged forward. Then the heart did break, and the indicators went dark. Only one engine remained now.

"What now?" Tahiri whispered. "Did we make it?"

"I don't know yet. We're right at the break point."

"Maybe we should all go stand on the side of the ship nearest Zonama Sekot," Tahiri said.

"Funny," Corran said, and without even thinking he reached over and mussed her hair.

She jerked away as if he had attacked her.

"Sorry," he said.

"No, it's my fault," Tahiri said, going red. "It's just—" She broke off helplessly.

"The head," Nen Yim explained. "In Domain Kwaad, we do not touch the head."

Corran regarded the snakelike coils on hers. "Yes, I guess not," he said.

I have to let go, he thought. *Whatever she is, Tahiri isn't Anakin's little friend anymore.*

Of course, that happened even without Yuuzhan Vong interference. He wasn't even sure what sort of music Valin liked these days, but it probably wasn't what he remembered.

Yes, when he got back from this he was going home, for a long time.

Or, rather *if* he got back . . .

He looked at the instruments. "Oh, *yes,*" he said. "We made it." He pointed at Zonama Sekot. "We're falling that way now."

"You did it," Tahiri said.

"The ship did it," Corran replied. "Of course . . ."

"What?"

He flashed her a smile. "Of course, we are still falling,

and while the jolt at the end won't be quite as hard, it's still going to smart."

"It's always going to be something with you, isn't it?" Tahiri said. "You've got a dovin basal left."

"For how long? If we can't find Luke—"

"I'm trying," Tahiri informed him. "I've been trying since we got here. But all I can sense is that planet. It's so strong in the Force it drowns everything else out."

"I'll try, too," Corran said. "It may be our only hope. Shaper, if there's anything you can do for that last dovin basal . . ."

"I will attend to it," Nen Yim replied.

They watched the moon grow. Both Jedi continued to reach out through the Force, but if Jacen and the rest were there, Tahiri certainly couldn't sense them. It was like listening for a voice in a sandstorm.

"Perhaps it isn't the right planet," Harrar suggested.

"It *is* the planet," the Prophet averred. "The planet of prophecy. Can't you feel it?"

Harrar frowned. "I feel—" He snapped his head side to side. "No, nothing."

"This ought to be the place," Corran replied. "The ship certainly thinks it is."

He checked his long-range sensors again. Whatever was orbiting the planet had moved behind the horizon now. He wasn't sure, but the last read on it had looked suspiciously like an Imperial frigate.

Luke had been escorted by an Imperial frigate, or so Kenth had told him. If he could somehow make orbit a little lower and faster than the ship, they could eventually catch it.

And maybe get blasted out of space. Unless he could hang some sort of sign out declaring his peaceful intentions. The Imps still might shoot him down just for the fun of it.

Looking at his trajectory, he suddenly realized that he didn't even have a choice.

"Ah, Sithspit," he grumbled.

"What is it?" Tahiri asked.

"Remind me to never fly a ship that has a mind of its own, especially a homesick one," Corran said. "It's got us on a landing vector."

"That is what we want, is it not?" the Prophet asked.

"Yes, but it would be nice to land near our friends," Corran replied, "especially since I've a feeling we won't be taking off again—not in this ship."

"I suggest survival is our first priority," Yu'shaa answered.

"Point. Okay, folks, we're about to say a close hello to Zonama Sekot. I suggest you all strap back in. The slow part of this trip is over."

He hit the atmosphere too steeply, and had to apply a hard push from the dovin basal to correct. The ship winced, but did its job, and they whistled down through the upper atmosphere. He felt the skin temperature climb, and again cut the engine in, trying to stay above terminal velocity. Burning up would be no better than crashing.

Water and jungle whipped by beneath, and Corran had to agree with Harrar—it looked like any of a hundred worlds. But it *felt* different. Tahiri was right—the Force was strong here, but strange, and put up a sort of white noise he couldn't filter through. Now and then he thought he might feel Luke, but it was never more than a glimpse or a glimmer.

He had more important things to worry about. The tree-tops were coming up fast. It was time to brake for real.

He engaged the dovin basal and felt it falter almost immediately, and then kick back in. Their airspeed dropped, but not nearly quickly enough. He couldn't push the engine any harder even if he wanted to, though. He'd diverted all its ability to cancel inertia in the cabin so he could use it to fly, and the g's were already mounting to his own tolerance level, which was pretty high. He cut the angle harder, traveling closer and closer to horizontal to the ground, wishing the Sekotan craft had wings, so if the dovin basal failed entirely he would at least have a chance.

A hundred meters from the ground, he still wasn't level. Fifty, almost there . . .

They mowed a swath through treetops and the dovin basal went suddenly off-line. Unpowered, the ship was a hollow rock thrown by a giant, and without an inertial compensator they were going to be pasted all over the inside of it.

There's the unity we're looking for, he thought grimly. *Yuuzhan Vong and human, all mixed together in one nasty—*

They hit something very hard, and then, desperately, he reached out through the Force, felt Tahiri reaching out too, and then—

Then he felt Sekot, immense, powerful, and indifferent. But something happened, a connection, and they were suddenly falling like a feather—

For just a second. Then free fall returned, and instants later they came to ground, hard.

"Interesting landing, *Jeedai* Horn," Harrar remarked.

"How is everyone?" Corran turned painfully in his seat to survey his companions.

The return chorus assured him that everyone had made it through.

Everyone but the ship, that is. The glow was going out of it, and the little voice in his head was a whisper, fading.

Sorry, he sent through the Force. *But you got us here. Thank you.*

Then he felt it go.

He looked out through the viewport at a forested landscape.

"Well," he told the others, "we seem to be here. I suggest we see if the hatch will open, and find out just what we came all this way for."

PART THREE

TRANSFIGURATION

NINETEEN

"No, not again," Han snapped as the *Falcon* dropped suddenly from hyperspace. "This is really starting to get old." How many times was he going to get pulled out by Yuuzhan Vong interdictor analogs? There weren't even supposed to *be* any Vong here.

He threw the ship into a series of evasive maneuvers. "Okay, where are you scar-faced clowns?" he growled.

"It's not Yuuzhan Vong," Leia said. "Look."

He did look, and had to resist the temptation to rub his eyes. For there, silhouetted against the bright stars of the Core, was an Imperial interdictor.

He noticed the comm was buzzing for attention. "Put 'em on," Han managed.

A moment later, a terse voice filtered into the cockpit. "Unidentified vessel, this is Captain Mynar Devis of the Imperial cruiser *Wrack*. Identify yourself immediately."

"Some things don't change," Leia murmured.

"Easy, honey. I think it's kind of romantic. Takes me back. Anyway, it has to be part of Pellaeon's bunch."

He keyed to answer. "Wrack, this is *Millennium Falcon*. Looks like you're a little lost. The Imperial Remnant is about twenty parsecs from here. Do you mind telling me whose orders you're under?"

There was a gravid pause. Then the voice returned.

"Captain Solo, I presume. You're every bit as insolent as I'd heard."

"Now, listen—" Han began, but the captain cut him off.

"And it's a great pleasure to meet you." Devis suddenly sounded very young. "I thought I recognized *Millennium Falcon* from the holos, but I couldn't be positive. How can I be of service?"

"Ah—" For a rare moment, Han was speechless. "Well, nice to meet you, too," he said. Not exactly what he'd been expecting, even with the recent alliance. He had a *fan* in the Empire? "But I suppose I still need an answer to my question before we continue this little love fest."

"Of course, sir. I'm here under orders from Grand Admiral Pellaeon."

"In connection with Operation Trinity?"

"Yes. I—ah—wasn't informed you were involved, sir."

"I just got drafted. In fact, I'm on the way to meet with the Grand Admiral. What are you guys doing, watching the back door?"

"Excuse me? I—oh, I see. Yes, sir. The Grand Admiral placed interdictors on all the major routes leading to the fleet's location."

"Smart," Han said. "Someone comes along and you yank them out of hyperspace and send a warning to the fleet. Dangerous position. What happens if a whole Yuuzhan Vong flotilla jumps in here?"

"We're to delay any forces that arrive here as long as we can, then jump. Unfortunately, our mission has been impacted by some sort of trouble with the local HoloNet relay. We can't get a message through to Grand Admiral Pellaeon."

"It's not just the local relay," Han informed him. "The whole thing's going down. Some sort of new Vong weapon, we think. Communication has been lost between the fleets—that's why we're here. Have you sent any couriers?"

"Yes, Captain Solo. We had an incident not long after we

lost communication. We sent a courier to report it and receive orders."

"Incident? What sort of incident?"

"We pulled a ship out of hyperspace. We gave pursuit, but it launched some sort of weapon that disabled our forward gravity-well generator."

"Vong?"

"I don't know. What sensor readings we got made it as organic, but it didn't match any known profiles of Yuuzhan Vong ships."

"That's no surprise," Han said. "Every time you turn around, they've grown something new."

"Their escape vector didn't put it going anywhere near the fleets, but it must have reported us. The courier returned and told us to hold our position."

"That's good," Han told Leia. "That means Pellaeon hasn't pulled out of the whole thing. He's still waiting on word from Wedge."

"Which we don't have," Leia said.

"Right. To get that, we'd have to go to Bilbringi."

"Which is not what our orders were," Leia reminded him.

"True," Han said. "And I'm such a stickler for orders . . ." He opened the channel again. "Captain Devis, could you do me a favor and send another courier?"

"Yes, of course."

"Thanks. Tell the Grand Admiral we're going to see what's going on with Alpha. As soon as we know something, we'll report back directly to him."

"Yes, sir. Captain Solo?"

"Yes?"

"If Alpha is fighting without backup, things may be pretty hot there. May I send an escort with you? I could spare a few TIE defenders."

"I don't—"

"Han," Leia said. "He's right. And if we get stuck, one of the TIEs might be able to slip out with a report."

Han nodded reluctantly. "As long as they don't get in my way," he said. He opened the channel. "Thanks—the help is appreciated."

"It's easily given. I've been following your career since I was five years old, sir."

"Well, let's hope there's plenty more for you to follow," Han replied.

"I'll see to it," Devis said.

A few moments later, three TIE defenders came streaking their way.

"Hi, fellows," Han told them. "I'm sending jump coordinates. Try to keep up with us."

"We'll do our best, sir," the flight leader replied.

Han wrinkled his brow. "Devis?"

"Yes, sir?"

"Since when does the captain of an interdictor trade down for a starfighter?"

"Since interdiction duty is boring, sir. I'll sort it out with the Grand Admiral later. Easier to beg forgiveness than to ask permission, as they say."

"Okay," Han said. "Looks like the interdiction field is down. Let's go do this."

TWENTY

A shock ran through Nen Yim as she stepped onto the leaf-littered soil of Zonama Sekot. It went from her toes to the tips of her tendril headdress and left her gaping. She remembered the first time she had set foot on a real planet of stone and soil and biosphere—it had been the moon of Yavin 4, just before her elevation to adept. She had been filled with wonder, fascination, and trepidation. To appearances, Zonama Sekot was not much different from Yavin—vegetation towered in a high canopy above her, and strange sounds of insects and animals created a steady drone. And yet—yet it was different. Yavin 4 had been utterly alien to everything she had ever known, and even Yuuzhan'tar, now bioformed with plants and animals from the lost homeworld, felt *wrong*.

But this place felt *right*, as even the worldship she had grown up on never had. It was as if a piece of her had been cut off and, until it was replaced, she hadn't even known to miss it.

She realized her mouth was open and closed it. She glanced at her companions, all of whom had come out of the ruined Sekotan ship by now. Harrar and the Prophet looked stunned, as she must. The two *Jeedai* looked curious, but the planet clearly hadn't had the impact on them that it had on her. Of course, she found human faces difficult to read, despite their similarity in structure.

She tried to shake the feeling off so she could observe objectively. Could there be some sort of pollen in the air, some microbe that affected Yuuzhan Vong but not humans?

Possibly. Something that lulled the thinking mind and created feelings of belonging. Such drugs had been used on the worldships in the deeps of space to keep the population from going mad in the long dark.

"I must begin immediately," she said.

"This *is* the place," the Prophet asserted. Oddly enough, he sounded surprised. Harrar said nothing, but the look he shot the Prophet could only have been described as respect.

Suddenly annoyed, Nen Yim went back into the ship to get some of her tools. After a moment, she realized Yu'shaa was following her.

"What do you want?" she asked.

"I would like to assist you."

"I need no assistance from—" She didn't finish.

The Prophet pulled himself up before her. "A Shamed One?" he said. "Come, Nen Yim. You are a thinker, and, I think, a heretic of a sort. Can't you see past my disfigurements and understand that you and I are here for the same purpose?"

A hot, unfamiliar feeling passed through her, and her tendrils twitched in consternation.

"Very well," she said. "This ship is no longer suitable to function as a laboratory. I wish to move my apparati outside and contrive some sort of shelter. You may help with that, if you wish."

"You will not regret this, Master Yim."

She nodded, and continued toward the back of the ship. It bothered her, speaking with a Shamed One, but she knew it should not.

Corran wiped the sweat from his brow. "After this," he said, "our next priority is to find Luke." He sliced his lightsaber through the base of another sapling and added it to the pile. Nearby, Tahiri did the same.

"There. That ought to be enough for the frame."

"I don't know about you, but the planet is still interfering with my senses. How do we find Master Skywalker without the Force?" Tahiri asked. "It's a big planet. We can't just start walking and hope to run into him."

"No, but this place is supposed to be inhabited—by Ferroans, if I understand correctly, and they ought to be able to help us get in contact with the others."

"I haven't seen any signs of civilization," Tahiri said.

"Neither have I," Corran admitted. "But tomorrow I'll start looking. Just short searches, and maybe I can talk Harrar and the Prophet into going with me."

"What about me?" Tahiri asked. "What do I do?"

"I want you to keep an eye on the shaper. You know her better than I do. What I don't want is any of them left to their own devices for too long."

"Okay," Tahiri replied.

Corran slung the poles over his shoulder and started back toward the clearing near the ship where Nen Yim was depositing a variety of weird biots.

"What have you done?" Harrar asked when he saw them. His tone was dense with reproach.

"Nen Yim said she needed a shelter," Corran explained. "The ship is pretty twisted up and probably won't be very pleasant when its organic components start to deteriorate, so that means building a hut. These will furnish the frame."

"You killed living things to build a shelter? We're to stay in deadlife?"

"Unless you brought the means to grow your own, yes. I don't know about you, but I don't want to sleep in the rain. Unless you have a better idea."

"I—Consider," the priest pleaded. "We came to this place following the legends of a living planet, a planet like no other. If these legends are true, is it best we begin by killing things? What if the planet is angered?"

"I never thought I would hear a Yuuzhan Vong say anything remotely like that," Corran said. "You guys started this war by wiping out not just a few saplings but entire ecosystems. Remember Belkadan? Remember Ithor?"

"Yes," Harrar said, stonily. He seemed to want to say more, but he didn't.

Corran glanced at the saplings. "Unfortunately," he confessed, "you're right, I wasn't thinking. Which means, I suppose, we need to find some sort of natural shelter. A cave, maybe, or a rock shelter. There might be some in the high ground to the east of here. Would you care to accompany me, Harrar?"

"I would," the priest said. "And—thank you for considering my words."

"What about you, Yu'shaa?" Corran asked, hopefully.

"I'm about to go on a collecting expedition," Nen Yim said. "He will accompany me."

"That sounds neat," Tahiri said. "Can I go?"

Aces, kid, Corran thought.

The shaper shrugged noncommittally.

Tahiri shared a quick mental smile with Corran. He was amazed at how quickly she had turned a misstep into an opportunity, solving their immediate problems rather neatly. He wished she could deal with social situations as conveniently.

Nom Anor watched Nen Yim move among canelike plants, stroking them with her shaper's hand and occasionally recording cryptic entries in a portable qahsa. The Jedi brat sat on a log some distance away, pretending not to be interested, but she was watching them, nonetheless.

The shaper had been "collecting" for hours, but so far as Nom Anor could see, she hadn't collected anything. She had examined trees, shrubs, moss, fungi, and arthropods with singular intensity. She hadn't shared anything of what she was thinking, though the expressions that flitted across her usually impassive face indicated that she found much to think about.

One thing had come clear, though—Shimrra was right to fear this planet. He had seen the faces of his Yuuzhan Vong companions, knew they felt the same affinity for this world that he did. When he'd made his prophecy, he'd been mining a few scraps of intelligence and some very old—and strongly forbidden—legends. He hadn't believed it himself, of course. He'd been trying to give his followers a ray of hope in otherwise dark times. Give them something specific to fight for—a homeworld, and redemption.

Now he had to revise all of that. Zonama Sekot was real, and it seemed not at all impossible that it could be the planet of legend.

Of course, in the legends it was taboo. The legends forbade even entering the galaxy where such a planet was found. What did that mean? Had the Yuuzhan Vong battled with Zonama Sekot in the past, and lost? Had Shimrra known about the planet's presence here even before the invasion began? There had been rumors that Quoreal had balked at invading. Then Quoreal was dead, and Shimrra ascended to the throne. Had the Supreme Overlord gone against prophecy, against the gods themselves?

Or was the legend somehow wrong? Zonama Sekot certainly did not *feel* taboo.

It didn't matter. This was his moment. With his prophecy proven true, more and more Shamed Ones would flock to him. His army would grow, unstoppable, until Shimrra fell, and Nom Anor rose—

Yes. Rose to govern not the glorious Yuuzhan Vong, but a state of Shamed Ones.

Ah, well. Better than death, and better than nothing.

A gasp from Nen Yim cut short his reverie. He looked and saw her bent over yet another plant, one that consisted of long filamentlike fronds. Or perhaps it wasn't a plant, for the fronds seemed to be moving of their own accord.

"What is it?" he asked.

"A lim tree," she murmured. She looked stunned. "Or a very close relative."

Nom Anor had never heard of a lim tree. Before he could ask what one was, and why she seemed so surprised, she turned to him, her eyes nearly ferocious.

"Do you truly believe this is the planet of your prophecy?"

"Of course," Nom Anor replied. "Why else would I risk the perils involved in finding it?"

"From whence came this prophecy?" she demanded.

"From a vision I had—of this world, shining like a beacon, like a new star in the skies of Yuuzhan'tar."

"In the skies of Yuuzhan'tar?"

"That was my vision," he said. "But prophecy is not always literal. We are in the sky of Yuuzhan'tar, though at such a vast distance that even the star this planet orbits is probably unseen. I believe it meant that Zonama Sekot was here, in the stars, waiting only for us to find it and be worthy of it. And so we have."

"And you believe it will redeem the Shamed Ones?"

"Yes. But not just the Shamed Ones. Once they are redeemed, all of us are."

"But this vision," she persisted. "Where did it *come* from?"

"I do not know the true source of my visions," Nom Anor said carefully. "Only that they are always true. Perhaps the gods send them. Perhaps this planet itself sent them. What does it matter?"

"Because that is a lim tree," she said.

"I do not understand you."

"The lim tree was a plant of the homeworld. It has long

been extinct except as a code in the Qang qahsa. I grew one for myself, to adorn my apartment at Shimrra's court."

"And now you find one here. Curious."

"No, not curious, impossible."

He waited for her to explain further.

"These other things," she said, "these plants and creatures around us, they share much with our own biota at the cellular and molecular level. That is one thing I came here to confirm—the Sekotan ship might have been a fluke, a false similarity that arose from similar engineering. But this life you see all around us evolved naturally, or at least most of it did. It does not bear the mark of shaping. And though, as I said, there is reason to believe we are biologically related to all of this—no other species I have seen here corresponds on any one-to-one basis with the extinct life-forms of the homeworld."

"And yet this lim tree is one of our species."

"Yes. The differences between this tree and a lim are small enough that they must have shared a common ancestor only a few millennia ago."

"I still don't understand the significance."

She gave him an exasperated stare. "Relationship at the molecular level could be explained by a common ancestor millions or even billions of years ago. In all that time, it is not so far-fetched to believe that somehow life from our home galaxy was brought here—by a long-extinct space-faring race, or merely as spores, riding the faint push of light and currents of gravity. But something as complex and specific as a lim tree cannot be explained in that way. It indicates more recent contact between this world and our own."

"Perhaps Commander Val left one behind."

"When I accessed the Qang qahsa for my lim tree's genetic code, it had not been accessed in a thousand years. The plant is of no use to a spacefaring race."

"How do you explain it, then?"

"I can't. Perhaps there was an earlier ship—a worldship that left our galaxy long before the main fleet. Perhaps they came here—" She stopped. "No, that can only be conjecture. I need more data before I begin to talk like this."

Nom Anor smiled. "But I must say it is enjoyable to hear you talk like this. Your passion is obvious. You are a credit to our people, Nen Yim. You will find the right path for us."

That got a smile from her. "I thought that was your job."

"I had the vision, but you are the one realizing it. I am little more than a passenger on this trip."

"Your insight has been interesting, however."

"I wish I understood enough about your work to be of real aid."

"You can be, if you're willing to learn."

"I'm eager to," he said.

"Good. You carry the qahsa and record what I tell you. I'm going to collect a few live specimens of the arthropods living in that rotten log over there."

And with that, she placed a world of information into Nom Anor's hand. He stared at it, feeling he had won a victory, not quite sure what to do with it.

TWENTY-ONE

"Ah," Harrar said. "Success at last."

"Looks like it," Corran said. "So long as somebody doesn't already call it home."

They were facing up a long, rocky ridge that showed a number of pronounced overhangs. Corran tried to hide his disappointment—their search had carried them less than a kilometer from the downed ship, during which time he'd seen no signs whatsoever of civilization. Of course, it was hard to search thoroughly when you refused to take your eyes off your search partner. He was a very long way from trusting Harrar. Or any of the Yuuzhan Vong, for that matter, but especially a priest. A priestess of the deception sect had very nearly succeeded in wiping out a good portion of the Jedi.

He started up the slope, keenly aware of the man beside him, fighting reflexes that told him to draw his lightsaber *now*.

"Is your home like this?" Harrar asked.

"My home?"

"Your planet of origin."

"Oh. Not really. I mean, it's got forests and fields, but for the most part it's pretty civilized." He frowned.

"It is covered in cities?" Harrar asked.

"If you're thinking about Coruscant when you say that, no."

Harrar made a peculiar face. "For us," he said, "the world

you called Coruscant represented the ultimate abomination. A world entirely covered in machines. It is because it represented everything we despise that we chose it for our capital, to remake it in the image of our lost homeworld."

"Yes, I'm aware of that," Corran said curtly. "If you have a point to make, make it."

Harrar's eyes seemed to harden a bit. "I am searching for a point, I think," he said. "I have had little opportunity to speak with infidels when they weren't being sacrificed or tortured."

"You're not scoring big with me right now, Harrar," Corran pointed out. He let his hand drift toward his lightsaber.

Harrar cocked his head, and a grim smile played across his scarred features. "Do not think I fear you, *Jeedai*. I do not doubt that you—the slayer of Shedao Shai—could best me in combat. But you would remember the fight."

"Is that what you want?" Corran asked. "To fight me?"

"Of course not."

"Fine. Then we won't."

They had reached the rock shelter now. It looked good— dry, protected, no caves leading off to the lair of who-knew-what.

"But I would like to ask you something," the priest said, settling cross-legged upon a stone.

"Ask, then," Corran said.

"I mentioned Shedao Shai. When you dueled him, you risked your life for the planet Ithor, correct? Those were the only stakes?"

"Yes," Corran said. "The Yuuzhan Vong were going to poison the planet. Shedao Shai agreed that if I won the duel, it wouldn't happen. If he won, he got the bones of his ancestor back."

"And yet, from what I have been able to determine, Ithor

had no real strategic value, no valuable minerals for your machines. So why did you do it?"

Corran frowned, wondering where Harrar could possibly be going with this. "Three reasons," he said. "The first was that I couldn't stand aside and let Ithor be destroyed if there was something I could do about it. And there was—Shai had a vendetta against me. I was the only one around who could tempt him with such a duel with such stakes. The second reason was that I had something of a vendetta against him, as well—he murdered my friend Elegos when he tried to make peace with your people."

"That last I can understand," Harrar said. "Revenge is desirable."

"Not for a Jedi," Corran said. "It was foolish and dangerous of me to fight Shai with those feelings in my heart. If I had been fighting primarily for revenge, rather than for Ithor, it would have been wrong."

"I have heard it said that *Jeedai* avoid the strong emotions. I have never understood it. Perhaps another time you can explain it to me."

"I can try."

"Good. But for present, I don't want to lose the scent of this hunt. I still don't understand your motives. And not just yours—many of your people died defending Ithor. You fought for it from the start. Were you protecting the secret of the pollen that destroyed our troops? Surely you could have replicated it elsewhere."

"We were never actually able to replicate it," Corran said. "But no, we fought for Ithor because it was one of the most beautiful planets in the galaxy, and because the Ithorians are a peaceful people who never harmed anyone." He crossed his arms. "And because it was one of *our* planets."

"And yet you personally suffered disgrace for defending it."

Corran stiffened. "You know a lot about me," he said.

"It is a famous story," Harrar said. "Shimrra was delighted at your treatment. It was then that he began to understand that the best way to destroy the *Jeedai* was merely to turn your own people against you, something that was remarkably easy to do."

"Yes, wasn't it," Corran said. "All Tsavong Lah had to do was promise not to wipe out any more entire planets if we were handed to him for sacrifice. Some people were frightened enough to do it."

"There must be more to it than that," Harrar said. "Perhaps some are jealous of you and resent your powers. Perhaps because some *Jeedai* may abuse that power?"

Tricky, Corran thought. *He's trying to pump me for information on our weaknesses.*

"Think what you want. The reason for my disgrace after Ithor was because a lot of people hadn't quite figured *you* guys out. They didn't realize that you weren't planning to stop until every last one of us was dead or enslaved. They couldn't imagine why anyone would poison an entire planet—a planet that, as you say, had no military or commercial value—just because they could. They thought it must have been because the Jedi put up a fight and angered you. A lot of people figured that Ithor was destroyed *because* I killed Shai rather than in spite of it." He realized, suddenly, that his voice had been rising, and that he had just delivered a genuine diatribe. He hadn't realized how much bitterness lingered in him.

But this was the first time he had really discussed the matter with one of *them*.

"Here is my dilemma," Harrar said. "I do not understand how a people who placed such value on Ithor could also hold dear the abomination that was Coruscant."

Corran snorted. "And I don't understand how a people who claim to worship life would destroy a pristine planet," he replied.

"So you've said once already. But since you said it, I've been thinking about it. You may be right. There may be a contradiction there."

"*May?*" Corran studied the Yuuzhan Vong's face for signs of mockery. The near-human visage suddenly seemed more alien than ever.

"Understand," Harrar said, "all life ends. Killing is in itself no wrongdoing. Even here, in this forest, plants are eaten by animals, animals devour one another, the dead form the food for the plants. My earlier concern for the saplings you cut was that the planet might take it as an attack, since we are from outside, not because I felt it was wrong on some intrinsic level for you to cut them. In the end, every living thing dies. Planets die. But life itself should go on. Your technology threatens that—ours does not. A world like Coruscant proves that a world could exist without forests or true seas. And if the living sentients in its belly were replaced by the machines-that-mock-life you call droids, there could be completion. Machines could spread without benefit of life. They could replace it. That, my people cannot—would never—allow. We would fight until all of us were dead to prevent it, even the Shamed who now rise against us."

"But—"

Harrar raised a hand. "Please. Allow me to finish answering your question. When we destroy life—even an entire planet, as with Ithor—we replace it with new life."

"Yuuzhan Vong bioformed life."

"Yes, of course."

"So you think that makes it okay?" Corran asked.

"Yes," the priest answered.

Corran shrugged. "So if that's your view, where is the contradiction?"

"Because in my heart," Harrar said, pronouncing each

word carefully and distinctly, "I feel the destruction of Ithor was wrong."

Corran regarded the priest for a long moment, wishing the Force could help him decide if he was lying or not. Of course, before he'd learned to know the Force, natural suspicion and CorSec training had served pretty well. To those ears, Harrar sounded sincere.

"What do you want from me?" Corran asked, finally.

Harrar steepled his fingers together. "I've spoken of the contradiction in my people. I want to understand the contradiction in yours."

"Oh. That's simple—we're not really one people. There are thousands of 'peoples' in this galaxy, and often we don't have a whole lot in common. If there's one thing you can say about 'us,' it's that we're a diverse lot. There are some cultures that probably would have made Ithor like Coruscant or a wasteland like Bonadan. There are beings in this galaxy who don't value life at all, and others who worship it to the exclusion of all else. Most of us fall somewhere in between. Believe it or not, technology and 'life' really can coexist."

"That is what I'm struggling with. You believe that. My people do not. Whatever Zonama Sekot represents, whatever promise it holds for my people, I do not know that it can ever bring peace between you and me. I do not think the Yuuzhan Vong could ever make peace with machines, especially thinking ones—or the people who use them."

"That's an interesting thing to tell me," Corran said. "You mean that you and I may have to fight after all?"

"Not you and I—not unless it is by your choice. But our peoples . . ." Harrar shook his head. "I see no end to the war here."

"Well, we've only just arrived," Corran said. "Maybe there's something neither of us is seeing."

"Perhaps."

They sat in silence for a moment, Corran slipping into reverie of the battle for Ithor and the terrible thing that the Yuuzhan Vong had done to the garden of the galaxy.

What if Harrar was right? What if there was no way to make peace with the Yuuzhan Vong?

He sighed, rose, and looked around the edge of the cave until he saw what he was looking for—a slope that kept going up.

"Where are you going?" Harrar asked.

"I want to check out what's up above our happy-home-to-be," Corran said. "Don't want any nasty monsters or giant bugs coming down to eat us in the night."

"You've more experience with wild planets than I."

"Doesn't seem too wild to me, this planet," Corran said, not entirely certain what he meant.

"Well. *Natural* planets then. Nonbioformed worlds."

"I think this world *is* bioformed," Corran replied. "I think it bioformed itself."

"Then you believe the planet itself is alive, sentient, as Yu'shaa claims?"

"That's the rumor. That's what your shaper is here to find out, right?"

"Among other things. I'm not entirely certain I understand Nen Yim's interests."

Three different castes, three different agendas, Corran thought.

They reached the top of the ridge in a few moments, which gave them an excellent view of the valley below. In fact, Corran could see the wrecked Sekotan ship, which was good. If anyone came looking from the air, that's what they would spot, and they would be near should such a search come.

But not *too* near if the searchers were unfriendly.

"What is that?" Harrar asked.

Corran turned and looked the other way.

The priest wasn't pointing. He didn't have to. Rising from the forest were three gigantic identical metal vanes. They looked to be at least three hundred meters tall. They were utterly familiar, but it still took him a long moment to recognize them. When he did, he felt suddenly light-headed.

"I'm not sure," he lied.

"Perhaps we should investigate." Did Harrar sound suspicious?

"Not today," Corran said. "It'll be dark in a few hours, and we'll want to have the important stuff moved up here by then."

"Very well."

He was just delaying the inevitable, he knew. But given Harrar's little speech just now, when the Yuuzhan Vong did figure out what those vanes were, they weren't going to be very happy. Not happy at all.

He wanted a little time to prepare for that.

TWENTY-TWO

Wedge had a hurried conference via hyperwave transceiver with his commanders, and then began transmitting battle plans. Their only hope now was to do the very thing they had begun as a feint—knock out one of the interdictors. If they tried to run, the ships would just follow them.

"We'll line up for the outsystem interdictor," he said. "Spoke formation. We'll cut a fire lane and hope some of the starfighters can get there in time. Pick your squadrons, commanders."

"Wedge, do you see that?" Pash Cracken asked excitedly.

He had, and he didn't believe it. More than half the approaching insystem force was dropping away from the fight. The interdictor was still there, and a healthy force to guard it, but now the fight was suddenly more or less even.

What were the Yuuzhan Vong up to?

"Five minutes until maximum firing range, sir," Cel reported.

"Very good," he said, still staring at the monitor.

The retreating ships increased their speed and suddenly vanished into hyperspace.

"What in the space lanes—?" he wondered.

Suddenly he felt a little smile carve itself on his face, and he vented a brief laugh.

"Sir?" Cel asked.

"This worked better than we ever dreamed it would," he

explained. "They're so convinced this is a feint they've sent half their ships someplace else."

"I wonder where?"

"Who cares? The odds are almost even, now. Attack groups, lining up for an insystem run. *Ithor*, you take the outside."

The massive ships began turning their backs to the outsystem forces, which were now greater than those toward the shipyards.

"Accelerate half speed," he said.

"New estimation for maximum firing range, two minutes," Cel said.

"Thank you." The Yuuzhan Vong in the outer system seemed to be holding their ground, perhaps suspecting he wanted them to abandon the interdictor. That was fine; he didn't want a two-front battle.

He continued to study the tactical readouts, and saw something else strange. Some of the coralskippers were breaking formation, streaming toward the insystem interdictor, probably anticipating his push for it.

Then he saw that wasn't what they were doing at all. They were dropping into its artificial gravity well at steep angles.

"They're doing the Solo Slingshot!" Lieutenant Cel exclaimed.

Even as she said it, the first of the skips slingshoted around the massive spicule, whirling with terrific speed toward the Alliance battle group.

"Minimum range."

"Fire when ready. Clear a lane to the lead capital ships."

Laserfire stretched out between the two fleets, and plumes of plasma rushed to greet them. The coralskippers, meanwhile, were arcing in with unnatural speed on parabolic vectors that did not cross the fire lanes being opened. That meant the enemy starfighters were going to be in the heart of the fleet in just a few moments.

"Tell the starfighters to drop formation as needed. I don't know what they're doing, but it can't be good."

"I'm never going to let Dad forget this," Jaina grumbled. "He taught them a new trick!"

And not a bad one. The skips were screaming down into the middle fleet, and at twice their usual speed, speeds the starfighters couldn't match, with the possible exception of the A-wings. In the squadrons under her command, that meant the Scimitar Squadron.

"Is that some new sort of skip?" Alema Rar asked. "Something looks strange about them."

"Look like plain old skips to me," Jaina replied.

She watched as a clump of skips tore past Wraith Squadron, hammering them hard and zooming past them before the Wraiths could get off more than a couple of shots. And now their trajectory was bringing them into Twin Suns territory, where they were escorting *Mon Mothma*.

She did a quick calculation.

"Twin Suns, on my mark, turn to point oh-oh-seven-one and go full throttle. Scimitar Leader, we're only going to get a few shots at them as they go past. Then they're yours, if you can catch them."

"Turn our tails to the enemy?" Ijix Harona asked incredulously.

"They'll overshoot you before you reach full acceleration," Jaina explained. "Then you'll be behind them at almost matching speed."

"Copy, Twin Leader," Harona replied. "I understand. Shouldn't have asked."

"What about our tails?" Twin Two asked.

"On my mark, tendi maneuver. Three, you're the fan."

"Copy."

"Copy," Jag said. "We've got it."

Now they were building toward full acceleration, flying along the projected flight path of the fast skips. She could almost feel them coming up behind. Three, two—

"Go!" she said.

Three cut his jets and flipped around, firing. Since she and Two were still under acceleration, he was quickly positioned as a shield between them and the approaching skips. After the skips got past him, they had time for a single quick shot at Jaina and her wingmate. She, on the other hand, had built up speed approaching two-thirds that of the skips, so she had the leisure for quite a few shots at them once they were past her and before they were out of range.

She got one in her sights and used a proton torpedo while it still made sense, then needled it with laserfire until the torp got there and blew it into molten slag.

Jaina narrowed her eyes. There *was* something strange. The vessel she had just destroyed looked like every other she had ever put her sights on—except that something was trailing behind it.

"Twin One," Rar asked, "did you see what that was attached to it?" Her tone very much said, "I told you so."

"Don't know," Jaina replied. "I didn't really see it until the detonation. Looked like a tail."

"Skips don't usually have tails," Rar responded.

"It might have been a cofferdam."

"Mine's got one, too," Jag said. "I thought I saw something bleeding out of it."

Stifling an uneasy feeling, Jaina used lasers as the skips pulled ahead, and nailed one right through the dovin basal. In the flare she saw that this one had a tail as well. Or a big sack of some sort, now empty.

Several more skips flared as they approached the A-wings. Now the skips had a choice. They could either retain their speed, but end up with A-wings on their tails, or they could—

"They're slowing down," Jag said.

"Yep. Scimitars, break off. You don't want them behind you now. Come back to the party."

"Copy, Sticks," Harona confirmed.

The A-wings peeled out of formation and scattered. Jaina dropped in behind a skip and started firing, lasers only. The skip juked and jinked, its dovin-basal-generated voids absorbing her shots. So intent was she on getting the skip firmly in her sights that she almost didn't see the thing in time. Her reflexes did, though, yanking at the stick as what she thought was a half-meter-wide chunk of rock was about to smash through her cockpit. She rolled, and it scraped centimeters from her screen.

It kicked as it went by.

Cursing silently, she chinned her microphone. "Be advised, *Mon Mothma* control. The skips are dropping grutchins."

Grutchins were insectlike creatures the Yuuzhan Vong had developed that could survive for a time in vacuum. Their mandibles secreted a solvent that could cut through hull metal.

"That explains the suicide runs," Jag said. "There must be grutchins everywhere, and the fleets haven't even engaged. They're probably going for the Star Destroyers."

"Advised," the voice of control said.

Jaina, meanwhile, had flown straight into one of the release trails. She kept up a steady stream of laserfire, blazing any of the bugs that got in front of her. The remaining skips suddenly broke formation, curving up from her operational horizon.

Something thumped against her hull, and Cappie, her astromech, reported a grutchin on the hull. Snarling, Jaina pulled the stick, hard, and pushed the drive to maximum, then rolled like crazy, trying to detach it before it could start making a meal of her starfighter.

Why couldn't the Yuuzhan Vong use normal weapons? Concussion missiles, lasers. Why did it always have to be miniature volcanoes and giant bugs?

To her satisfaction, her particular bug-nemesis of the moment lost its grip and fried on the way through her ion trail.

In the meantime, of course, one of the skips had taken the opportunity to latch onto her tail, so now it was volcano time . . .

"We've got close to two hundred grutchins on the hull, sir," Cel informed him.

"Electrify it," Wedge said.

"They've already tried, sir. It's not working."

"Not working—great." Yes, the Yuuzhan Vong were adapting. Not good.

"Seal off the outer sections and get people in vac suits with blasters in there."

Of course, that wouldn't stop them in the engine areas.

The Yuuzhan Vong capital ships had drawn up in a defensive formation and were no longer pushing forward. Wedge had his ships nearly stationary as well, and both sides were keeping their starfighters close, the grutchin carriers aside. For the moment, it was a long-range game. That would probably change soon—the Yuuzhan Vong were waiting to see how well their grutchin stunt had worked. When they knew, they would renew their attack.

That meant his starfighters would be free for a short time.

"Have some starfighters make close runs on our capital ships," he told control.

"Sir, with all due respect, the grutchins are attached to us. Some of the pilots are bound to miss, and they could easily do as much damage as the bugs."

"I don't want them firing. I want them to singe the things off with their exhaust."

The officer's eyes widened. "That will take some pretty precise flying."

"Then pick the squadrons well. And fast, because soon we'll need them against skips."

"I have him, Twin Leader," Jag said. Even as he did so, glowing chunks of yorik coral bloomed out into the void.

Jaina breathed a sigh of relief. That pretty much did it for the fast-skip wave.

"Thanks, Four." She glanced down at the new battle orders scrolling.

"Uh, guys," she said. "You aren't going to believe this, but . . ."

TWENTY-THREE

Nen Yim glanced at Yu'shaa. He'd been working quietly on the task she had given him, entering the genetic sequences of various flora and fauna into her qahsa. Now he seemed to be having trouble.

"What is it?" she asked.

"It ceased granting me admittance," he said. Somewhere in the distance, something mewled, and another something chattered a response. The sky was clear and the air still.

"Did you try to access data forbidden to you?" Nen Yim asked.

"Not too my knowledge, Master Yim. I was merely attempting to enter the freman signatures you asked me to."

"Pheromone," Nen Yim corrected. "It may be my security prohibitions were too broad. Let me see it."

He handed her the bulbous living memory in compliance.

"No," she said. "Because it is not keyed to you, after a time it rejects your entry." She examined a bit further. She could reset his temporary access, but would only be forced to perform the same task again in a few hours.

She could key him to the qahsa, but she hesitated to do so. She had stored the protocol data on Sekotan biology in it. In the wrong hands—

But the Prophet had proved himself useful, and only someone well versed in the shaper's arts could understand what they found there, much less use it. By the pattern of his rejected implants, she gathered that before being Shamed, Yu'shaa had been an intendant.

Time was of the essence. With Yu'shaa performing the simple tasks, she was making great progress with the more complex analyses. "Come here," she said. "I will make you familiar to it."

That done, she was able to work for a time in peace.

Until Harrar came, standing rather imperiously waiting for her attention. She reluctantly gave it to him. If he knew anything about shaping—and he certainly did—then he already knew she was a heretic. If she was to do her work, there was no hiding it any longer.

"Yes?" she said.

He gave her an uncomfortable little bow of recognition. "I was wondering where your researches were leading you," he asked. "Whether you've come to any new conclusions."

Always that question. What did he think conclusions were, fruit to be pulled from a tree? "It's premature to say anything definitive," she said.

"I understand that," he replied softly. "But I'm hoping you will keep me apprised of new developments."

She could tell this approach pained him a bit. Harrar was used to giving orders, not cajoling. After all, short of Shimrra, the priests were the voice of the gods.

"There have been a few developments," she allowed, "though they are at the level of data rather than conclusion."

"Go on, please. Anything new must be worth hearing."

"But the telling costs me time, when I might be reaching those conclusions you desire."

Harrar's expression flattened. "*Jeedai* Horn tells me it may be a long while before anyone finds us. I shouldn't think the hurry is so great you can't spare a few words concerning your progress. After all, I did arrange this trip."

"Yes, I've been meaning to ask you something about that," Nen Yim said.

"Perhaps if I answer your questions, you can answer mine," the priest said.

Nen Yim leaned away from her work, forcing her tendrils to relax into a neutral posture.

"When we first met, you said that you could not arrange my escape yourself, for fear of being noticed."

"That is true. An escape engineered by me would have failed."

"Yet here you are; you came along. Won't that be noticed?"

Harrar seemed suddenly to relax, as if he had expected another question, a more difficult one.

"I am believed to be on the Outer Rim, meditating over our conquest where it began. A subordinate of mine took my ship there. I should not be missed. You arranged to make your abduction appear as a kidnapping as well, yes? We have both covered our trails."

"I give my deception only a small chance for success," Nen Yim replied. "When I return to Yuuzhan Vong space, I fully expect I will be executed."

"And yet you plan to return."

"Of course. Our people must know what has been discovered here."

"What Ekh'm Val discovered has been quite effectively repressed," Harrar pointed out. "What makes you think your discoveries will fare any better?"

"I will find a way," Nen Yim assured him.

Harrar crossed his arms and looked at her with approval. "You mean what you say. You see no personal gain in this at all. I believe you may be one of the most admirable people I have ever known."

"Please do not mock me."

"I do not mock you," he said, his voice suddenly a bit angry. "I am trying to express respect. If you reject it, the respect remains all the same. Each caste seeks to elevate itself over another, each domain competes with the others, individuals betray and murder one another in a blind, groping desire for elevation. In the galactic deeps, it nearly tore us apart. I hoped when we had a real enemy to face, we could turn that aggression outward, and so we did, but now it comes to haunt us again. It has become more than a habit; it has become how we live."

"Are we not taught that competition breeds for strength?" Nen Yim asked.

"Of course," Harrar answered. "But only to a point, if there is not also cooperation."

Nen Yim twisted her tendrils into an ironic mode. "And there is the lesson of Zonama Sekot," she said. "The lesson you and I both seem to agree our people must learn."

Harrar relaxed again.

"Take a seat," Nen Yim said. "I will explain what I see here as best I can."

Harrar settled into his usual cross-legged position and waited.

"The diversity of species here is quite low," she began. "Much lower than one would expect in a natural ecosystem."

"What could cause such a thing?" Harrar asked.

"Mass extinction, for one. Some catastrophe or series of catastrophes that served to wipe out many of the species."

"That's an interesting fact, but—"

"No, it's more than an interesting fact," she averred. "The ecosystem *functions* as if it were fully diverse. Species have filled roles they were not designed for."

"I'm not sure I entirely understand."

"After any mass extinction, many ecological niches are opened, and species take advantage of these empty niches, adapting through natural selection to fill them and benefit from them. Eventually, after millennia, a ravaged ecosystem becomes healthy again, and as diverse as the one that was impacted."

"Isn't that what you said is occurring here?" Harrar asked.

"No. Not at all. For one thing, the extinctions here are very recent. There hasn't been enough time for the sort of adaptation I speak of to take place. For another, species here are not adapting to fill ecological niches—they remain adapted to their own niches, the ones they evolved to fill, and yet they also perform the environmental tasks of extinct species—for no benefit to themselves."

She waited a moment to let him absorb that, enjoying the sudden breeze and the smell it brought, a sort of dusty golden scent.

"Perhaps an example will help," she began again, "There is, for instance, a plant with a kind of tubular blossom. The only possible way for it to reproduce is for an arthropod or other small creature to enter the tube of one plant, and then enter that of another, carrying with it the sticky secretions of the first. The plant entices this insect with an edible fluid, nourishing to the insect—and, I suspect from certain clues, important to that insect's life cycle."

"That makes sense," Harrar said.

"Yes, except that I can find no insect that feeds on the fluid. Yet I have seen them pollinated, by another insect whose primary role in the ecosystem is feeding on carrion. Its life cycle, from egg to nymph to adult revolves entirely around carrion. Yet they make time to enter these flower tubes with enough frequency to pollinate them, at no benefit to themselves."

"Perhaps you have not yet discovered the benefit."

"If this were the only example of such behavior, I might agree with you. However, I find more than half the animals I have examined play roles in this life-web that are plainly unrelated to their life cycles and physical design. More interesting yet, I have discovered that each species practices some form of reproduction control. When a particular sort of moss becomes scarce due to its consumption by a kind of beetle, the beetles begin disposing of their eggs without fertilizing them. In other words, the ecosystem of this planet is homeostatic—it seeks to remain in absolute balance. It manages to do so even after enormous extinction events."

"That sounds reasonable."

"For a worldship, yes, because each life-form is engineered to play a certain role and the system is guided by intelligence—by a rikyam at one level, and by shapers at the next. Mutations are eliminated, as is undesirable behavior. But in the natural ecosystems I've studied from data collected in this galaxy, that's not how things normally work. Each individual organism fights to maximize the number and survivability of its *own* offspring. Mutations come along that have advantages and are perpetuated. Such systems are in a constant state of flux; they are not—cooperative. The evidence is that this world was once like that—like a wild planet—but it is no longer."

Harrar pursed his lips. "You're saying that this planet has something like a dhuryam, some intelligence that links all these organisms together and prompts them to perform harmoniously."

"I can think of no other explanation."

Yu'shaa, who had remained absolutely silent, suddenly spoke up. "As I prophesied," he said, "and as the *Jeedai* said. This is a living planet, one large organism, more than the sum of its parts. Like a worldship that made itself. Don't you see what this planet can teach us? Harrar, you were just decrying the competition that destroys us. It is that blind fight to ascend that leads us to treat so many of our people as Shamed."

"Can this be?" Harrar asked Nen Yim. He seemed to be ignoring the Prophet.

"We are seeing it," Nen Yim replied. "However, I can find no clues as to the mechanism that binds the individual life-forms to one another. There are no chemical exchanges that might explain it. The flora and fauna here are not equipped with communications organs like our villip, or anything even remotely similar."

"It's the Force," Tahiri interrupted. "I can feel the ties, feel a sort of constant chatter among—well, everything."

Nen Yim focused on the young Jedi. "I have heard that you *Jeedai* possess telepathy like our villips," she said. "But the ones I've taken ap—examined showed no signs of specialized organs, either."

"No, of course not," Tahiri said, her voice suddenly dark. "The Force binds everything together. Some creatures communicate through it. I can feel what Corran is thinking, sometimes. With Anakin it was even stronger, like . . ." She trailed off. "Never mind. You'll have to take my word for it."

"And—using this Force—you can impress your will upon others, yes?" Yu'shaa said.

"Yes, on the weak-minded," Tahiri replied. "But I get no sense that anything here on Zonama Sekot is being coerced into anything. It's like every living thing just *agrees* to do things this way."

"I cannot see this Force, measure it, or test it," Nen Yim said. "I cannot credit it with the effect you assert."

A stone suddenly rose from the ground, floated toward Nen Yim, and fell near her feet.

"You may not know what it is," Tahiri said, "you might not be able to see it or feel it, but you can see the results."

Nen Yim conceded that with a small nod. Then a thought struck her with the force of a baton. "Assuming you are correct," she said, "*you* are connected to this Force—as no Yuuzhan Vong is. And yet, in part, you *are* Yuuzhan Vong. What does your Force tell you this place is? To us?"

"I've been thinking about that a lot," the young woman

replied. "I've never been able to quite put it into words until just now."

"And?" Harrar asked.

Tahiri took a deep breath. "This is where we are from," she replied.

That got even Nom Anor's attention. While the three were absorbed in the conversation, he'd been exploring Nen Yim's qahsa, and had run across some very interesting things. He'd made his little speech so as not to break character, not because he was interested. But now he stared at the young Jedi just as Harrar and Nen Yim did.

"That's not possible," Nen Yim said.

"You asked me what I felt," the girl said. "That's it. But didn't you say that only a few thousand years at most separate the life of this planet from Yuuzhan Vong life?"

"In the case of one plant only," Nen Yim replied. "And several thousand years ago we were very far from here. Moreover, the Qang qahsa contains abundant data regarding the homeworld, and this is not it."

"Was the homeworld like this one? Living, like an organism?"

"There are some legends—" Harrar began.

"Whatever the legends may say," Nen Yim pronounced, "the *facts* are that the homeworld was an ecosystem of unchecked competition and predation. Would a creature like the vua'sa have evolved on a world were all of nature was in cooperation? No. The vua'sa was a vicious predator that at times multiplied so quickly, it left deserts behind it. This competition among ourselves you speak of is the *legacy* of the homeworld."

"But perhaps that was after we lost the grace of the gods," Harrar said.

Nen Yim blinked at him, and Nom Anor saw what he

was certain was barely concealed disgust in the shaper's expression.

"In any event," the shaper said, apparently dismissing Harrar's suggestion, "this conversation will not bear the fruit that further work will. We speak of things we do not have the data to support."

"You asked the question," Tahiri said.

"Yes, and now I'm sorry that I did. If you will all please allow me to go back to my work . . ."

Nom Anor expected Harrar to snap back, but instead the priest nodded and looked thoughtful.

What in the world was going on here? Were they actually starting to believe his prophecy? Was he?

No, because he knew the source, and the source was a lie. Yes, the planet was a curiosity, but many planets in this galaxy were curiosities. And everything the others saw here was informed by his crèche-tale of a planet of redemption. That filter was causing them to see things in a very strange light.

Would they turn against Shimrra? They might. If Harrar did, he might be able to muster a great deal of support from the priesthood, and with this shaper . . .

But no. If Harrar turned against Shimrra, it would be to put not the Prophet of the Shamed Ones on the polyp throne, but himself. And he was in a better position to do it than Yu'shaa.

Especially if Yu'shaa never left Zonama Sekot.

And there was also the chance that Harrar already knew Nom Anor's true identity. He had caught more than one suspicious look from the priest.

"Yu'shaa?" Nen Yim said. "What are you doing?"

"I am sorry, Master," he said. "It is just that today's revelations—I must ponder them."

"You've been of enough help today," Nen Yim told him. "In fact, I would rather be alone for a time."

"In that case, I will meditate in the splendor of this world."

He left the clearing and began wandering vaguely uphill.

There were other things to consider. From what he had seen in her qahsa, Nen Yim had come here in fear of Zonama Sekot, prepared to destroy it if necessary. She had protocols that might be useful in that, though they were obviously untried. They were in the shorthand and symbolism of the shapers, so she probably thought he couldn't understand them.

What she didn't know was that he had done quite a bit of shaping himself. As she was no ordinary shaper, he was no ordinary executor. He was certain he could understand and use the information if he had to. Though why he would want to destroy the planet, he couldn't say, except that it would please Shimrra.

That stopped him in his tracks.

It would please Shimrra a lot.

If into that bargain was included the deaths of Corran Horn, who had so embarrassed the Yuuzhan Vong at Ithor, and Tahiri Veila, who had used her dual nature to betray them more than once, and a rogue priest and master shaper even now plotting against not only Shimrra but the very nature of everything Yuuzhan Vong . . .

Shimrra might be so pleased he wouldn't have the one who delivered him these things executed, no matter what he was wanted for. So pleased that such a one might actually be elevated to a higher station than he had held before his disgrace.

Musing on that, he continued up the hill. Harrar had mentioned something strange on the horizon.

He stopped when he reached the summit, staring at the enormous made-objects climbing into the sky, and was suddenly shaken to his very core.

Harrar had not spent enough time with the infidels, un-like Nom Anor, who had flown on their lifeless ships and lived in their lifeless stations. Harrar would naturally not understand what he was seeing.

But Nom Anor knew hyperdrive field guides when he saw them, even if they were a thousand times larger than they should be.

But then, they would have to be, to move a planet.

Something clicked into place for Nom Anor. He sat on a stone, listening to the sounds of the strange world for a moment. He was alone, for the first time since they had crashed. With a sigh, he released his face from the grotesque masquer that hid it. His contention that it was difficult to remove had been, of course, a lie.

He reached into the living pouch beneath his arm and re-moved the thing he had brought with him. He must have known, somehow, in the back of his mind, that it must al-ways come to this.

He stared at it, turning it over in his hands. It was a dedi-cated villip, linked to one other, far away. He had not used it in a very long time, since before the disaster that had led to his exile.

He stroked it to life.

After a moment, the face of an intendant appeared on its surface, one of his former subordinates.

Even through the medium of the villip, Nom Anor could see the surprise.

"You were assumed dead," the man said.

"I greet you as well, Phaa Anor," he told his crèche cousin.

"You might as well be dead," Phaa Anor told him. "Shimrra has called for your skin. I will have to report this conversation, of course."

"Of course. I want you to. In fact, I want you to see that your villip comes before Shimrra himself."

"Before Shimrra?" Phaa sounded incredulous.

"Yes. Send him the message that you have heard from me. Tell him I am on Zonama Sekot, and that I have found his missing shaper. He will listen to you then. When you gain an audience, present him with your villip."

"Why should I do this for you?" Phaa asked.

"Consider. I have information so important that I believe I can redeem myself in the Supreme Overlord's eyes. Not only that, I believe I will be elevated for my efforts. Do you not think you will benefit as well, he who brings these tidings?"

Phaa Anor seemed to consider that for a moment.

"I will do it," he said at last.

"Do it quickly, and tell no one anything I have said save those whom you must convince to grant you an audience with Shimrra."

"Yes, yes," Phaa replied. Then the villip returned to its natural state.

He had probably just doomed Phaa Anor, he knew. Shimrra would have him killed simply for knowing the planet existed and was in this galaxy.

Sacrifices had to be made, however, for the good of all. And for the good of Nom Anor.

He sealed the villip back into dormancy and its airtight container, returned it to its resting place beneath his arm, and went back down the hill.

TWENTY-FOUR

Jaina throttled down and made another run on *Mon Mothma*, dropping to within a meter of the Star Destroyer's skin. Suddenly she seemed to be skimming above a vast, white, slightly curving plane. An irregular dark lump appeared ahead, and she angled toward it. At the last instant she hit her repulsors and nosed up, washing her exhaust over the grutchin, which released its hold. Its charred body drifted off to join the other twenty or so she had flashed.

"This is actually kind of fun," she said. She would have to ask Uncle Luke if going after womp rats was anything like this.

"Speak for yourself," Twin Two said. "I just banged a stabilizer."

"Just watch yourself. If you plow into the hull, you'll do more damage than any grutchin."

"Don't make me weepy with your concern for my welfare," Two replied.

"Hey, I've got a big heart . . . Okay, I think we're almost through here."

"Just in time for the *real* fun," Rar said.

"I see that."

The big ships were closing again, and space was alive with light as they pummeled each other. And now the rest of the skips were arriving, not coming in as fast as the advance guard, but twice as hot. Jaina checked the new orders.

"All right," she said. "Let's vape some skips."

* * *

"They really don't want us to get away," Wedge muttered. He'd thought about making a hard push for one of the interdictors so they could clear out, but the Yuuzhan Vong were keeping them far away and under heavy watch. That was good, in a way—it gave him near parity in the actual combat. Even though they had ships behind him, they weren't using them for anything but to prevent him running that way. Nor did they have enough ships to try an encirclement.

Still, slugging things out nose to nose was an iffy proposition when numbers were this even. He hadn't come here for a fair fight—the Alliance couldn't *grow* new ships like the Yuuzhan Vong could.

But a run for one of the interdictors would be suicide at this point.

"Sir," Lieutenant Cel said. "I think I've found one of the Golans."

Wedge raised his eyebrows in surprise. He'd asked her to hunt for any of the battle stations the Empire had once stationed here—or anything else that was operational—but he hadn't really expected her to find anything. The shipyards were virtually gone, food for a growing Yuuzhan Vong fleet, and the stations had all been around the shipyards.

"Where is it?"

"Way off its orbit, if it's one of the ones we had on the charts. And its present orbit is eccentric."

Wedge glanced at the display. "That *is* out there," he said. "It may have been drifting all this time, or maybe the shipyards put it there for some reason. Still, it's odd the Vong missed something that size."

"I don't know, but we missed it on the first pass, too. As you said, sir, it's way out there."

"Is the power core still active?"

"Yes, sir."

"Then it might still have guns. We'd better check it out—we might need it."

"Are we taking the fight out there, sir?"

"Not unless I know it's working. Are the Twin Suns done with their clean-up duty?" he asked.

"Yes, sir. They're on their way to cruiser-designate *Olemp*."

"Get me Colonel Solo."

"Yes, sir."

Jaina's comm chirped. Much to her surprise, it was General Antilles, on a closed and heavily coded channel.

"Sir?"

"I've got a task you might find a little more exciting than bug burning," Wedge said.

"I'm about to have my hands full, General. What do you need?"

"I need you to find Admiral Kre'fey for me."

"Admiral Kre'fey, General?" What was Wedge talking about?

"Something's wrong with the HoloNet," he explained. "We were the advance for two more fleets. We can't contact them, so they haven't shown. I need you to find him, fast, and bring him here. Have *him* send someone to find Pellaeon."

"Sir, won't they come when they realize it's the HoloNet and not something gone wrong here?" Jaina asked.

"They're not supposed to. For all they know—for all *I* know—the downing of the HoloNet is cover for an attack on Mon Cal or the Imps, and this battle group is already starfood. I need you to let him know we're still kicking."

"General, you want me to leave the battle?" What was her squadron turning into, an odd-job unit? There was real fighting to do.

"A few starfighters can get out of the interdiction cones. Our capital ships can't. Still, I doubt they're going to make it easy for you, so I wouldn't worry about lack of action. Anyway, there's another part to this deal, if you really don't fancy leaving the Bilbringi system. Our long-range sensors indicate that one of the Golan Two Battle Stations may still be operational. If things go badly here, we might be able to use it as a rally point, but I need it working. If it's not, and can't be made to, I need to know that as well. Send one of your flights to find Kre'fey and secure the station with the other two."

"Yes, sir."

"We're all counting on you, Colonel."

Are you sure you aren't just trying to get me out of the action? she wondered. The numbers looked pretty even to her, since the mass jump a few minutes before. What was Wedge so worried about?

That wasn't her concern, she decided. She had her orders. It wasn't the first time she hadn't liked them; it wouldn't be the last.

She changed frequencies. "Twins, we just got new orders. Scimitars, you're on your own. Good luck."

"Copy, Twin One."

"Twins, follow my lead." She led the squadron straight up from the plane of the ecliptic and then made a hard break for open space.

"We're running, Colonel?" Jag asked, the surprise more than evident in his usually reserved voice.

"Not exactly," she said, though it felt that way.

"We've got a head start," Eight reported. "We've got pursuers, but they're pretty far behind."

He should have sent Scimitar, she thought. *A-wings are faster.*

"They'll catch up, Eight," she said. "Before they do, I want some distance from the fleets. We're splitting up. Jag, as soon as we're out of range of that interdictor, you're taking

Five and Six to the coordinates I'm sending you. We'll cover you until you've made the jump."

"Jump, Colonel?"

"Yes. I don't know how secure this channel is, and I'm sure somebody's paying a lot of attention to us just now. Make the jump and contact your superior there. Tell him it's all go. Do you understand?"

"Copy. What about you?"

"We've got another job to do."

"Understood," Jag said.

They were nearly clear to jump when the first of the skips closed to firing distance.

"Okay," she said. "Let's give them the distance to jump. Good luck, Four."

"Copy." Jag didn't sound happy. She sighed and switched to a private channel.

"Jag, I need someone I can rely on, someone with command experience. Can you do this, or not?"

"I don't like it. I don't like leaving you behind."

"Then go do your job and hurry back, okay?"

"Yes, Colonel."

Plasma bursts started whipping past her. "No more time to talk," she said. "Go."

She rolled to port and came around. Two skips were following close on Three. She dropped in behind one and started firing, meanwhile jinking to confuse her own pursuer. She hit one of her targets with a torp and flew straight into the expanding mass of plasma and coral. When she couldn't see anything, she pulled on the stick, arcing up and back—

And dropped in behind her tail. Grimly she got him in her sights. She slipped a few shots through his void defenses, but apparently none hit anything important, because he continued on after Jag and his wingmates, firing constantly.

She had picked up two more on her tail, and her wingmates were busy elsewhere. The X-wing rocked as its shields took a heavy hit, and for a moment she lost the skip in her sights. Cappie squealed.

The skip was going to catch Jag before he jumped.

She fired her last torpedo and escorted it in with stutterfire. A void appeared and the torp exploded before being sucked in, as it was programmed to do. Her laserfire riddled the skip, which erupted into an expanding ring of ions.

Two more were coming up from the side. She wasn't going to be able to hold them all back.

Then Jag and his wing were gone.

Take care, Jag, she thought.

She cut hard starboard and under horizon, now more concerned about the skips behind her than any in front. She nearly ran into one she hadn't seen. He was right in her sights, and she let him have it. The skip didn't explode, but it rolled off, obviously injured.

"I've got you, Twin Leader," Eight said.

Two explosions behind her, and she was suddenly clear again. The odds were starting to even.

"Form up," she said. "We have to stay together, or they'll pick us off." Nine, in particular, was a long way from the fight. "Nine, that means you, too."

"Sorry, Colonel. Can't do anything about it. I've lost an engine and my stabilizers are shot."

"Hang on, then, we're coming for you."

But it was only a few seconds later when his X-wing flashed out, struck by fire from three coralskippers.

She watched, feeling hollow and numb. Then she shook it off—they were even more outnumbered now than before, and she realized Wedge had been right. She saw on the long-range scanners that even more skips were coming her way, these slingshotting around the interdictor.

We'll be lucky if any of us survives.

She no longer felt so bad about leaving the main battle.

She could see the Golan now. It was still a long way away, near the edge of Bilbringi's wide asteroid belt.

"Let's take 'em through the rocks, people."

Moments later, they were dodging asteroids from the size of pebbles to genuine monsters. They forged in deep, and slingshotted skips changed course to follow. Most had the common sense to slow down when they saw where they were going. A few didn't, and Jaina had the satisfaction of seeing them pulverized against oversized rocks. Strangely, Jaina began to relax—this was what Twin Suns did best, fighter-to-fighter combat in dodgy circumstances. The yammosks handling the big fight had clearly cut these fellows loose to battle on their own. Bad for them.

Another advantage was that X-wing shields repelled the small asteroids. Yuuzhan Vong voids actually attracted them. It wasn't a huge problem for the Yuuzhan Vong, because any space rock small enough to be attracted by the pinpoint singularities could also be eaten, but if they hit a big one, the singularities sometimes stuck them to it. So the Twins flew tight, dodging in and out, letting the skips eliminate themselves.

Jaina's optimism grew stronger, but she knew the victory was more illusion than anything else. They still had to reach the Golan station and bring it on-line—if they could outrun the twenty skips still after them, which didn't seem likely, even with them slowing down to get through the asteroids. If they really pushed it, they might get there with a few seconds to spare, which wouldn't give them time to do much of anything with the station, assuming the antique still worked. It was nowhere near the shipyard, so it probably hadn't been used since the days of the Empire. The guns and everything else useful had likely been scavenged while she was still in diapers.

She clicked her comm. "Okay, Twins, here's what we're

going to do. Our primary objectives were to see if the station is operational and to bring it on-line if it was. I don't think General Antilles figured on half the fleet following us out here, though. We're going to get there a few seconds ahead of them. The rest of you will cover me while I enter the docking bay, then you're going to punch to the outer system."

"Are you saying we're supposed to *leave* you, Sticks?"

"With any luck, they won't see me drop in. They'll think I jumped with the rest of you."

"With all due respect, Colonel, that's crazy," Two said.

"General Antilles needs to know the status of this station, and he needs to know soon. If any of you can think of a better plan, tell me now."

"Same plan, but one of us stays behind," Three said. "It doesn't make sense it being you, Colonel."

It makes plenty of sense, Jaina thought. *I won't send any of you on what's probably a suicide mission.*

She didn't say that, though.

"It's the way it's happening," Jaina said. "The last thing I need right now is an argument."

"Yes, Colonel. Understood."

She had it about right—the skips were just catching up when they reached the station. The others fell into combat formations. She pretended to, and even squeezed off a couple of shots before making her run for the docking bay. She'd picked up a couple of friends by then, however. Three was right behind them, but there were four skips on her. Jaina's heart sank. It wasn't going to work. Even if she made the docking bay, they were going to notice.

She was grimly reaching to turn when her cockpit strobed in a flash of green light, and another.

In her headpiece, Twins Eight and Nine were cheering.

Jaina made her turn and saw why. Gigantic beams of

TWENTY-FIVE

In the night, Nom Anor felt the villip move against his chest, signaling an incoming communication. He lay quietly, wondering if he could leave the rock shelter unobserved. The Jedi slept lightly, and so did Harrar—besides, despite the fact that they hadn't seen any animals more dangerous than a dhillith, the older Jedi insisted on keeping watches, and Tahiri was on watch at the moment. His own shift would begin in a few hours—why couldn't the signal have come then?

Cursing silently, he lay there until the villip ceased quivering, but did not sleep again. Shimrra did not like to be ignored or delayed, and excuses rarely got one far with the Supreme Overlord. He felt his last, best chance at reconciliation slipping from him.

If he could kill Tahiri without waking the others . . .

Yes, and if a wish was a dha'eh, the maw luur would all be choked.

So he stayed there, trying to keep his muscles from twitching.

When at last his watch arrived and he took Tahiri's place on the outjut above the cave, he still dared not reply to the other end of the connection until enough time had passed that he could be relatively certain she was asleep.

Finally, more than an hour after he took the post, he climbed a little higher up the hill to be sure he was out of earshot of anyone who might be awake, and once again unsealed the bag and stroked the creature to life.

For long moments, nothing happened, but then a face appeared, a hideous, distorted face.

With a faint shock he realized it was Shimrra's jester, Onimi.

"Nom Anor," the jester burbled. "Nom Anor, Nom Anor, your reputation we deplore, the bumbling failed executor—"

"I must speak with Shimrra," Nom Anor whispered fiercely. "Quickly, before our enemies discover us."

"*Our* enemies?" Onimi burbled. "What fortress will we ever stand in together, ever, whether, sever again?"

"Tell him it concerns Zonama Sekot. Tell him—" The face suddenly melted, and a new, infinitely more terrifying one took its place. Nom Anor shivered, and for an instant he wanted to crush the villip, throw it in a deep pool, and return to his role as Prophet.

He thought about his disciples, his diseased, pathetic, gullible—

"Nom Anor," the villip growled, unable to actually convey the profound, bone-shivering bass of Shimrra's voice but suggesting it well enough. "Most unworthy and perverse of my servants. What could you possibly want?"

"Only to serve you, Lord."

"You would have served me best to have given yourself over to sacrifice after the disaster you caused on Ebaq Nine."

"I could not, Great Lord," he said. "I was captured, captured by the *Jeedai*. I have been their captive since that time."

"Indeed. It was very considerate of them to allow you the use of a villip."

"I secreted it upon my person. It went undiscovered."

"Then why did you not use it earlier?" the Supreme Overlord rumbled.

"I was observed, always observed. But I have won their confidence now."

"Enough," Shimrra snapped. "You mention Zonama Sekot. That world has been destroyed."

"It has not, Dread Lord. I am upon it, along with the shaper Nen Yim and the priest Harrar. They have allied with the *Jeedai*, Lord Shimrra. Against you. Against *us*."

"Harrar? You would have me take *your* word that Harrar is a traitor?"

"Summon him, my lord. You will find him absent from Yuuzhan'tar, and indeed from Yuuzhan Vong space. As is Nen Yim."

For an interminable period, Shimrra said nothing.

"Go on," he finally said.

"With me are also two *Jeedai*—Corran Horn, who slew Shedao Shai, and Tahiri, the one-who-was-shaped." He took a deep breath. "Lord, Luke Skywalker is also here, the chief of them all, and Mara Jade Skywalker."

"On Zonama Sekot." The Supreme Overlord's tone carried an almost unimaginable tinge of fear.

It almost stopped Nom Anor from going on. But he tightened his resolve and plunged ahead. "Yes, Dread Lord. They have come to persuade the planet to join them against us."

"So. So." Shimrra's voice rumbled away. It returned a moment later. "You know how to reach this planet?"

"My villip can be made to serve as a tracer. You may use Phaa Anor's villip to find me. A shaper can make the necessary modifications."

"Lead me to Zonama Sekot, Nom Anor, and you will find the gods smile on you again. *I* will smile on you again."

"That is my only wish, Dread Lord. To serve you as I once did."

"I should hope you will serve me better." Shimrra paused. "Based on our past experiences, it will require overwhelming force to destroy this cursed planet. Much of our fleet is presently engaged. Indeed, I consider it possible, Nom Anor, that you may yet be a traitor trying to lure my fleet there so the infidels can take Yuuzhan'tar."

"No fleet is necessary, Dread Lord. There is an Imperial frigate above this planet, and doubtless Skywalker has a ship. Send one ship to deal with them, and a landing craft to find me. That is all that is required."

"Fool," Shimrra grunted. "The problem is not with infidel ships, but with the planet itself."

"The planet will not present a problem, Lord Shimrra. I have the means to sabotage it. By the time your ships arrive here, it shall be occupied with its own death."

TWENTY-SIX

Jaina's comm registered a hail, not on the battle frequencies. She switched over.

"There you are," a voice on the other end said.

"Yes," Jaina replied. "Thanks for the assist just now. But if you don't mind my asking, who in the galaxy is this?"

"My name is Erli Prann," he replied. "I'm in charge of this battle station."

"You realize you're in Yuuzhan Vong–held space, and have been for a long time."

"Yes. It's a long story. What's going on out there?"

"Just what it looks like. We're retaking Bilbringi. But things haven't gone exactly according to plan, and the general sent me out to see if this station is still operational. Looks like it is."

"It's in pretty good shape," Prann said proudly. "We'd be glad to be of any assistance we can. If you want to come aboard, I'll show you what we've got."

"That's great," Jaina said. "Just assign me a berth."

"What about the rest of your pilots?"

"There are still Vong out there. I expect they'll be headed this way after that display you just put on. I think I'll keep them out there to help with the defense."

"Copy," Prann said. "Come on in. Berth Seven—you'll see the beacon."

*   *   *

Jaina slipped her X-wing into the docking bay without a mishap. She waited as the doors closed and the area outside was pressurized, then unsealed her cockpit and stepped out onto the deck. The bay was massive, but her ship was the only one she saw. It looked a little lonely in all that space. On the far end she noticed a lot of carbon scoring on the walls, as if there had been an explosion of fire.

"Welcome aboard!"

Jaina looked over to see her reception committee—two humans and a Rodian, all wearing the uniform of the old Bilbringi defense force—dark blue slacks and military-style blue jackets over gold-colored shirts.

The male human, a fellow she guessed to be about as old as her father, with hair that might have once been red but had faded to auburn and silver, came forward with his hand out.

"I'm Lieutenant Prann," he said as he shook her hand. "We spoke a moment ago. These are my associates, Zam Ghanol and Hiksri Jith."

Ghanol was the other human, an older wiry woman with gray hair and a crooked nose. Jith was the Rodian. Both shook her hand.

Prann flashed her a big smile. "I really can't say how glad we are to see you—" He glanced at her insignia. "—Colonel? . . ."

"Solo," she replied.

"Solo? Not the one from the holos? Jaina Solo?"

" 'Fraid so," she replied. "And I hate to be rude, but could we cut straight to the situation? I need to assess this station and report to General Antilles as soon as possible."

"Of course," Prann said. "It's just such a surprise and such an honor. If you'll follow me, please?"

"If you don't mind me asking, Lieutenant Prann, what in blazes are you people doing here?"

He uttered a short chuckle. "I suppose that does require a little explanation, doesn't it? We were part of a crew sent out here to overhaul the station." He paused as the turbolift came and they stepped into it. "You might have noticed it's way out here."

"Yes," Jaina said. "I was wondering about that."

"In fact, we didn't know it was here for years. It was cloaked, you see."

"Cloaked?"

"Yep. The theory is that Grand Admiral Thrawn cloaked it for some reason, back when he cloaked all of those asteroids to blockade Coruscant. It showed up missing in the later inventory, but nobody could find it. When a Yuuzhan Vong invasion looked imminent, however, we wanted every advantage we could get, of course. One of the brass guessed it might be cloaked and sent us out here with an old crystal grav-trap to find it. As you can see, we did, but—our bad luck—the invasion started while we were out here. We had taken the cloak down, but didn't have the shields working. A flight of skips came out here and pretty much fried our transport—you may have noticed the damage to the docking bay."

Jaina nodded. The lift opened, and Prann gestured for her to step out into the fire control area, where several other sentients waited—two more humans, a Twi'lek, a Barabel, and a Toydarian. Over banks of controls, through a broad viewport, she could see the distant battle as a series of tiny winking lights. The seeming smallness of it didn't fool her— a lot of people were dying back there. It made her itchy to be so far away.

"Anyway," Prann went on, "we managed to get one of the turbolasers on-line and the shields up. We gunned down the skips and put the cloak back on—it was the only thing we could think of to do. There was a whole fleet out there. The Vong apparently thought we'd gone to hyperspace— seems they don't know Golans don't usually come equipped for that."

"But that was more than a year ago," Jaina said.

"You're telling me. We've just been waiting, tinkering with the station. Everything works fine, by now, at least those things we had the parts to fix. This thing has a terrific power core—had to, to run the shield for so long. We floated a small probe out on an insulated cable so we could see what was going on, which as you've probably guessed wasn't much that was helpful to our situation—just the Vong setting up shop."

His grin broadened. "This morning, though, we swept and saw your fleet. We dropped the field, hoping you would spot us. We've got limited sublight communications, but no hyperwave or HoloNet." He grinned again. "And here you are."

It was about then that Jaina understood something was wrong. The feeling in the Force that she took as relief at the end of a long, dangerous isolation was there, but seething beneath it was something hungry.

She was reaching for her lightsaber when something hit her, hard. Her hand, midway to her weapon, suddenly refused to obey her commands, and the room spun dizzily. She tried to focus and use the Force, but the dizziness got worse, and she was vaguely aware that her legs weren't holding her up anymore. She didn't feel the deck when she hit it, but she had a strange view of boots and legs moving her way. She heard faraway sounds that resembled thunder, but which she understood to be speech. Then—

Then she woke, strapped down to a table with some sort of webbing, her head pounding, and everything still doing a slow spin.

"Sorry about that," she heard Prann say. "Sonics leave you with a terrible hangover without the benefit of ever having the fun."

He was standing a meter away. The Toydarian stood across the room with a blaster trained on her.

"I hear Toydarians are more resistant than most species to Jedi mind tricks," Prann said. "I hope we don't have to test that. I'd like to see all of us walk out of this healthy."

"Prann, what's going on?" she managed. "Who are you really?"

"Oh, that name's as good as any."

"What are you, Peace Brigade?"

His eyebrows squinted together. "Colonel Solo," he said, "now you're hurting my feelings. That pathetic bunch of collaborationists? Hardly. I'm a liberator."

"Of what?"

"Technology, actually."

"Ah," Jaina said. "You're a thief and a smuggler."

Prann shrugged his shoulders. "What I do is more like emergency salvage. I haven't taken anything the Vong wouldn't have destroyed anyway. Remember Duro? We got some good stuff there, in hit-and-run raids after New Republic forces pulled out. If we hadn't it would have been wasted. The Vong sure weren't going to use it."

Her head was starting to clear. "So you came here after the Vong took Bilbringi?"

"Nope, this job was a little different. Most of my story was true—except that it was Vel, here, who discovered the missing station in the shipyard databanks. I'd heard a story that one of the Golans disappeared right before the New Republic forces invaded. A few of us got jobs in the shipyards, and Vel managed to slice into the old Imperial records." He beamed. "One of the best slicers in the business."

"Ah, just average," the Toydarian replied. He didn't take his gaze off Jaina.

"He's very modest," Prann added. "Anyhow, he found an old encryption that suggested the station *had* been cloaked—apparently Thrawn was keeping it in reserve as a little surprise, but when Thrawn died the station was lost, because he obviously didn't share the information with his command structure. We were able to reckon a general sector and calculate for drift and then we sort of—um— *borrowed* a crystal grav-trap detector from the Bilbringi dry docks to find it. After that, the story is more or less the one I already told you."

"So what do you want with me?" Jaina asked. "Why did you stun me?"

"Well, frankly, Colonel Solo, I don't want anything from *you*, especially trouble. But I need to borrow some parts from your X-wing."

"You can't all escape in a single X-wing."

"No, we can't. We're going to escape in the station itself."

"Come again?" Jaina said. "I thought you said it isn't equipped with hyperdrive."

"No, I said Golans aren't *usually* equipped with hyperdrive. This one wasn't, either. But how do you think we were planning on salvaging a space station without the Bilbringi authorities noticing?"

"You brought your own drive," Jaina realized.

"Yes. We almost had it installed when the Vong showed up and torched our transport. Unfortunately, the motivator was still *on* the transport. No motivator, no hyperdrive." He held his palms out. "So—we've been waiting."

"You can't use an X-wing motivator to jump a station this size," Jaina pointed out.

"No, but we can cobble one together from seven."

Jaina jerked at the webbing. "Leave my squadron alone!"

"Hey, calm down," Prann said. "They're all okay. We hit them with ion beams, hauled them in with tractor beams, and stunned them with sonics. And that wasn't easy—not with the Wookiee and that crazy Twi'lek. Look, I'm not trying to make any enemies, here."

Jaina could only stare at him in the face of such an absurd statement.

"We were hoping you would all dock," he continued,

"and make the whole thing easier, but we've been working out contingencies for a while now. Not a lot else to do here, you know."

"Look, Prann," Jaina said, "General Antilles *needs* this battle station."

Prann laughed. "I'm sorry, Colonel, but we've all invested a *little* too much in this baby to just hand it over to be destroyed. Do you know how much I can get for the cloaker alone? No, forget it. In a few hours we'll be ready to jump. Meanwhile, we've put the cloak back on."

"And what about me?"

"You're a bit of a problem. I know enough about you to know that the longer I keep you around, the better the chance you'll be able to use those Jedi powers of yours to—well, I don't *know*, do I, and that's the problem. On the other hand, I don't want to kill Han Solo's daughter. I mean, I respect the guy, and I know he's already been through a lot."

"You're just afraid he would hunt you down and kill you," Jaina said.

"Yeah, that, too. Look, I'm a businessman—this is business. Once we've got the hyperdrive working and jump out of here, we'll put you all off someplace safe—*with* your starfighters. Okay?"

"No," Jaina said, "*not* okay. Who are you going to sell your cloaker to, Prann? The Vong? Because they're going to be the only ones around to buy it if you don't help us here."

"That's a little dramatic, don't you think?" Prann said. "I mean, there's still plenty of market for this sort of thing in the Corporate Sector—heck, in lots of places. A small planetary government is what I'm looking for, one afraid they'll soon need negotiating power. If this battle here goes sour, it'll only make the market that much better."

"Until there *is* no market," Jaina snapped. "Until the Vong have everything, because Huttoads like you are still trying to make a profit rather than doing what they can to help us win."

Prann's smile vanished. "We sat out here for a *year* surrounded by Vong," he said angrily, "in constant fear that they would find us. Sure, they can't see us when we have the cloak on, but we can't see them either. Every *single* time we pushed out the probe we all got the shakes. And who knew what the Vong have that might detect us at any second? Do you know what it's like to be surrounded by that kind of pressure every day for a year and not be able to do a single thing about it?" His face was getting redder, and his voice was rising. "After what we've been through—sister, you can *keep* your platitudes. I'm taking this station, I'm selling it, and I'm going to take my share and retire to some little backwater so far away the Vong won't reach it in my lifetime and sip cool drinks on a hot beach."

"There's no place that far away," Jaina said.

"I'm willing to look," Prann replied.

Jaina focused the Force on the Toydarian. "He's crazy," she told the Toydarian. "Stun him and help me out of this."

The Toydarian blinked, looked briefly confused, and then laughed.

Prann smiled, too, his tirade apparently over. "So it's true, then. Good. Now, if you'll excuse me, I'm going to help get those motivators coupled together. Vel, I've changed my mind. Take her to fire control and watch her there. I can't spare you just to be a guard during this. Just—keep an eye on things, and don't let her talk to anyone."

"I want to see my pilots," Jaina said.

"After we've made the jump," Prann told her. "Not before."

With that he left the room.

TWENTY-SEVEN

"Nothing," Corran grumbled, folding down to rest on a log. "I must have looked for ten kilometers in every direction, and there's no sign of natives."

"Maybe there aren't that many," Tahiri said, reaching up to pick an oblong fruit with a serrated corona of leaf at the top. They had dubbed it a pingpear, and it was one of the eight fruits that Nen Yim had identified as edible and nutritious. Since their food stores were limited, Corran had insisted that they eat native food when possible. The gathering expeditions also gave them an opportunity to talk away from the Yuuzhan Vong without leaving them too long unobserved.

"Or maybe we had the misfortune to crash in the one uninhabited region they have left," Corran said. "It doesn't matter—we can't stay here forever. I've been trying to think of a way to attract the attention of that Imperial frigate, if nothing else."

"Any thoughts on how to go about that?"

He nodded. "Yes. I'll have to go to the one place I've been avoiding."

"Oh. The giant hyperdrive."

"Right."

"Which you don't want the Yuuzhan Vong to know is a giant hyperdrive because you're afraid it will disillusion them somehow."

"You get two marks," Corran said. "But it's the only sign of civilization around. There might be someone tending it. Failing that, there might be other things—a hyperwave, for instance, or even a subspace transceiver. And Harrar's been after me to check it out, anyway."

"How do you think he'll react when he finds out what it is?"

"You tell me."

She thought about that for a moment, trying to recall how she had felt when she'd gone to the top of the ridge a few days before.

She held up the pingpear. "It's like discovering a perfect piece of fruit has a nasty worm in it—after you've already taken a few bites."

Corran nodded. "That's what I figured. Still, we have to do something, and I can't imagine he'd let me go without him, not as curious as he's been about it."

"How far away do you think it is?"

"I eyeball it at about twenty klicks."

"Yeah, that's what I figured, too," Tahiri said. "So when do we start?"

"*We* don't," Corran replied. "Harrar will go with me. I need you to stay and look after the other two."

"Again? I'm sick of baby-sitting. Don't you trust them yet? They're completely moon-eyed over this place, both of them. Harrar is the one we ought to worry about."

"I do worry about Harrar. That's why I'm keeping an eye on him. But the other two—they're still the enemy, Tahiri. No matter how well we seem to be getting along with them as individuals, we can't lose sight of the fact that our goals might be quite different."

"I understand that. It's just that Nen Yim and the Prophet are *boring*. All they do is poke at bugs and twigs all day. Why don't you let *me* go and you stay here, if you think someone has to?"

"Because this is how I want it, that's why. Brush up on your meditation technique and practice your lightsaber footwork."

"That's all I've *been* doing for the past week."

"Well, life is hard," Corran said, more sarcastically than he needed to. "Sometimes you actually have to spend a week *without* going into battle. I'm sure you can handle it."

"Yes, sir," Tahiri replied, unenthusiastically. She felt a knot of hurt and resentment in her belly. Why was Corran treating her this way? Couldn't he see it hurt?

"So Harrar and I will start in the morning," he went on. "It shouldn't take us more than a day or a day and a half of walking, but I can't say how long it will be before I figure out if there's anything useful there—maybe an hour, maybe days. I need you to stay alert here."

"For what? Vicious fruit?"

Corran looked up, his eyes sharp. "I don't know," he said. "But the longer we're here, the itchier I feel."

"Maybe you're bored, too."

"It's more than that. I've got a bad feeling about this whole deal. But there's nothing I can do about it until I have some way to contact Luke."

"If he's still here."

"I think he is. I get occasional glimpses."

"So do I," Tahiri said, "especially of Jacen. But the Force doesn't care how far away they are. They could be back on Mon Calamari."

"That's not how it feels," Corran said. "You're going to have to trust I've learned a thing or two over the years."

The angry tone startled her. "Corran, I *know* you're a more experienced Jedi than I am."

"Not the impression you give."

"I'm sorry if I—" The knot, growing since she had first seen him again, exploded. She felt warmth on her face and realized to her utter shame that she was crying.

"Sometimes I don't express myself very well, I think," she said. "I mean, I've just integrated two personalities. I don't have this all worked out yet."

"Hey, easy," Corran murmured. "I misunderstood you, that's all."

"No, no—Corran, you're my *hero*. Ever since that time when you and Anakin and I—I thought we were friends, and then—" She stopped. She was just sounding stupid.

"Look, Tahiri—"

"I need more training," she blurted out. "Special training. Can't you *see* that? Why haven't you ever offered—I mean you know so much more than I do . . ." She trailed off, both horrified and relieved that she had finally said it.

He just stared at her for a second. "I never imagined you wanted anything like that from me."

"Well—" How could someone so smart be so stupid? "Why wouldn't I? I need some sort of guidance, Corran. I might seem like I know what I'm doing, but I don't."

"I'm not a Master, Tahiri," Corran said gently. "There are Masters who would be happy to train you."

"You have half a chance of understanding me," Tahiri said. "They don't."

"I think you're selling them short."

"Maybe." She thrust her chin out defiantly. "Does that mean you don't want me?"

"No," Corran said. "But it's not that simple. We'd have to ask Master Skywalker. And at the least it means you'll stop talking back and do what I say. Do you understand that?"

"You mean you'll take me on?"

"Provisionally, since there are no Masters around, and until I get Luke's yes or no on the matter—if you agree to those conditions."

She wiped her eyes with the back of her hand. "I agree, then."

"Good. Then you stay here with Nen Yim and the Prophet. The end."

"Okay."

Nen Yim examined the thing she had grown. It was, to all appearances, a qahsa. The differences between it and the usual item were invisible to the naked eye. She reached for it, but the faint sound of approaching footsteps gave her pause.

It was the shaped Jedi, of course. She was never far from Nen Yim, always watching. It had been a source of irritation, at first, but now it seemed somehow less of a bother. The young human's insights had proven valuable, and had even prompted this experiment.

"Hello," the shaper said.

"You seem in a good mood," Tahiri replied.

The corners of Nen Yim's mouth turned up. "That may change in a moment. I'm about to try something new. It will probably fail."

"Is it dangerous?"

"I don't see how it could be, but anything is possible."

"Maybe you should wait until Corran and Harrar get back," Tahiri suggested.

"They only left a few hours ago," Nen Yim said. "They could be gone indefinitely. I think this should be safe."

Tahiri turned a curious eye toward the experiment. "What is it, exactly? It looks like a qahsa."

"It is, so far as it goes. But I grew it with modifications."

The Jedi sat cross-legged near her. "What sort of modifications?"

"Your talk of the Force binding the life of this world and serving as its means of intercommunication interested me. And yet, since Yuuzhan Vong life does not appear in the Force, I could think of no way to test that possibility. However, it occurred to me that if the ecosystem of this world is truly self-regulating, it must have some sort of memory—it needs to know what happened yesterday and last cycle to plan for tomorrow. Furthermore, that memory must be shared somehow by all of its constituents."

"I'm with you so far."

Nen Yim indicated a ten-legged arthropod she had enclosed in a nurturing membrane. "Even if the memory were stored at a molecular level, a creature this size could not possibly carry enough to be useful, so I reason the planet's central memory core lies elsewhere, but that any living thing—even a cell—must be able to contact it, perhaps through this Force of yours."

"Interesting. And you've found a way to test that?"

"I think so." She glanced up at the young Jedi. "To explain, I may have to speak of things that will upset you."

Tahiri's eyes narrowed. "This concerns my own shaping, doesn't it?"

"Yes."

"Go on."

"There is a protocol—the protocol of Qah—which is used to integrate manufactured or borrowed memories into the brain tissue of Yuuzhan Vong life. We use it often, mostly for rather mundane purposes—teaching ships to fly, for instance. But we also use it at times to enhance our own memories, to gain skills or knowledge without having to learn them. In the past, on rare occasions, we've used the protocol to replace entire personalities."

"Which is what you tried to do to me."

"Exactly. But the protocol of Qah did not work on your human tissues, naturally—Yuuzhan Vong and human tissue are not sufficiently compatible for that. So instead we used your own brain cells to create a sort of human Qah cell, but filled with Yuuzhan Vong information. It was a hybrid cell."

"And that worked," Tahiri said.

"Correct," Nen Yim said. "In terms of your brain tissue, you are quite literally half Yuuzhan Vong. We did not implant merely memories, but also the cells that carried them."

Tahiri's eyes narrowed. Nen Yim had learned that was a sign of danger.

"Do you want me to stop?" she asked.

"No. I mean, yes, but it's like picking a scab. In fact, there's something I've been meaning to ask you."

"I attend," Nen Yim said, cautiously.

"I need to know—was there a real Riina?"

Nen Yim blinked. What an interesting question—but of course she would be curious about that. "I'm sure there must have been," she said. "The name was probably changed—names are easy to change—but the details of your childhood undoubtedly came from a real person. Such memories might be generated, I suppose, but there would be no reason to when they could be donated by any living Yuuzhan Vong."

"Is she—dead?"

"I've no idea. Mezhan Kwaad supplied the memory data. Only she could know who the donor was—and of course, she's in no position to tell you." Her tendrils curled with curiosity. "Did it truly work? You remember being in a crèche, and so on?"

Tahiri nodded. "Some things like crystal, others muddier. I remember once, my crèche-mates—P'loh and Zhul—we took one of the scrubbing korsks and put it in the communal food area. It—"

"Ate all the i'fii," Nen Yim finished, feeling a strange twisting in her.

"Yes," Tahiri said. She frowned. "How did you know?"

"Do you remember an incident involving a damaged fighting n'amiq?"

"I—wait. You mean those lizard-bird things the warriors

used to fight against each other? I . . . I found one once. One of the warriors had abandoned it in the grand vivarium because it wouldn't fight. It was injured and I nursed it back to health. Then one of my crèche-mates took it and fought it—I got there in time to see it die. It was torn to shreds. I thought it kept looking at me, pleading for help."

The chill deepened.

"What's wrong?" Tahiri asked.

Nen Yim sighed. "Those are *my* memories."

Tahiri stared at her for a long moment without speaking, as if trying to see through her skin. Nen Yim was glad for that, because she had to collect her own thoughts. *Mezhan Kwaad,* she thought, *may the gods devour you twice a day.*

Tahiri finally dropped her lids over her green eyes. She seemed to be trying to compose herself.

Or perhaps she was about to kill Nen Yim. The thought of her onetime tormentor sharing the same childhood memories might well be too much for her.

But when Tahiri looked back up, her gaze held only curiosity. "Whatever happened to P'loh?" she asked.

Relief spread down Nen Yim's backbone. "She was assigned to Belkadan, and killed there," she replied.

"And Zhul?"

"Zhul is an adept on the worldship *Baanu Ghezh,* and so far as I know is well."

"And the young warrior who watched our dormitories in primary shaping?"

We, Nen Yim noted. *She said* we, *as if . . .* "Killed taking Yuuzhan'tar. They say he died bravely, crashing into an infidel ship even as his own disintegrated."

Tahiri rubbed her forehead. "He was nice," she said.

"Yes, if such can be said of a warrior."

"As if I wasn't confused enough," Tahiri murmured. "Now I find out I have friends on both sides of the war who died. Maybe I even killed one of them."

Nen Yim didn't have a response to that.

"I have a lot of questions to ask you," Tahiri said. "But now isn't the time. I need—I need to absorb this."

"As do I. I knew no more than you."

Tahiri looked up. "I forgave you, you know. Even before I knew this."

"I didn't ask for that."

"I know."

"But I'm glad."

For another stretched moment, they sat together. Tahiri was the first to speak.

"Uh . . . you were telling me about the qahsa."

Nen Yim nodded, happy to return to a subject she could get a grip on. "I extracted nerve cells from Sekotan life and modified them as your cells were modified. It was an easier task, because Sekotan life is genetically similar to our own. I hope, through them, to gain access to the memories of this world, as I might access a qahsa."

"But if those memories are transmitted through the Force, and Yuuzhan Vong life is outside the Force—"

"Consider, Tahiri. Your brain contains Yuuzhan Vong implants. Yet you still sense and use the Force."

"Yes!" Tahiri said. "And when my personalities were integrating, Riina used a lightsaber, like a Jedi." She peered at the qahsa. "So this could work."

"It could. If one of the many assumptions I've made doesn't turn out to be false. But I suppose now I shall see."

"May I watch?"

"I would be honored."

Nen Yim hesitated no longer, but reached for the qahsa and joined with it.

For an instant, there was nothing, and then the world seemed to shatter. Images and data roared through her mind, stars and vacuum, the feel of life on her skin, the tear of wind across her polar regions. Feelings—fear, pain, despair, joy, all on a scale that dwarfed the tiny Yuuzhan Vong brain trying to interpret it. The images came faster, running together, burning in her, casting light into every corner of her brain.

Please, slow down, this will kill me, and I will never understand.

It was something like trying to access the eighth cortex, but both less painful and, she understood, more dangerous. Her thoughts were disintegrating under the onslaught. Nen Yim was vanishing. Something else was hollowing her out. A god was eating her from the inside.

Nen Yim clasped the qahsa and a look of vast surprise twisted her features. Then her body jerked strangely and she fell over, convulsing, the qahsa still gripped between her fingers.

"Nen Yim!" Tahiri cried, starting forward. She reached to help her, to pull the thing from her hands, but stopped.

She didn't know what was happening. Anything she did might make it worse.

Of course if she did nothing, Nen Yim might die, she thought, as the shaper's convulsions grew more and more violent.

Carefully, she reached out in the Force. Nen Yim herself was a blank slate, as usual, but in the qahsa, something was happening. It was buzzing and humming with power—Tahiri could feel the flow of it from all around her, a million voices speaking at once.

Black blood began to dribble from Nen Yim's nostrils.

Okay, Tahiri thought. *I have to do something.* Breaking Nen Yim's bond with the qahsa couldn't make things worse—it was already killing her.

She reached for the qahsa, hoping the Force would guide her.

When she touched it, a world struck her down.

*   *   *

Suddenly, the stream of sight and smell and tactile data slowed and distilled. The noise dropped away, and Nen Yim found herself in the middle of a quiet moment, a totality rather than a sequence.

She found herself *understanding*.

And she knew the secret of Zonama Sekot.

She felt like laughing and crying at once.

When Tahiri came to, Nen Yim was daubing her forehead with some sort of damp tissue. It smelled minty.

"What happened?" she mumbled through a tongue that felt like a bloated grysh-worm. Her head hurt. Her whole body hurt.

"I'm not certain," the shaper admitted. "When I ceased contact with . . . when it was over, I found you unconscious."

"I was trying to help you. I touched the qahsa, and there was this light—that's all I remember." Her eyes held concern. "Are you okay?"

Nen Yim nodded. "As I have never been."

"So you made contact with Zonama Sekot?"

Tahiri's words seemed slow, after what Nen Yim had just been through. The whole world seemed slow, and wonderful. "Not with the living consciousness, no," she said. "I think you are correct—one must have some connection to the Force for that. But the memories—the memories alone nearly overwhelmed me." She stood. "I must beg your indulgence. I must meditate now. But I think—I believe I have the solution."

"To what?"

Nen Yim felt her mouth pull in an unaccustomed smile. She still felt as if in a dream. "Everything that concerns us," she said.

TWENTY-EIGHT

Nom Anor drew himself quietly deeper into the forest above the cave. Neither of the females had noticed him. From his angle he couldn't see them, but he'd heard most of their conversation. If only he'd understood more of it.

What did Nen Yim mean when she said that she had learned the secret of Zonama Sekot?

As he watched, the shaper walked into view, carrying her qahsa, and then out of view again, into the deep boles of the bottomland.

Tahiri did not appear, apparently respecting Nen Yim's desire for solitude.

After a moment, Nom Anor slipped up the ridge, traveled fifty meters or so in the direction he believed Nen Yim had gone, and then descended the hill after her.

Nen Yim gazed at the trees around her, immersed herself in the lisping of wind through their leaves and the insistent purr of insects and chatter of animals. She felt something tight in her relax, release her inhibitions and prejudices, and saw the living world, at last, as *alive*. Finally she felt *herself* as alive.

For so many years, she had been the quintessential observer. Even her actions—even the extreme actions that had brought her to this place—had merely been in the service of observation. And yet she had never thought of herself as part of what she observed, as a piece of the great mystery that was the world. She was always outside—outside her people, her caste, her companions.

But now she felt in the center, as everything was its own center, and she was . . . happy.

"It's what we always should have been," she murmured to herself. "Zonama Sekot is—"

"Am I interrupting you?"

She shook herself from her reverie, and then smiled. It was the Prophet.

"You knew all along," she said. "Somehow, you knew all along."

"You have discovered something," the Prophet said.

"Something wonderful," Nen Yim replied. "I'm eager to share it with all of you."

"Is it about our redemption?" he asked. To her surprise, she thought he sounded mildly sarcastic.

"It is," she assured him. "And not merely for the Shamed Ones, but for all of us. But it will not be easy. Shimrra will resist the truth."

"You're beginning to sound like me," the Prophet said.

"I suppose I am," she replied. "But when you know the truth—"

"Truth is an entirely relative thing," the Prophet said, stepping a little closer. "And sometimes not even that." He reached toward his face.

"Why are you removing your masquer?"

"If this is the day of revelation, let us all stand before Zonama Sekot as we truly are. But you've interrupted me. I was speaking of truth. My truths, for instance, were all carefully crafted lies."

His voice had harshened as the masquer unpeeled from his face. "What?" she asked. But then the masquer dropped away to reveal, not the face of a Shamed One, but the perfectly normal face of an executor, except that one of his eyes—

She gasped, and flung up her shaper's hand. In an instant, the whip-sting hissed from her finger toward the face, but he was faster, much faster, bringing his arm up so that the sting drilled through it. He gasped, snarled, and quickly rotated his arm, wrapping the whip-sting around it so she could not withdraw for another strike.

Then he set his feet and yanked her toward him. She saw the pupil of his eye dilate impossibly wide, and then it spit at her.

Plaeryin bol, she had time to think, before the poison struck her.

Her muscles contracted instantly, and she felt her heartbeat roaring in her ears as she thudded to the ground in what seemed like slow motion. The sounds of the forest seemed, conversely, to rise in pitch, and she saw everything as through a distorted sheet of mica. Her body flopped until she was on her back, and she found the executor standing over her. She could no longer make out the features of his face.

"Know you . . ." she managed.

"I'm flattered," he replied. "We met only once, I think."

"Why?" Her lips were numb, the words torture to form, but she knew if she could keep him talking, the reagent implants in her body would manufacture an antidote to the toxin. She noticed he had released the sting from his arm.

"Why?" he repeated, moving away, apparently searching for something on the ground. "You don't have long enough for me to explain it, my dear."

"But Zonama Sekot. I . . . the answer."

"I really couldn't care less," the false Prophet said. "You've gone mad, you and Harrar. Whatever future you would launch from here, I don't think it would be one I care for. There is only so much a people can change before they lose themselves."

"Already . . . lost." She needed to make him understand.

The Yuuzhan Vong had lost their way long before coming to this galaxy.

"I really don't think that's your judgment to make," the Prophet said diffidently. She remembered his real name, suddenly. Nom Anor. "After I'm done with you," he continued, "Zonama Sekot won't be far behind. You see, you gave me access to your qahsa, and contrary to what you probably think, I am well able to understand its contents."

"No. You're mad." She was feeling a little stronger. Sensation was returning to her extremities. She felt her whipsting, trailing on the ground, unretracted.

He reached down for something and picked it up. A rock.

"You'll have to excuse me if I'm humble enough to doubt that a poison of my manufacture will kill you, Nen Yim. You truly are a genius. You are a terrible loss to our people."

He came toward her, hefting the rock in one hand. Her heartbeat blurred into a steady vibration as with every bit of strength she had left she thrust her sting at him.

He swung the rock down, and something thundered, and one side of her head felt *huge*.

The second blow seemed softer. She saw again the rush of images that Zonama Sekot had shown her, the beauty of a world in harmony, a harmony so sublime that the Yuuzhan Vong had no word for it—though once they must have.

She saw the back of her own hand, the normal one, the one she had been born with. She was suddenly very young, back in the crèche, noticing it for the first time, fascinated that she could make the little things on it move.

Does Tahiri remember this, too? she wondered.

She wiggled the fingers, trying to guess how they worked. She could not seem to move them very much.

Nom Anor gasped as the sting ran him through, but used the pain to drive the rock into Nen Yim's head a second time. The forest floor was already black with blood, and he was spattered with it. He could taste it, somehow, though he hadn't remembered opening his mouth.

He hit her a third time and fell back, pulling at the thing in him, wondering if she had managed to kill him, too. He'd been stupid—he should have killed her more quickly. He was lucky the plaeryin bol venom worked at all, upon reflection. He was never more grateful that he had chosen to replace his lost implant.

He was relieved to discover the sting had gone through the meat of his side. She had missed any organs, and he didn't think the sting was poisoned. Still, it hurt, as did the hole she had made in his arm. He'd been lucky—if he hadn't surprised her, things might well have gone very differently.

Ignoring his oozing wounds, he reached down and picked up the qahsa, examining it with a critical eye. Was this her original qahsa, or the thing she had used to contact the memories of Zonama Sekot? He fervently hoped it was the former, and that she had brought it along to record her new discovery. If it was the other one, he would have to go back to the cave and face Tahiri. That was a very risky proposition—he would have to take her from behind. He had only a partly depleted plaeryin bol and a rock, no match for her Jedi powers and a lightsaber. She could take his rock from him and club him to death with it from ten meters away.

To his relief, it was the qahsa he sought—the one Nen Yim had keyed him to. He took it and left the clearing, quickly climbing back up the ridge. Over the last few days, he had stolen the other components he needed to carry out his plan—the only thing lacking was the protocol itself, which was too complicated to memorize. Now he had it.

He faced out toward the gigantic hyperdrive guides. He still had challenges ahead. There were still Corran and Harrar to deal with, and Tahiri would surely come after him.

And he had little time. In less than a day-cycle, the ships

sent by Shimrra would be here. By that time, Zonama Sekot had to be dead, or at the very least crippled. He intended to see it done.

When sundown drew near and Nen Yim hadn't returned, Tahiri went looking for her. She hadn't seen the Prophet in a while, either, and suddenly worried that Nen Yim's performance had been just that—a ruse to create an opportunity for their departure.

She went in the general direction the shaper had taken. Above her, clouds were gathering, and the tall boras creaked in a quickening wind. Leaves whirled and danced, and a scent like electricity and resin crackled in the humid air.

She found Nen Yim in a small clearing. A trail of blood showed that she'd crawled a few meters before collapsing. As Tahiri knelt beside her, she saw the shaper's head was a messy ruin. Her one remaining eye was still open, however, if unfocused. Her breath came in faint wheezes.

"Nen Yim," Tahiri said gently. "Who did this?"

"Prophet. He's not—" She quivered at the effort of saying the words. ". . . Nom Anor."

"Nom Anor?" Tahiri looked quickly around, her hand grasping for her lightsaber. Nom Anor, the one who had tried to kill them at Yag'Dhul, had been right under her nose? A sick chill ran through her.

Nen Yim shivered and gasped.

"I—I have a medpac back at the camp," Tahiri said. "Just hang on, and I'll be back."

"No—I've stayed too long already. I can't—He thought I was dead. He's going to kill Sekot. You have to stop him."

"Kill Sekot?"

"Has my qahsa. I brought protocols, in case Sekot was a danger to us."

"Where's he gone?"

"He will seek—drive mechanism. The center that controls it can be sabotaged to make the drive fail cataclysmically. Probably made-thing drive, if the ship is an example. Stop him."

"Of course I will. But you have to help me."

"No." Nen Yim's hand came up. "Leave me here. Let me become a part of this."

Tears were blurring Tahiri's vision. She wiped them away with the back of her hand.

"You *are* a part of this," she said.

"So are you. And part of me. Don't forget." Nen Yim gasped and her body seized. "Wanted to tell you about Sekot. It's what—" But that was the last thing she said. Her mouth kept working for a time, but no words came out. A few moments later, her pulse was gone.

Tahiri stood grimly, anger and grief coursing through her. Jacen had said you could draw power from anger without turning to the dark side. That evil was praxis, not the emotions that drove it.

But there had to be a trick in that. Because what she wanted most to do at that moment was cut the Prophet's heart out—and not too quickly.

He would be headed to where Corran and Harrar had gone. Was Harrar in on this?

Then there would be two hearts to carve.

TWENTY-NINE

Corran stood gazing up at the immense metal vanes, trying to imagine the engineering job that had produced them. Now that they were near, he could see more of the engines—three vast pits that must be the exhaust vents of ion or even fusion drives.

It smacked of the Empire, when everything came in deluxe sizes. Was this whole planet some sort of super-weapon? It had destroyed the better part of a Yuuzhan Vong fleet, after all, not the easiest thing to do.

"You know what these are, don't you?" Harrar said in an accusatory tone. "They look like made-things."

Might as well get it over with, Corran thought. "Yes. These are part of a hyperdrive engine."

"A hyper—the planet can be moved?"

"It *has* been moved. It took the Jedi quite some time to find it because it had left the system where it was last recorded."

"I see now why you avoided bringing me here," Harrar said. "No, don't deny it—it was clear that you wished to keep this from me for as long as possible."

"I don't deny that," Corran said. "I thought it might—cloud the issue of Zonama Sekot."

"You underestimate my ability to reason," Harrar said. "Do you think all Yuuzhan Vong react without considera-tion? You insult me."

241

"I'm sorry," Corran said. "No insult was intended."

Harrar shrugged. "You should have told me sooner, but you did not. Now I know. The issue is moot—unless you are still holding information back." He looked out over the nearest pit. "We move planets," he said. "But we use dovin basals. There is no—how would you say it? Push-back?"

"Counterreaction," Corran said.

"Yes. How can a planet stand the stress of the sort of engines you use?"

"Not without cost, I would think." A sudden thought occurred to him. "Nen Yim mentioned recent mass extinctions. Using this engine may have been the cause of them."

"The danger they were fleeing must have been great," Harrar said.

Corran laughed. Harrar gave him a puzzled look.

"We think they were fleeing you," Corran explained. "The Yuuzhan Vong."

The priest seemed to absorb that. "Shimrra fears Zonama Sekot," he said. "Zonama Sekot fears the Yuuzhan Vong. What can be the explanation?"

"I've no idea."

"Nor do I understand how this planet's consciousness, if it indeed has one, can countenance this—*thing*—driven into its very surface."

"Perhaps Sekot believes that life and technology can coexist peacefully," Corran suggested.

"Perhaps," Harrar said dubiously. "Or perhaps the infi— the sentients who dwell here have enslaved the planet and imposed this technology upon it."

"That's also a possibility," Corran admitted. "But as Nen Yim might say, we're not going to find the truth by merely speculating."

"What was your reason for coming to this place, if you already knew what this was?"

"I'm looking for a communications device, so I can contact the Ferroans or the ship in orbit. Otherwise, we could be stuck here for a very long time."

"You could have told me that, too," Harrar said. "Did you think I would object?"

"To falling into the hands of the enemy? Maybe."

"I *placed* myself in your hands," Harrar reminded him. "I trust you have enough honor to make certain we are not made prisoners, but will be paroled to return to our people."

"I promise to do the best I can," Corran said, "but the matter might be taken out of my hands. Anyway, are you sure you *want* to go back? I doubt that Shimrra will be very pleased with you."

"That risk is mine," Harrar said, "and that of the others if they choose to take it. I feel that you would do the same in my place, Corran Horn."

"Probably."

Harrar searched about with his gaze. "Where do we look for this communications device of yours?"

"I don't know. I figure there must be some sort of maintenance access to the hyperdrive core. I'm hoping we'll find something—or someone—there. If not, I'm fresh out of ideas."

"Where should we look? Down one of those pits?"

Corran chuckled wryly. "Climb down the exhaust vent of an engine big enough to move a planet? No, thanks. It should be someplace obvious, say at the base of one of these vanes."

They found that access with relatively little trouble—a large metallic dome was half buried in rock about twenty meters from the northernmost tower. Corran could see that the top was built to open so that large parts and equipment could be shuttled in and out. A more modest ground-level entrance wouldn't open for them, but Corran was able to solve that little problem after a few minutes with his light-saber. He hoped the Ferroans would go easy on vandals, if they had good cause.

Within, they found an enormous shaft plunging straight down toward the planet's core. Faint track lights illuminated the floor as they entered.

"The maintenance area will be down there," Corran said, gesturing down the shaft. "This could take a while, if it's as big as it looks."

"I suggest we begin, in that case," Harrar said.

Nom Anor watched the entrance to the huge hyperdrive for a long while before starting down. It was clear that the Jedi and Harrar had gained entrance using the Jedi's weapon. What wasn't clear was where they were exactly, and what they were doing. Still, it was convenient for him that they had opened the way.

He entered and listened carefully, but heard only the wretched hum of machinery. Perhaps they were not within, after all, but had moved on, or were returning to camp by a different route. Darkness was falling, and a storm coming. He could not wait forever.

He'd replaced the masquer on his face. If he met them, he would simply say he had followed out of curiosity.

So determined, he entered the building and began searching for a way down, where logic dictated he might find what he sought.

He found a series of lifts not very different from those he had encountered on a dozen infidel worlds. He stepped in, found the control that would send it down, and reached for it.

At that moment, he heard another lift arrive, coming up from below. He froze, wishing he had a cloak of Nuun to make him invisible.

The door to his lift closed just as the other opened, and he heard the voices of Harrar and Corran. He quickly stabbed his finger at the control to pause his descent.

"I might be able to piece something together with this stuff," Corran was saying. "But it will take a while."

"Perhaps we should fire the engines," Harrar said. "That should get their attention."

A chill went up Nom Anor's spine. From his tone, Harrar was clearly joking, but that was insane for two reasons. The first was that Harrar never joked. The second was that *no* Yuuzhan Vong would casually jest about using machine technology. There was no possible humor in that.

Which meant that what he'd told Nen Yim was true— the planet was driving Harrar mad. No wonder Shimrra feared it.

When the voices had faded beyond hearing, he touched the descent control and the lift began to whir down its shaft. It took what seemed a long time, so long that the air actually seemed to get thicker. He was beginning to wonder if he would simply continue on to the other side of the planet when the car finally arrived in an immense room. Banks of machines and control panels gleamed in the faint light from the floor.

He called all the lifts down, wedged them open with some crates he found stacked nearby, and began his search.

He had very little technical knowledge concerning hyperdrive cores, but he didn't really need any. What he was looking for was an interface, something where the biosphere of Sekot met the cold metal of the infidel machines.

He sat cross-legged on a console and took out Nen Yim's qahsa, searching through it for the data on the Sekotan ship. There was a long entry on the engine moorings, the analog of which was certainly what he was looking for.

The ship had been grown around a sort of neural net. The

hyperdrive was probably connected to something similar. So where would that be?

He suspected he had a long search ahead of him.

Halfway back to the camp, Corran heard a rustling in the underbrush and saw Tahiri, moving at a fast trot. She had her lightsaber in her hand, and he could sense her anger like a torch in the high wind.

"Tahiri," he called.

She whirled at the sound of her name. Her eyes looked wild.

"What's happened?" he asked.

"Nen Yim is dead," she said, her voice as heavy and flat as a sheet of duracrete. "The Prophet killed her."

"The Prophet?" Harrar asked. "Are you certain?"

She turned on Harrar almost as if she meant to attack him. "She told me so herself, before she died," she snapped. "She'd just made some sort of discovery about Sekot, something important. She told me she wanted to be alone and think. She was gone for a long time, so I went looking for her. I found her. He'd done a pretty good job on her head with a rock. But she managed to tell me that he's planning on killing Sekot."

"Killing? . . ." Corran began, then put his hands on her shoulders. "Okay. Slow down. Tell me everything she told you. And start with this discovery of hers."

He listened carefully as Tahiri went through the story. Telling it again did not seem to calm her down.

"But the Prophet believes this planet is the salvation of his followers," Corran said. "Why would he want to destroy it?"

"Because he isn't the Prophet," Tahiri replied. "He's Nom Anor."

"Nom Anor?" Corran and Harrar repeated in unison.

Harrar closed his eyes and ground his knuckles into his forehead. "Nom Anor," he muttered. "Of course."

Corran certainly knew who Nom Anor was, and not just by reputation. The executor had very nearly killed him—and Tahiri and Anakin—in the Yag'Dhul system.

"What do you mean, *of course*?" he asked.

"Don't you see?" Harrar said. "Nom Anor *is* the Prophet."

"I don't see at all," Corran replied. "Nom Anor was the agent behind half the Yuuzhan Vong invasions in this galaxy. Why would he be a Prophet of the Shamed Ones?"

"Because he failed too often," Harrar replied. "After the disaster at Ebaq Nine, Shimrra called for his sacrifice—after which he vanished."

"And became the Prophet of the Shamed Ones, maybe in a bid to take the throne by revolution," Tahiri guessed. "What does it matter? We have to find him."

"No, wait," Corran said. "Harrar, you acted as if you should have guessed his identity."

"I didn't know, if that's what you mean," Harrar replied. "But—he did not act like a Shamed One. I could tell he had once been an intendant, and suspected he wore the masquer for fear Nen Yim and I would recognize him from his former life. And he seemed, at times, familiar. I can't believe he made such a fool of me."

"He fooled us all," Corran said. "The question is—why would he want to destroy Sekot?"

"To win back Shimrra's good graces," Harrar snarled.

"But he'll be stuck here, with the rest of us," Corran said, then immediately felt stupid. "No," he said. "They're coming after him, aren't they?"

"The lump under his arm," Harrar said. "If that was Nom Anor, it was no disfigurement. It must have been a villip."

"But Nen Yim released a virus to destroy anything like that," Tahiri pointed out.

"She did?" Harrar said. "I shouldn't be surprised. She was resourceful, that one. But if it was sealed in a q'et—a sort of living bag for preserving other organisms—it may have survived."

"Which means we have to find him *fast*," Tahiri said. "So what are we waiting for?"

"For you to calm down, for one thing," Corran said. "I'm not having an apprentice of mine run into battle in your state."

"I'm okay," Tahiri said, defensively.

"No, you're angry. Remember our deal. Especially the part where you have to do what I say."

She nodded, then took a deep breath. "I'll try. It's hard."

"The Yuuzhan Vong belief in revenge is very strong," Harrar said.

"I'm aware of that," Tahiri said. "Sometimes it doesn't feel right to fight it."

"Anger always makes you feel good at the time," Corran said. "Makes you feel bigger than yourself, makes you feel that everything you do is justified. But it's a trap."

She closed her eyes, and when she opened them, she looked calmer. "Thank you," she said.

"Good." He scratched his beard. It was no longer neatly trimmed, but sprawling all over his face. "We didn't see the Prophet or anyone else at the hyperdrive assembly."

"He might have easily slipped past us," Harrar said. "While we were searching for a communications device."

"You're right. We'd better go back."

It was beginning to rain as they swept the area around the vanes, and then entered the repair complex, lightsabers ready. They didn't find anyone at the entry level.

But they did find the turbolifts jammed.

"He's down there," Corran said.

"Well, we can't wait for him to come back up," Tahiri said. "By then, it'll be too late."

"Do you have any idea what he intends to do?" Corran asked.

"None," Tahiri said.

"Nen Yim once spoke of protocols already in the possession of shapers that seemed intended for use against the biology of this planet," Harrar said. "I've no doubt she developed weapons of her own, as well."

"Are you saying *Nen Yim* planned to destroy Sekot?" Corran asked.

"I think she initially believed, like Shimrra, that Zonama Sekot was a threat to our people," the priest said. "As did I. But I believe that both of us came to a different conclusion." He sighed. "I wish I could have spoken to her about her new discovery."

"She said she had the solution to all our problems," Tahiri said.

Corran noticed her eyes were damp. "Maybe she thought that solution was killing Sekot," he ventured.

Tahiri shook her head. "I don't think so, Master."

"Right, well, there's only one way to really find out, isn't there?" Corran peered down the shaft. "There ought to be a manual way down, in case the power cuts out, but I don't see anything."

"They probably use some sort of flitter or hoverlift," Tahiri pointed out. "That's too far down to go by ladder."

"Yes, it is," Corran said, eyes still searching. "But I think I do see a way. It's just not one I like."

To Nom Anor's delight, the search was not nearly as long as he feared it would be. In fact, the object of his search was so large and obvious that he overlooked it at first.

In the center of the chamber was a knob about twice as tall as he was, and about the same in diameter. At first glance, it seemed to be wrapped in some sort of rough fabric, but a closer inspection showed that it was heavily wound in very fine threads. At the base of the thing, the threads spread out like fine roots and dug into the damp, exposed stone of the floor.

He'd found it, as easily as that. The threads were precisely like the filaments of the neural net on the ship. There were just more of them—many more.

He quickly unpacked the incubator, a wet, fleshy device about the size of his hand. He linked it to the qahsa and accessed a protocol that was both a genetic and developmental blueprint. A stream of chemical and telepathic data moved from the qahsa to the incubator. The latter quivered and began to vibrate ever so slightly. Nom Anor allowed himself a smile. The incubator was already transforming genetic blueprints into living organisms. The result would be a soldier virus that would invade the neural integuments and corrupt their ability to carry data. The result should be a feedback explosion in the core. That would not only render the planet unable to travel, but sear a third of the biosphere away, as well. If that did not kill Sekot, it should at least distract it long enough for him to get away. Shimrra could send a small number of ships to finish the job.

He had only to hide the incubator and leave.

He pushed experimentally at the filaments. They were too tough to break, but they pushed readily aside, so that he was able to bury the organism deep within. When he was finished, the filaments slowly returned to their places, leaving no sign of what he had done. Even if the Jedi were following him, they would have to not only know what he had done—and he couldn't imagine how they could—but also find the incubator, a task that might take hours.

By then it would be too late—the microbes would be leaking out and invading the strands. Ten hours after that, things would start going very wrong for Zonama Sekot. But by then, Nom Anor would no longer be on the planet.

He removed his disguise, produced his villip, and stroked it. A moment later, the fierce visage of a warrior appeared.

"I am Ushk Choka," the villip informed him. "You are the one I have come for?"

"Yes," Nom Anor replied. "What is your present position?"

"In high orbit around the planet your signal emanates from. We seem to be undetected."

"Send a lander for me," Nom Anor said. "You may follow the villip's signal."

"Yes, I have your position," Choka confirmed. "All you have promised Shimrra is done?" He sounded skeptical.

"Yes, Commander."

"Nothing seems to have changed. The planet is there, and very much covered in life."

"Things will change soon," Nom Anor said, "but I assure you we do not want to be here when they do."

"I risk much, to send a lander now," Choka grunted. "I have been informed of the planet's defensive potential. You promised it would be negated."

"And it will be," Nom Anor insisted. "It will not be able to prevent our escape."

"But it might prevent the landing."

"By the time the lander arrives," Nom Anor said, "the planet will be thoroughly preoccupied." Or so he hoped. But he had been unable to concoct another scheme that would both destroy Zonama Sekot and allow him to escape with his life. The window would be narrow, but it should be there.

"In any event," he continued, "what is risk to the mighty Ushk Choka? Only a chance to show your bravery."

The warrior grunted angrily, and Nom Anor knew he had hit the right nerve.

"Of course," Choka said. "The lander will be there in seven hours."

"You're looking at that superconducting cable, aren't you?" Tahiri asked.

"Yes." The cable was smooth and just small enough that his hands could fit around it. It looked like it went all the way down, and hung ten centimeters away from the wall.

"I'm game," Tahiri said.

Corran shook his head. "No. If Anor hears me coming down, he'll just come back up on a turbolift. You have to be here in case he does that. Harrar doesn't have any weapons." *And maybe Harrar wouldn't stop him if he could. The two of them might still be in on this together.*

Which meant he could be leaving Tahiri in a bad position. There was nothing he could do about that, though. This was too important.

He took his jacket off. Outside, a steady pounding began as the rain came. Thunder crashed nearby. He reached out and touched the cable experimentally, then wrapped the jacket around it, getting a firm grip. He swung himself over the guardrail and reaffirmed the grip.

"This should be fun," he said.

"It looks like fun," Tahiri said. "Be careful. I'd hate to have to explain to Mirax what happened to you."

"Just watch those lifts," Corran reminded her.

Then he let his body slide out into the air.

For the first few seconds, he was in true free fall, accelerating toward the bottom of the shaft at the exponential speed of gravity. Then he began to tighten his grip, creating friction against the cable. His rate of fall slowed, but his arms complained, and the jacket warmed quickly. He relaxed again, clamped down again, alternating.

Above him, the top of the shaft had already diminished to

a circle so small that Tahiri's face was barely visible. Below him, the light strips on the walls still met together in a point.

He had a *long* way to go, and proceeding like this he wasn't going to make it. His arms would wear out long before he reached the bottom, or more likely the jacket would burn through. He'd known that from the start, but had needed to experiment with the cable for what he was about to do.

He closed his eyes, feeling the air rush past, feeling the living Force around him, the great pulsing life of Sekot, the unseen floor, his own body, all one in the Force—

And relaxed. He kept his hands loosely around the cable, but put no pressure on it. He was really falling now, his body tending horizontal as the atmosphere pushed against it. Fear tried to rise up and take him, but he batted it away. There was nothing to be afraid of—he knew he could do this.

Of course, he'd always had a little trouble with levitation . . .

He had to get the moment exactly right, and he had to trust the Force to let him know when it was.

It came. He clamped down on the jacket, and his arms felt like they were coming out of their sockets. The smell of scorched synthleather filled his nostrils, and he felt the floor coming up, still too fast. He pushed, pushed in the Force—

—and slammed into the ground. He let his knees buckle, released the jacket, and rolled.

"Ouch," he murmured.

Nom Anor heard something strike the floor, not too far away, and without even having to look, he knew the Jedi had somehow found a way to come down the shaft after him.

He cursed under his breath and ran for the lift. They couldn't catch him now—he would either have to help them reverse his sabotage or die along with them, neither of which figured very prominently in his plans. He was still unarmed, except for the plaeryin bol.

The lift came in sight, but he heard running footfalls behind him. He lurched to a stop in front of the car, pushed out the crate that was blocking it, and punched at the ascent control.

Only then did he look up to see how close his pursuer was. Corran Horn was just rounding a bank of equipment, his lightsaber blazing. He was coming fast, but not fast enough.

"Nom Anor!" he shouted. "Fight me!"

Nom Anor actually laughed at that. "I wouldn't fight the Solo brat at Yag'Dhul," he shouted, as the door closed. "Why in the galaxy would I fight you?"

The lift started up.

Now he had a few seconds to think. Horn would unjam a lift and follow him, but he hadn't seen Tahiri. She was probably still at the top, waiting for the lift door to open. Maybe Harrar was with her. Could he take them both?

He had to, obviously, or all of this would be for naught.

They already knew his identity. The shaper must not have been as dead as he thought she was.

He spent the next few seconds marshaling his strength, knowing this would either be his moment of triumph, or another failure.

The door opened.

THIRTY

Thunder seemed to rumble through *Mon Mothma* as the ship turned ponderously broadside to bring her guns to bear on the lead Yuuzhan Vong destroyer analog. The destroyer, already in a position to fire, held its ground and unloaded, pounding the deflectors mercilessly. Wedge could almost hear the Yuuzhan Vong commander's triumphant gloat—by the time the *Mothma*'s main batteries were in position to strike at him, its shields would have failed.

Which was why it was good that that was not really what Wedge had in mind, after all.

"Now," he said quietly. "Engage the tractor beam."

The entire ship jolted and hummed as its structure tried to compensate for suddenly being attached to another mass of even greater size. Both ships suddenly began to pivot in ponderous slow motion.

"They've broken the lock, sir," Cel informed him.

"That was plenty," Wedge replied, repressing a grin. They had managed to roll the destroyer right into the path of a Yuuzhan Vong Dreadnaught, effectively blocking fire from it to either the *Mothma* or the heavy Mon Cal cruiser *Vortex Wind* that was coming up behind. The Yuuzhan Vong ship not only was serving as a shield for them, but was now exposed to fire from both Alliance ships, as well. Wedge watched in satisfaction as huge chunks of the vessel went white, fading through blue to red, then black. A seam of internal explosions ran down the spiny length of the destroyer, ripping it apart.

Cheers went up from the bridge crew.

That put them ahead of the game, in terms of numbers.

"Continue as planned," Wedge said.

The *Vortex Wind* nosed over the dying hulk of the destroyer, swinging broadside as she did so, and caught the next ship hard with its batteries as it came from behind the eclipse. Wedge took *Mon Mothma* to starboard and down, relative to the *Vortex Wind*, joining *Memory of Ithor* in a bombardment of a smaller frigate-sized ship. He'd been working his way through the Yuuzhan Vong formation with a series of these bait-and-switches, using one ship to draw the attackers into the line of another. It was almost too easy, but they had clearly expected him to make a hard, straight push for the interdictor. Instead, he was plowing around the flank farthest from the huge dovin basal vessel, shredding it pretty effectively. They'd finally analyzed his plan and were bringing around the largest ship in the center, but they were slow, and he'd already managed to take out three of their capital ships without losing any of his own, though the Ranger was in pretty bad shape.

The starboard flank was theirs, now. He had the ships form a line and began laying down a corridor of fire that opened a lane to the approaching Dreadnaught, a monstrous kilometer-long cone of bone-white yorik coral. Maybe a hundred coralskippers flared out in the first few furious seconds, and Alliance starfighters rushed in to fill the gap, pouring toward the hulking Yuuzhan Vong vessels.

"Come and get us," Wedge said. "Come on, be the Vong I know and love."

Because now what remained of the Yuuzhan Vong flotilla was at a pronounced disadvantage. To continue the fight, they would have to fly straight into the combined firepower of six Alliance capital vessels.

Which, predictably, they began to do.

This was where the heavy slugging would begin.

"Sir, we report some activity from the Golan Two. It opened fire on the skips pursuing Twin Suns."

"Really?" That was good news. He hadn't really expected the battle platform to be functional after all this time. How had Jaina commandeered it so quickly?

"Yes, sir."

"See if you can raise Colonel Solo."

The Dreadnaughts were closing, and beginning to fire at extreme range. Wedge could already see them taking hits from the starfighters.

"Target dovin basals until they're in deep range," he said. "Lasers only, at your pleasure."

The *Mothma* and its sisters commenced firing.

"Sir?" Cel sounded distressed.

"Yes?" he asked mildly.

"We can't raise Colonel Solo. And there's something else."

"Well?"

"The Golan Two has disappeared."

"Disappeared? Destroyed?"

"It's hard to say at this range, sir, with this much interference, but there's no obvious sign of explosion or debris. It's more like it just dropped out of existence."

Gone, then here, then gone . . .

"Thrawn," he murmured. "Did you leave us a present?"

"Sir?"

"It's cloaked, Lieutenant. Keep an eye on that sector, and let me know the instant anyone hears anything from Colonel Solo."

He turned his attention back to the immediate battle. The Golan was still very much a wild card—he would have to work with what he had.

The lead Dreadnaught was taking terrific damage, but it

must have been mostly hull in the forward sections, because it was still coming. Wedge paced up to the viewport.

"Die, you ugly brute," he muttered.

But on it came, aimed at *Spritespray*, a medium cruiser. At this point, even if they managed to kill the dovin basal drive the ship would keep coming with enough momentum to wreck the cruiser and open a hole in his line. If the Dreadnaught retained any firepower, it would then be behind his line, forcing him to a two-front battle.

"*Spritespray,* let her through. *Vortex Wind, Justice*—execute rumble."

The three ships acknowledged. Wedge watched the Dreadnaught roar past, with far too much momentum to stop as *Spritespray* scooted aside and the *Vortex Wind* and *Justice* rolled above and below the gap. As the Dreadnaught went through the hole, they let the ship have it from both sides.

The Dreadnaught passed through the line with no drive and massive damage in all areas. Without power it continued on its last vector, out toward the system's rim.

Other ships were making for the gap, though. Wedge shifted his line to break and form on either side of the already damaged vessels.

"Sir!"

From Cel's frantic tone, he knew it would be bad.

Ships were decanting near the interdictor—Yuuzhan Vong ships. A thin chill lifted the hair of his neck.

"They've figured out we weren't a feint," Wedge said. "They're back."

That meant he had a whole new battle on his hands.

THIRTY-ONE

The door opened, and Nom Anor stepped out, smiling, his hands extended with open palms.

"Stop right there," Tahiri commanded.

"If I don't, will you cut me down?" Nom Anor asked. "I have no weapons."

"You wouldn't use them if you had them," Tahiri snapped. "Coward. You wouldn't fight Anakin at Yag'Dhul."

Nom Anor shrugged. "True enough. How is the young Solo brat? No—didn't I hear he died? Yes, that's right, he did. And you two were close, were you not? What a pity."

"Shut up," Tahiri said. The hatred was welling up in her, urging her to do exactly as he had suggested, cut him down and slash that murderous smug leer from his face.

"You're angry," Nom Anor said. "I thought you Jedi weren't supposed to get angry."

"I make an exception for you," Tahiri said.

"How flattering," the executor purred. "You would turn to the dark side just for me?"

"You have no idea what you're talking about," Tahiri said.

"Wrong," Nom Anor replied, taking a step out of the turbolift. "I have studied your ways, Jedi. I know that if you strike me down in anger you will have committed the most terrible sin your kind can commit."

"You won't care about that," Tahiri said. "You'll be dead."

"Will I?" He took another step.

"*Stop*," Tahiri commanded.

"Very well. I will do as you ask." He stopped, less than a meter away, staring at her. She felt her hands shaking—not with fear, but with the effort to control her passions.

"Kill him," Harrar said.

"He's not armed," Tahiri said. "I won't murder him."

"No!" Harrar said, leaping forward.

It distracted Tahiri for an instant and she looked away, noticing even as she did that one of Anor's pupils was growing—

Memory clicked—something Leia had said about that eye.

She leapt aside as the glob of venom spurted toward her, but she hadn't taken the guardrail into account. She hit it with her hip and agonizing pain jolted up her side. She tried to turn and managed to just in time to see Nom Anor side-step the priest and kick viciously at her. The kick connected, flipping her back. She dropped her lightsaber, grabbing wildly for the railing.

She missed and then she was falling.

Part of Nom Anor was amazed it had been so easy to deal with Tahiri. He turned on Harrar, and found the priest coming for him again, a snarl on his face.

Nom Anor hit him with a q'urh kick, then spun and snapped his fist against the back of the priest's head. Harrar faded with the blow, however, dropping and sweeping. He caught one of Nom Anor's feet, putting him off balance long enough to launch a powerful thrusting punch.

More by luck than from any design on Nom Anor's part, the punch missed. Nom Anor brought his fist up under Harrar's jaw with such force that the priest left the ground. Bits of shattered teeth sprinkled the floor as Harrar thudded to it, slid up to the wall, and lay still.

Nom Anor took quick stock of his situation and saw that

his day was getting even better. The Jedi had dropped her weapon. Quickly he picked it up. He had experimented with them before, and so found it easy to ignite. Then, remembering Horn, he severed the power conduits to the lifts, starting with the one in motion. He heard it drag to a stop someplace not far below.

Knowing that this might not be good enough—for all he knew Horn might cut hole in the wall and *fly* up—he left the building and struck off through the driving sheets of rain toward a high, flat spot he'd picked out some time before, shoving the now quiescent weapon under his sash.

Tahiri flailed in space, reaching desperately to grab something, *anything*, but nothing was in reach. From the corner of her vision she caught sight of the cable Corran had slid down, less than a meter away—which was still half a meter too far.

The Force, idiot, she thought. She reached out, tugging at the cable with the Force, changing her vector so she angled toward it.

She wrapped her bare palms around it, gasping as her hands burned. Her fingers tried to open reflexively, but she couldn't let them, or she would fall. Nom Anor would escape, Sekot would die—and she would let Corran down.

If the older Jedi was still alive.

She embraced the pain and focused beyond it, using the Force to further slow her descent. Finally, every muscle in her body shrieking in chorus with her palms, she came to a stop.

She looked up, and discovered she had fallen almost a hundred meters.

The anger was back, but now she needed it—not to fight, but to wrap her legs around the cable and pull herself up, though every centimeter gained brought a world of agony. She felt blisters rupturing on her hands.

At least it makes them stickier, she reflected. Her hands conformed to the cable now, as if they were made of tal gum.

Nom Anor went carefully up the narrow path, choosing his steps in the freeze-frame moments that the lightning created as it limned the world white and blue, then left it again in darkness. The rain was a steady drum, and the wind gusted like the laughter of an insane god. His route was a broken spine of stone with yawning pits of darkness on either side. He came to particularly narrow footing and stopped for a moment, realizing that he was actually afraid. It was as if the planet itself was trying to do what the Jedi had been unable to.

As perhaps it was. If Nen Yim was correct, and the planet was sentient, perhaps it had witnessed his act of sabotage. Perhaps it sought revenge.

"Do your worst," he snarled into the wind. "I am Nom Anor. Know my name, for I have killed you."

As he said it, he finally knew with absolute conviction that he had done the right thing. Zonama Sekot was like a tonqu flower—attracting insects with its sweet scent, tempting them to alight upon it—where they found themselves cloyed, watching the long petal roll up. Part living, part machine, and somehow part *Jedi*, it was an abomination—more so than Coruscant, more so than anything in the galaxy of abominations.

Quoreal had been right. They should never have come here.

But Nom Anor had set that to rights.

He crossed the narrow area, stepped over a gap in the next lightning flash, and saw that the way widened a bit ahead.

But from the corner of his eye—

Someone crashed into him, chopping viciously at the side of his neck. The force of the blow knocked him sprawling, and his chin grated against stone. With a roar he kicked back and rolled. A foot caught him under his savaged chin, but he managed to catch it and twist. His attacker fell heavily. Nom Anor scrambled back, trying to regain his footing, but found himself teetering on the edge of a cliff. Lighting ripped the sky, and he saw a silhouette rising against it. Another flash came, this one behind him, and he made out Harrar's face, terrifying, as if the very gods had put their light of vengeance in him.

"Nom Anor," the priest shouted through the rain. "Prepare to die, perfidious one."

"This planet has driven you mad, Harrar," Nom Anor snapped. "You side with Jedi against *me*?"

"I side with Zonama Sekot," Harrar said. "And you— you are accursed by Shimrra, you honorless qorih. I would have killed you anyway."

"Zonama Sekot is a lie, you fool—a tale I told my followers so that they would obey me."

"You know nothing," Harrar said. "You know less than nothing. Do you think you know the secrets of the priesthood? Do you think we share all we know? It is Shimrra who has lied to us. Zonama Sekot is the truth. If you would be of service to your people, you will tell me what you have done."

Nom Anor felt the lightsaber in his hand. Harrar was advancing, and a single kick would be enough to send Nom Anor plunging to his death. He dared not use the plaeryin bol—even if it still contained poison, the rain would at best deflect it, at worst wash in onto *him*. The Jedi weapon was his only chance.

"Telling you will do no good," he sneered at Harrar. "Nothing can reverse the damage now."

"I believe you," Harrar said, his face twisting as he took a quick step toward Nom Anor.

Nom Anor pressed the stud on the lightsaber and the cutting beam blazed out, hissing and trailing steam in the downpour. It felt strange, a weapon with no weight other than its grip. He cut at the priest's knee, but his position and the unfamiliar blade made the cut awkward. At the appearance of the blade, however, Harrar tried to stop his forward motion and jerked his leg away from the attack; he slipped on the wet rocks and stumbled, falling past Nom Anor and over the cliff.

His howl of rage and frustration was quickly cut short.

Panting, Nom Anor rose, extinguished the lightsaber, and continued on his way. The gods were with him again, it seemed. Certainly they were no longer with Harrar.

When the turbolift jarred to a halt, Corran ignited his lightsaber and cut through the roof of the car, stepping aside as the circle of metal clanged to the floor. After waiting a few seconds for the plating to cool, he leapt up and caught the edge of the hole, then drew himself up into the shaft.

In the dim emergency lighting, he could see the door some ten meters above. The lift was magnetic, so the walls were glassy smooth, and the power cables were buried in them. There were no rungs and nothing to give purchase. He could cut handholds for himself and climb, but that would take a long time.

He dropped back down into the car and examined the control panel. He didn't know the language. The up and down icons were obvious, but the others would take a little figuring out.

Nom Anor must have cut the power from above somehow, but the car hadn't fallen—presumably there was an emergency battery system to prevent that happening. But would the emergency system be able to finish the ascent, or was it doing its best just to keep him from falling?

He pushed a red button with two vertical lines and a triangle, with no result. He tried a few of the others, again with no result. Frustrated, he tapped the up key.

The car started moving, though much more slowly than before. He felt like pounding his head against the wall: the emergency system was separate from the normal one—he needed only to tell the car where he wanted to go.

A few minutes later, he emerged from the lift, ready to fight—but there was no one to fight. The room was empty. There were light spatters of black blood on the floor, but other than that, no clues as to exactly what had happened.

He was about to go outside when he heard a faint noise behind him, in the maintenance shaft. Peering over, he saw Tahiri pulling herself up the superconductor cable, about twenty meters below.

"Are you okay?" he shouted.

"I'm fine," she called back up, her voice shaking. She seemed to be having trouble climbing. "Nom Anor got away," she added. "You have to stop him—I'll join you when I can."

"And leave you dangling? No. I don't think so. You just hang on there."

He went back to the lifts. Someone had indeed cut through the power couplings—with a lightsaber, it appeared. He reached cautiously inside and grabbed a rope-sized fiber-optic conduit and began to pull it out. When he thought he had enough, he cut it with his weapon and then tied a loop in the end.

Tahiri hadn't made much progress in the intervening time. He threw the loop end down to her.

"Put your foot in that," he said, "and hang on with your hands. I'll pull you up."

She nodded wearily and did as instructed. Bracing his end of the rope over the safety rail, Corran hauled her up.

When she had pulled herself over the rail, he saw her hands.

"Let me see those," he said.

"They're all right," she protested.

"Let me see them."

They were badly friction-burned, but it looked as if her tendons were undamaged, which was good. The scar on her old amphistaff wound had torn a bit and was leaking blood, but not too much.

"Well, at least you got to slide down the cable," he said. "Was it as fun as you imagined it would be?"

"That and loads more," Tahiri said.

"What happened here?"

"I let my guard down," she said. "Nom Anor has something in one of his eyes that shoots poison."

"Did he hit you with it?"

"No. But when I dodged, I hit the rail, and then he knocked me over it."

"And Harrar?"

"I don't know. He attacked Nom Anor, I think. Maybe he's gone after him. Which is what we ought to do."

Corran peered outside at the dark and the rain. "I agree. But how to track them in this, without the Force?"

"I have my Vongsense," Tahiri said. "If he hasn't gone far, I might be able to sense him."

Corran produced a small glow rod, and in its light they found muddy, water-filled footprints leading back toward the heights. They followed the prints until they came to a narrow ridge of stone.

"At least there's only one way to go," Corran said.

As they ascended, the lightning reached a crescendo, striking in the valley where they had been staying every few seconds or so. The roar was so steady they couldn't hear each other speak. Then—rather abruptly—it was over. The rain slacked off, and then ended, and the wind subsided to a clean, wet breeze.

The ridge continued until it joined a larger one, ascending the whole time.

"He's going for high ground," Corran said. "Can you sense your lightsaber?"

"No," she said. "There's something interfering—more than usual."

"I feel it, too," Corran said. "It's Zonama Sekot. Something's wrong."

"We failed," Tahiri said. "Whatever Nom Anor was going to do, he's already done it, I'm sure of it."

"There may still be time to stop him," Corran replied. "Concentrate. Use your Vongsense."

She closed her eyes, and he felt her relax, reaching out to someplace he couldn't go.

"I feel him," she said at last. "Up ahead."

By the time the east was gray with dawn, they had reached a broad, upland plateau that showed signs of recent convulsion. The stone beneath the soil had split in places, rearing up to reveal its strata. The soil was black and ashy, and the vegetation was low when there was any at all, though the charred trunks of larger boras still stood here and there, like the columns of ruined temples.

"I've lost him," Tahiri said, a tinge of despair in her voice. "He could be anywhere up here."

Corran agreed. Where there was soil, it was spongy with a dark green web of grass that resisted tracks.

"We'll keep going in the same general direction," Corran said, "unless—"

Far above, they heard a faint report, like very distant and brief lightning.

"Sonic boom," he murmured, searching the skies with his gaze. The clouds had cleared away, leaving only a few thin ones very far up.

"There," Tahiri said. She pointed to a swiftly moving spot, high above.

"Good eyes," Corran told her. "I'll give you one guess where that's going."

"Wherever Nom Anor is."

The dot was descending rapidly toward the plateau. Corran peered along its projected path and caught a hint of motion near a copse of low trees.

"Come on," Corran said. "If we run, we might get there in time."

"We *will*," Tahiri swore.

Nom Anor was watching the ship approach when the ground beneath his feet suddenly shuddered. It lasted for only an instant, but he knew it was only the beginning. He looked off toward the still-visible field guides and saw a white plume curling up toward the sky. He curled his lip—if he had timed this wrong, if he died in the explosion he had caused, how the gods would laugh.

The grass off to his left rustled, and from the corner of his eye, Nom Anor glimpsed unnatural color. Turning as if in a dream, he beheld Corran Horn stepping into the clearing, his eyes full of death.

Nom Anor glanced up at the approaching ship. It was only moments away, but that was longer than it would take for the Jedi to kill him. He touched his hand to the stolen lightsaber—

And ran, into the low-sprawling copse of trees behind him. He need only buy enough time for Choka's ship to land and dispatch warriors.

Corran Horn shouted and ran after him.

Nom Anor dodged through the trees, leaping an old fissure, then bore to his left, hoping to circle back to the clearing. The ground trembled again, not enough to upset his footing, but almost. He glanced back over his shoulder, saw Horn gaining on him, turned to redouble his pace.

Just in time to see the blade of a foot, level with his eyes. Behind the foot was an airborne Tahiri, her body horizontal to the ground.

The kick caught him above the nostrils, snapping his head back and knocking him completely off his feet. He crashed into the trunk of a tree, and half of the wind blew out of him. He clawed for the Jedi weapon he'd thrust in his sash, but it was missing.

In fact, it was in Tahiri's hands, the energy blade already on.

"This is *mine*," she said.

Corran had come up behind her. "Don't kill him," the older Jedi said.

"I won't," Tahiri replied, but Nom Anor heard the tone in her voice. It was not a human tone at all—although she was speaking Basic, every nuance of her speech was Yuuzhan Vong. There was no mercy in it, but promises aplenty.

"I'm going to cut off his feet, though," she continued, stepping nearer. "And then his hands. Unless he tells us how to stop what he's done to Sekot."

"Do what you will," Nom Anor said, forcing as much contempt into his voice as he could. "It has already begun. You cannot stop it."

"Where's Harrar?" Corran asked.

"He's dead," Nom Anor replied. "I killed him." He watched the tip of Tahiri's blade dip toward his foot, and then winced as she traced a shallow burn across the ankle.

"Tahiri, no," Corran commanded.

Her eyes narrowed further, then she withdrew the blade.

"Yes, Master," she said.

"Get up, Anor."

Nom Anor began coming slowly to his feet.

"The ship's landing, Corran," Tahiri said.

"But he's not going on it," Corran said. "You have a villip, don't you, Nom Anor? You'll call them off, now, or I'll cut your head off myself. And that, my friend, is absolutely not a bluff."

"They will not obey me," Nom Anor said.

"Maybe they won't," Corran told him, "but you'd sure better try to make them."

Nom Anor stared into the man's eyes and knew he was not lying.

He reached for the villip beneath his arm, thinking furiously.

Then Zonama Sekot tried to throw them all into space.

The ground bucked beneath them and an anguished cry exploded in the Force, filling Tahiri's head with such agony that she hardly noticed when she thudded back to the ground. Desperately she tried to shut out the world's pain and regain her feet, but the will behind it was too strong. She felt as if a trillion needles were growing from her heart, pushing through her heart and lungs and bone. She clutched at her head, screaming with Zonama Sekot's voice.

Through her blurred vision, she saw Nom Anor running off through the crazily tilted trees.

No! Sekot, he's the one doing this to you!

She was never sure if Sekot somehow heard her, or if that gave her the extra strength she needed to push away the sick pain, but she levered herself to her feet.

Corran was up, leaning heavily against a tree.

"Corran—"

"Just a second," he said. "I—okay. I think I've got it under control now."

The two Jedi stumbled through the newly broken terrain. The ship was on the ground, and Nom Anor was running toward it. Tahiri ran as she never had before, drawing on the turbulent Force around them. Corran was just ahead of her. They were gaining on the executor. If they could reach him before the warriors on the ship could debark, they might yet be able to save Sekot. She clung to that hope, as the breath ripped at her lungs and her heart stuttered unevenly.

Without warning, Corran lashed out at her, sending her sprawling. Even before a sense of betrayal could register, she saw he was going down, too. Less than a heartbeat later, a swarm of thud bugs whirred through the space where they'd just been.

She suddenly understood that she and Corran must have been occupied with Sekot's pain for longer than she'd thought. The warriors had already come out of the ship and hidden themselves around the clearing. Corran and she were completely surrounded.

THIRTY-TWO

"Okay, folks," Han said as the reversion warning began sounding. "Hang on. If Wedge is still here, it's probably because the Vong have interdictors to keep him from leaving, which means we'll probably get pulled out early. Again."

"I hope he isn't here," C-3PO said. "I *so* dislike unplanned reversions. They cause an unpleasant resonance in my circuits."

"That's great," Han said. "All I need now is a hypochondriac droid."

"Sir, it is *quite* impossible for a droid to be a hypochondriac."

"If you say so, Goldenrod. Okay, here goes."

Han pulled back on the levers, and the *Falcon* decanted as effortlessly as she ever had—in fact, more smoothly than usual. "Well, whaddya know," he said. "We came out normally. Guess that means—"

"—that we're too far from the interdictor," Leia finished. "Just barely."

Leia was right. His instruments showed the gravitic profile of not one dovin basal interdictor, but two. The *Falcon* had flashed into existence marginally outside the field of effect of the nearest. If he'd been set to revert just a little farther in, he would have made good on his prediction.

"Oh, dear," C-3PO said. "It looks as if General Antilles *is* here. And not doing very well!"

"Yeah," Han agreed. "You can say that again." He looked sharply at the droid. "But *don't*."

The system was swarming with Yuuzhan Vong ships. The nearest was one of the interdictors, hanging in space like a sword with two blades and no grip. Beyond it was a stationary mass of skips and a few cruisers, apparently guarding the interdictor against attack. Farther insystem was the main battle, where ten Yuuzhan Vong capital ships—two of which were behemoths—were engaged with what was left of Wedge's battle group.

Which wasn't much—Han counted four Alliance ships of frigate size or larger. They were clustered together, trying to avoid being encircled, but—as C-3PO had pointed out—it didn't seem to be going so well.

Beyond all of that was another interdictor. It, like the one near the *Falcon*, was keeping its distance, moving only to keep the Alliance ships from going to hyperspace.

"Ouch," Han said. "He needs reinforcements, and he needs them now."

"It's a disaster," Leia murmured. Then she straightened and got that Jedi look in her eye.

"What?"

"It's Jaina."

He waited for her to continue, his heart frozen in his chest.

"She's alive," Leia said, "and I don't think she's injured. But something's wrong."

"If she's down there, I guess so," Han said, swallowing.

"There must be *something* we can do!" C-3PO wailed.

"There is," Leia told him.

"Yeah," Han said, looking at the interdictor. "There is."

"Whatever—sir, you're not going to attack the interdictor? We barely survived the last time!"

"They haven't noticed we're here yet," Han said. "They don't even have any ships on this side. We've got a good clean shot at them. With a little surprise on our side, a little know-how—sure, why not?"

"But our weapons aren't sufficient to incapacitate a ship of that size," the droid pointed out.

Leia leaned over and kissed Han on the cheek. "That's never stopped him before."

Han felt the lump in his throat swell, but he forced a smile. "This is just more of the usual, Threepio. Don't worry yourself."

He opened a channel to the TIEs.

"Captain Devis, can I trust you to advise Grand Admiral Pellaeon of this situation immediately?"

"I thought you were going to do that, sir," Devis replied.

"Pellaeon might not arrive in time. He might even decide not to come at all, given the situation. Heck, he might have troubles of his own. We're going to stay and take out that interdictor."

"That could be quite a task," Devis said.

"All in a day's work," Han replied. "Just hurry up and bring us a little relief, will you?"

"I'll send a wingmate," Devis said, "but I'm staying to help."

"I—" Han looked back at the battle, remembering that Jaina was down there, somewhere. "I would appreciate the help, Captain Devis. Thank you."

He laced his fingers together and cracked them. "All right," he said, "let's get this show on the road."

He turned to Leia. "Sweetheart, could you get to one of the turbolasers? Our Noghri friends are picking it up pretty fast, but in this situation, I'd rather have you—" He stopped, almost unable to continue, and most of the swagger went out of his voice. "I'd rather have you here, next to me," he finished. "But I need you in the upper turret."

She gave his hand a squeeze. "I know. I'll put Meewalh in the other."

She stood to go, but before she could leave the cockpit, he pulled her down for a kiss. "Be careful up there, huh?" he said.

"I always am."

He watched her go, wishing suddenly that they could just leave, go find Pellaeon, go watch a sunset . . .

But Jaina was here, and despite the fact that the odds were—

"Oh, great," he murmured. "I'm turning into Threepio."

"What was that, sir?" C-3PO asked.

"I said, I'm glad you're up here, Threepio."

"Why—thank you, sir. I'm really quite touched."

"Right," Han said. He opened the channel again.

"Okay, TIEs, we're going in—just hang back until they start throwing skips at us."

The interdictor was two spicular cones with their bases touching, and it was nearly the size of a Star Destroyer. Usually they were covered with skips, but this time the skips were elsewhere—either in battle or between the interdictor and the battle, guarding against a push in its direction.

Han dived the *Falcon* toward the thickest part of the vessel, knowing he would get only one good run before they were aware of his presence and set about a thousand skips on him. The TIEs dropped into formation on his port and starboard.

"Watch the gravity well, fellows," he warned them. "We want to mess up their paint job, but not by splatting all over 'em."

"I hear you," Devis replied. "Correcting."

Han tilted the ship to put the seam where the two cones met in the Money Lane and started in with the quad lasers. An instant later, the turret guns joined him. Voids appeared in spidery clusters, sucking the blasts into nothingness. Han launched a concussion missile to either side of the fire lane, and had the satisfaction of seeing both plow into the craggy yorik coral surface, rupturing it and sending shock waves crawling out toward the thin ends of the ship.

Then he was curving around the interdictor, his course bent by gravity. But instead of using the force to sling him away, he settled into a tight orbit, firing constantly, trying to dig a trench into the thing deep enough to do real damage.

The interdictor's plasma cannons began to fire, but one reason Han had picked the centerline as his target was that the ship angled away from it in every direction, making it tough to fire at him at all and impossible to put him in a cross fire. Nevertheless, a near miss roared by the cockpit, an eight-meter-wide explosion of superheated matter that grazed his shields and sent an ion jolt through the ship's protective circuitry.

Meanwhile, less than one in ten of his laser shots were getting through, and he had only a few concussion missiles left. His trench wasn't getting deep very fast.

"Skips coming in," Devis reported. "Six in the first wave."

"Can you keep them off us for another pass or so?" Han asked.

"Copy that, Captain Solo."

Han fired another pair of concussion missiles—one got through, the other exploded when it was about to be sucked in by a void. That happened near enough to the *Falcon* that the shock wave bounced him from his orbit and sent him away from the centerline. Suddenly he was no longer outside the interdictor's line of direct fire, but squarely in it. He stood the *Falcon* on her thin side relative to the interdictor to minimize his target surface, weaving through withering fire, dropping lower to keep the blasts from converging on him. When he was practically skating on the ship's surface, he turned abruptly up and out.

"Wow," he heard Devis say. Han's jaw nearly dropped—

the two TIEs had stayed with him the whole way. Behind them were only three skips of the original six. Han didn't have to wonder what had happened to the other three—not with pilots like that.

Even as he watched, the TIEs broke and came around, putting the skips between them and the big guns of the cruiser, and proceeded to take them apart.

"That's some pretty fancy flying," Han commented. "Good thing there weren't more like you when we were *fighting* the Empire."

"Thank you, sir," Devis said. "But we've got more company. A lot more."

Han glanced at the monitor. "We can make one more pass," he said. "After that it's going to be way too hot here."

In fact, he knew, this pass was going to be more than a little warm itself—probably fatally so.

"Wow," Prann said, gazing out through the Golan II's viewport. "Look at that. And you wanted us to help them."

"What?" Jaina said.

"Come here," Prann said.

She got up and made her slow way to the viewport. They had traded out the webbing they had bound her with for stun cuffs on her hands and feet and a slave collar around her neck. Moreover, the Toydarian was still sticking close to her. Prann didn't seem too worried that she would try anything.

She reached the viewport, and to her dismay saw what Prann was talking about.

"The rest of the Vong fleet came back," she said dully.

"Yep. In a few hours your fleet's going to be scrap metal, and even if we were inclined to lend a hand, I don't think we could do much good against that many."

"Don't try to justify your cowardice to me," Jaina said. "They're all going to die, and you're just going to watch."

"Watch?" Prann said. "No, I'm going to run. The hyperdrive is ready to go, thanks to your spare parts. Why do you think I dropped the cloak? But it looks like they've forgotten us out here, so we're going to finish running computer simulations. Our cobbled-together drive is a little quirky, and we don't want to end up in a star."

"Please," Jaina said. "If you'll just listen to me—"

"Solo, I said no. Hey, look at it this way: you're going to live to tell the uppity-ups what happened here, which no one else is likely to be able to do. You're going to live, Colonel—and it's not even your fault."

"What's that supposed to mean?" Jaina asked.

"It means," Prann said, leaning over her, "I've done a little fighting myself, in my time, and I know your type. Getting dead is your *goal* in life, and you'll keep throwing yourself into the fray until it happens. In the meantime, you live in constant disappointment."

"You don't know me," Jaina said. "Don't pretend you do."

"Whatever, kid. I'm not going to make an argument out of it. It's not worth it."

"Take this station into battle, now!" Jaina said, as dramatically as possible. Prann blinked at her. She felt the Toydarian tense.

"Well," Prann said. "Nice try."

Jaina let her face sag in defeat, but inwardly, she conjured a wicked little smile. She'd only lightly nudged Prann with the Force, just enough to let him know she was there.

Because, in the middle of their little discussion, she had found a plan. She wasn't sure it would work, but it had a better chance of succeeding now than it had a moment ago.

"Pash?" Wedge said.

"Get me General Cracken!"

He'd just seen *Memory of Ithor* take a series of hard hits, and sensors said its core was going critical.

"Here, Wedge," the general's tired voice said a moment later. "Sorry, we're not going to much help to you from here on out."

"Just get out of there," Wedge said.

"We're evacuating now," Pash said. "We'll have to take our chances in escape pods—we've got none here. I tried to aim her at one of the interdictors, but she's not going to make it, I'm afraid."

"Just take care of yourself, Pash. This isn't over yet."

"Good luck, Wedge. Cracken out."

A few moments later, the *Memory* flashed out of existence. Wedge hoped Pash made it out, but he didn't have time to dwell on it. The *Mothma* was limping itself, and it wouldn't be long before he was sharing his old friend's fate. Unless something changed, and quickly, they were all going down.

Millennium Falcon and her escort had picked up twenty skips by the time they came into firing range again. The TIEs were staying behind them, drawing fire in an effort to keep them from hitting the *Falcon*, but plenty of shots were getting through, making it an awfully rough ride.

"Captain Solo," C-3PO moaned from the copilot's seat, "I'm afraid our rear deflector is beginning to fail."

"See if you can reroute the power," Han said, wishing Leia were in that seat, despite what he'd said earlier.

"Can't keep them off," Devis said. "I've lost my shields."

"Thanks for the help," Han told him. "I can handle it from here. You just get clear." He fired off the last of his concussion missiles, blowing another gouge in the interdictor, and focused his quad lasers on the hole. Yorik coral churned and evaporated. He dropped even lower, hoping a void didn't get him, and continued to strafe.

An enormous explosion rocked the ship.

"What was that?" he asked of everyone and no one in particular.

"My wingmate," Devis replied. His voice had a rattling quality to it. "He took a direct hit."

"You're still back there?" Han snapped. "Get out! Make sure Pellaeon is coming!"

"A little late for that, I'm afraid," Devis said. "But maybe I can still be of service. It was a great honor flying with you, Captain Solo. Tell ... tell Admiral Pellaeon I did what I thought was best."

"Devis, what are you—"

But then the TIE came screaming by on his starboard. It was spinning as if it had lost a stabilizer, but somehow the kid had still managed to aim it. It smacked into the interdictor like a meteor, blasting off a chunk of yorik coral almost the size of the *Falcon* and leaving an incandescent hole. Atmosphere blew out into the void, along with a few figures that could only be Yuuzhan Vong.

Han pulled up, pulling a few skips through the explosion as he did so.

"Threepio?" he demanded.

"I'm sorry, sir," the droid said. "The interdictor is still functioning."

Which means it was all for nothing, kid, Han thought. He realized he didn't even know what Devis had looked like.

"Han, what's happening?" Leia's voice drifted up.

"Nothing," he said. "We've lost the TIEs and the interdictor is still on-line. If we make another pass, they'll bring us down for sure."

"If we don't—"

"Yeah, I know," Han said. "Even if Pellaeon comes, it'll be too little, too late. So we make another pass, right?"

"Right."

"Right." He spun the ship in a vicious roll that brought

the interdictor back into view. "I love you, sweetheart," he said.

"I love you too, you old pirate."

"Okay," Prann said, "looks like we're ready, guys. I'm laying in the final calculations."

This is it, Jaina thought. She reached out through the Force, subtly, not taking control, but instead substituting her own coordinates for the ones Prann thought he was entering. She didn't have much skill controlling minds through the Force, and like Jacen she didn't think much of the practice.

But this time there was no choice.

One-one-two, not aught-aught-two, she thought at Prann. *Aught-nine-one, not one-one-nine. Everything else is right, it's perfect, the best jump ever calculated, and then you'll be home, rich, safe from the Vong forever.* She couldn't change the jump much, or he would notice. But she didn't need to.

"Hey," the Toydarian said. He must have noticed her look of concentration. "What are you doing? Stop it, or I shoot your hand off."

"I'm not doing anything," Jaina said, desperately trying to keep up her monologue through the Force. "What could I be doing?"

"Doesn't matter anyway," Prann said. "Here we go."

He pulled back on the jump lever, and they went.

"What in the—" Han yanked back on the stick, pulling the *Falcon* out of her dive and just whispering by the huge object that had appeared in his path.

"Just when you think things can't get worse—"

"Sir! Sir!" C-3PO shouted. "It's a Golan Two Battle Station. Where in the galaxy could that have come from?"

"A Golan? . . ."

"We're saved!"

* * *

"What—what happened?" Prann shrieked.

"You tried to jump through an interdictor," Jaina replied. "It didn't work."

"I did not! I set the jump in exactly the opposite direction."

"Yes, well, obviously you didn't."

Prann leapt up, pulling his blaster. "*You* did this. Somehow you got in my head—"

"Listen to me, Prann," Jaina snapped. "You're interdicted. They have a solid read on you by now, so if you put the cloak up you'll not only be a sitting target, you'll be a *blind* sitting target. You've got just one choice now—take out that interdictor, or die. What's it going to be?"

Prann kept the blaster on her, his face contorted with fury.

"She's right, Erli," Ghanol said. "We have to fight our way out now."

Prann's finger twitched on the blaster contact—then he slammed it back into his holster.

"To the guns, then. But so help me, Jedi, you're going to pay for this."

Han cut hard in next to the station as the shields went on. The next instant, heavy laserfire began pounding the interdictor. Now his only worry was the dozen or so skips still on his tail, his own failing shields, and twenty other things that were going wrong in his ship.

"Hang on, everybody," he said. "This is going to be tight."

"Han," Leia called up.

"Little busy right now, honey," he said.

"Jaina's in that station."

"Really? There ought to be a good story behind this one—but hey, that's our girl."

"I don't think—Han, she's still in trouble."

"Oh, yeah?" He yawed and straightened, leading a skip through cannon fire. "Well, we'll see about that."

"Sir!" Cel shouted. "The Golan Two just appeared right next to the Interdictor. It's really giving it a pounding!"

Wedge looked at the display, not believing what he was seeing.

"How did they move it?" he wondered.

It didn't matter. "Change heading. When that field goes down, I want to be out of range of the other one. We'll take up the rear."

Ponderously and under heavy fire, what remained of his tattered fleet turned to obey. All except *Mon Mothma*.

The ships between them and the interdictor had realigned to deal with the battle station. His battle group had a clear run at it, but someone had to prevent that other interdictor from keeping pace with them. And since this was his fiasco, it looked like he was elected.

THIRTY-THREE

"Remember, you're supposed to be training me," Tahiri commented as she and Corran moved to stand back to back. "What does the wise Jedi do in a situation like this?" The warriors were advancing toward them in a tightening circle. In the distance, near where the tops of the field guides could be seen, the sky was a mass of white vapor.

"The wise Jedi avoids situations like this," Corran said.

"Oh," Tahiri said. "I don't guess I *know* any wise Jedi, then. Very disillusioning."

She counted thirty warriors.

"Right," Corran said. "And that's your lesson for the day—don't hang on to your illusions."

"I was hoping more for a crash course in 'how to kick butt when you're outnumbered thirty to two.' "

"Well, if you're going to be picky about what I teach . . ."

"Quickly!" Nom Anor shouted, from near the ship. "There is little time."

The circle contracted more rapidly. The ground trembled again, and pain pulsed through the Force. Pain and something else—something familiar.

She hadn't had time to sort it out when a track of green laserfire ran through the warriors on their right flank, then their left, and suddenly a gleaming spacecraft come into view. It dropped to hover a few meters off the ground.

"*Jade Shadow!*" Corran whooped. "It's Mara and Luke!"

Even as he said it, the landing ramp dropped down, and Luke Skywalker and Jacen Solo leapt out, followed by the hulking reptilian figure of Saba Sebatyne. Three new lightsabers flared to life. Then the *Shadow* leapt back up, turned, and began raining fire on the Yuuzhan Vong craft.

The remaining warriors shook off their stupor and charged, but Tahiri ignored them, tearing through one of the gaps cut by the *Shadow*. Nom Anor wasn't watching her—instead he was dodging laserfire, trying to reach the landing ramp of the Yuuzhan Vong ship. He made it there only a few meters ahead of her, but as soon as he was on it, it began to retract.

With a war cry, she hurled herself through the air, landing on the ramp, sweeping her lightsaber toward the executor's head.

Nom Anor ducked at the last instant and her lightsaber cut into the coral hull. He scrambled away from her, and she started to follow, but the ship suddenly bounded up from the ground, twisting as it went. Tahiri lost her footing and fell. She grasped at the edge of the retracting ramp and missed, but caught the edge of a plasma cannon with her left hand. Furiously, she cut at the hull with her lightsaber. It resisted the blow, and her weight suddenly tripled as the ship went into drive. She lost her grip and went whirling back to the ground, landing so hard all of the wind went out of her. She lay there, trying to recover, watching helplessly as the yorik coral vessel bored up through the atmosphere with *Jade Shadow* in hot pursuit.

Another wrenching wave of pain from the planet lashed at her, and again the ground shifted. Wheezing, she forced herself to her feet.

Corran, Luke, and Jacen were trotting toward her. Saba was standing at the edge of the clearing, staring out at the towers. The Yuuzhan Vong warriors all appeared to be dead.

"Tahiri," Jacen asked. "Are you okay?"

"Nothing broken, I think," she said.

He wrapped her up in an embrace that hurt almost as much as it felt good. Tears threatened again.

"I let him get away," she murmured. "After all that, I let him get away. And now Sekot will die."

"Die?" Master Skywalker said. "Do you two understand what's going on here? What's wrong with Sekot?"

Over Jacen's shoulder, Tahiri saw a shaft of blue light suddenly leap from ground to sky, appearing from somewhere near the hyperdrive. It lasted only a second.

"Down!" Corran shouted. "Cover your ears."

A heartbeat later, the shock wave came, followed by a wind so hot it scorched her back.

"What was that?" Jacen asked.

"The ship's drive," Corran explained. "Nom Anor must have sabotaged it somehow."

"Nom Anor?" Master Skywalker said. "What—?"

"That's a long story," Corran said, "one that I would like to tell. But I don't think I'm going to get the chance if we don't get out of this area, and quickly."

"Mara's already on her way back," Master Skywalker said.

By the time the *Shadow* dropped back low enough to pick them up, the surface of Zonama Sekot was vibrating like a plucked string, and in the Force, Tahiri could feel something building, something out of control. She followed the others aboard.

"I came back when I saw the plasma burst," Mara said. "Is it a weapon?"

"No," Luke said. "Get us out of here, Mara—fast."

"Sounds good to me."

"What about Nom Anor?" Tahiri asked.

"I alerted *Widowmaker*," Mara said. "They should have enough firepower to deal with the Vong ship."

The ground was dwindling, and the gigantic vanes of the hyperdrive were coming into view. The entire valley they stood in was black, and as she watched, three brilliant blue beams like the one they had seen a moment ago tore up through the atmosphere.

The shock wave hit, and the *Shadow* went into a crazy yaw, which Mara fought, cursing, into control.

"I appreciate the save," Corran told Master Skywalker as the ship leveled out. "But how is it you just happened by?"

"We didn't know it was you," Luke said. "Sekot was in pain—we came here to find out what was wrong, and saw the Yuuzhan Vong ship." He raised an eyebrow. "We were pretty surprised to find you here."

"Right," Corran said. "That explanation I promised you . . ."

Through the upward-angled cockpit view, Tahiri saw stars appearing as they left the atmosphere behind.

Then, abruptly, they streaked away.

Nom Anor was standing on the bridge of the transport vessel *Red Qurang*, watching the planet recede with a grim smile of satisfaction. *Jade Shadow* had broken off her pursuit.

"A large infidel ship is approaching," one of the subalterns growled.

"It's the Imperial frigate I mentioned to Shimrra," Nom Anor said. "You were supposed to occupy it with your other ships."

"There *are* no other ships," Ushk Choka growled. "Lord Shimrra had need of them elsewhere." He grimaced at the sight of the approaching ship. "It's too large to engage," he said. "Can we outrun it?"

"We will have to bear its first assault," the subaltern said. "After that we can outrun. Its mass will prevent it changing its vector quickly enough to catch us before we burrow into darkspace."

"Can we withstand?" Ushk Choka asked.

"Possibly," the subaltern said dubiously.

"Maneuver evasively, then."

Nom Anor was still watching the planet, feeling oddly calm, despite the danger he was in. He could still see where the hyperwave guides were by the boiling cloud, and as he watched, a brilliant blue cone suddenly appeared, then just as quickly vanished.

Something was wrong. The core was supposed to explode, not fire the engines. Had he failed? Was there something about Nen Yim's protocol he hadn't understood, or had he underestimated Sekot? Perhaps Skywalker and the other Jedi had managed to somehow reverse the damage he had caused.

The view swung away from the planet and was replaced by the night of space and a white wedge of abomination. It seemed Choka meant to run right into the warship's forward batteries.

"Keep our present course," Choka said. "Secure for bombardment."

"Entering range," the subaltern muttered.

The ship began rocking from the frigate's guns, but Nom Anor ignored them and stumbled his way back to the mica-like rear viewport analog, where Zonama Sekot was still visible.

Behind him, Choka and the pilot snarled at each other. Something exploded, and a haze of acrid smoke filled the air. Nom Anor dug his fingers into the spongy edge of the bulkhead, still unable to look away from the planet below.

The planet of his prophecy.

Not one, but three blue cones stabbed up through the atmosphere. It was a beautiful sight.

An earsplitting detonation snapped his face against the mica. He tumbled to the deck, black spots swimming before his eyes, but with grim persistence he dragged himself back up, noticing as he did that everything had gone eerily silent, though the ship still shivered beneath the Imperial frigate's attack. For a foolish instant he thought perhaps the ship had lost its atmosphere and he was in vacuum, but then he would be dead, wouldn't he?

He wiped blood from his eyes, realizing his forehead was cut, and gazed back out the viewport, just in time to see that they had made their run past the Imperial ship. Its drive section was just coming into view. It eclipsed his view of the planet as it began a ponderous turn, trying to come after them. It was still firing at them from its rear tower. Nom Anor noticed that *Red Qurang* was trailing a cloud of vaporized coral.

"We can stand no more of this," the subaltern said. "Another strike, and—"

Suddenly all the stars fell toward Zonama Sekot. The frigate quivered and twisted, stretched into a streak of light, and vanished with the stars. Nom Anor snarled, braced himself—

And the stars were back. In the distance, the orange gas giant rotated as always. Where Zonama Sekot had been was only empty space.

Not what I expected, Nom Anor thought as his body went light from relief. *Not what I expected, but it will serve.*

Still, for long moments he gazed at where the planet had been, blinking away the blood even though there was nothing to see.

He willed his muscles to relax. The truly dangerous part of his journey was yet to come. Ushk Choka and his men were surely doomed. Shimrra would probably execute them the instant they landed. Nom Anor would live longer, at

THIRTY-FOUR

The hull-breach claxon blared as *Mon Mothma* closed with the pursuing Yuuzhan Vong fleet.

"Deck Twenty-four, sir," Cel reported. "Contained. The damage is minimal."

"Get those deflectors back up," Wedge ordered. "Divert power from starboard, if necessary."

Mon Mothma ran port broadside to the approaching vessels, lasers and ion cannons thrumming in a steady rhythm, missiles and mines ejecting as rapidly as the ship's weapons systems allowed. Wedge knew he couldn't keep that up for long, but he wasn't worried about depleting the power core or running out of ammunition—they would be overwhelmed by the enemy long before that happened. In the meantime, however, his desperate maneuver was causing the lead capital ships to either slow or veer onto lengthier vectors— not so much from fear of the *Mothma*'s firepower as to avoid collision. That wasn't true of the entire advancing line, of course—the ships on the wings had simply gone around him. Those weren't the ones he was worried about; his central preoccupation was with tying up the cluster of the four ships flying point, because if they were slowed significantly, the second Interdictor would have to set a parabolic and hence longer, slower course to reach the rest of the Alliance ships. That would give the battle station that much more time to incapacitate the outsystem gravity-well generator and his fleet that much more of an opportunity to jump out of this thoroughly botched affair.

And, to his surprise, it was working.

The Yuuzhan Vong had been strange throughout this whole battle—tentative. The sudden appearance of the Golan II seemed to have made them more so. Even approaching his lone Star Destroyer, the Vong seemed almost cautious. It was almost laughable—Ebaq Nine must have really shaken them up if they thought the string of mishaps that constituted the Bilbringi offensive might actually be the setup for some ingenious trap.

Come to think of it, that might be why they were trying to stay relatively clear of *Mon Mothma*. Maybe they expected . . .

He blinked. It might work.

"Commander Raech," he said.

"General," *Mon Mothma*'s commander said.

"Evacuate the sectors adjacent to the power core and reduce the core shielding efficiency by two percent every thirty seconds."

"*Reduce* the efficiency, General?"

"That's correct," Wedge replied.

"Very well," Raech said.

"Give me reports on that as it develops, Lieutenant Cel."

"Yes, sir," the lieutenant said, clearly as puzzled as the commander.

Wedge turned his attention back to the battle. The largest of the ships had rolled up above his horizon and was pounding their upper shields from medium range, while a smaller frigate analog was coming in from below.

Wedge ordered a change in heading. Groaning, the ship turned its nose toward the Dreadnaught and the three cruisers behind it. *Mon Mothma* was now under fire from an entire hemisphere.

"Forward deflectors failing, sir."

"Steady," Wedge said. "Hold this course."

The pockmarked surface of the Dreadnaught grew nearer, resembling a badly scarred moon. The lights on the bridge went out, suddenly, and stayed out.

"Power core shielding down fifteen percent, sir," Cel said. "Sir, the surrounding decks are reporting contamination."

"Continue as ordered," Wedge said.

And hope the Yuuzhan Vong don't revert suddenly to form.

The interdictor cracked at its central seam and bled plasma in a white-hot fountain of lead. Spinning from the reaction, it rolled like some bizarre child's firework and then split, light flashing inside it like lightning in a dark thunderhead.

Jaina, still bound in stun cuffs, felt like cheering.

So did some of Prann's people, apparently, because they actually did.

Prann wasn't one of them. "Status?" he snapped.

The Barabel at system ops looked over. "We've sustained major damage to the southwestern deflector grid. Other than that, we're in pretty good shape."

"Good."

He looked over his shoulder at Jaina, his eyes smoldering, then finished the turn and took a few steps toward her.

"Well, Jedi," he said. "You got your wish. Now I get mine." He pulled the blaster out and pointed it at her head.

"Hey, wait, Prann," one of the humans said. "None of us signed on for murder, especially the murder of a Jedi. The station is still in good shape, we're no longer interdicted— let's just blast jets out of here, stick to the original plan."

"Unh-unh," Prann snarled. "Nobody gets inside my mind like that. It ain't right. And if we try to jump, she'll just do it again, drop us by the *other* interdictor. Once she's dead, *then* we jump."

"Just let me stun her," Vel said. "She can't do anything then."

"No, not until she wakes up. Then who knows what kind of mind tricks she'll pull? Better this way."

Jaina watched the muzzle of the weapon calmly. "Right now you guys look like heroes," she said. "Nobody knows you weren't planning to help. Nobody has to. Kill me, and all that changes."

"Hey, she's right," the Rodian—Jith—said.

"No, don't be a fool," Prann said. "We've got all those other pilots on board. Somebody will talk."

"Good point," Jaina said. "Are you going to kill them, too?"

"Prann, come on," Vel pleaded.

"I'd take his advice," an infinitely more familiar voice said, from behind her.

Prann jerked the gun up and fired as Jaina whipped her head around. She was in time to see a large, furry mass intersect the bolt with a blazing bronze lightsaber and send it whining into the bulkhead, missing its intended target—her father.

Lowbacca—the furry mass—growled and leapt toward Prann, followed closely by Alema Rar, whose lightsaber was also blazing. Then the air was suddenly full of blaster fire. Lowbacca slashed through Prann's weapon and then knocked him to the ground with an elbow strike; Rar leapt straight at the bridge crew. Her mother and father were suddenly in front of her, Leia blocking any shots coming their way and Han taking careful aim so as not to damage the consoles.

It didn't take long for Prann's people to give up in the face of the furious and unexpected attack. Within a few moments they were all disarmed.

Jaina let her breath out in a long sigh. "Hi, Dad, hi Mom. I was wondering how long you were going to take."

Prann was picking himself up off the floor, rubbing his jaw.

"We stopped to pick up reinforcements," Han told her, indicating Alema Rar and the rest of Twin Suns.

Leia moved to stand next to her. "Are you okay?" she asked, putting her hand on Jaina's shoulder.

"Never better," Jaina said.

Her dad was staring Prann down.

"Look, Solo," Prann said, most of his bluster suddenly gone. "I don't want any trouble from you."

"You were holding a blaster on my daughter. What do you expect from me, a kiss and flowers?"

"Oh—yeah." Prann muttered, almost as if to himself. "I was just—angry, you know. I wouldn't have really done anything."

"The rest of you," Han shouted. "I want you back at your posts, because this crate isn't going anywhere until every last Alliance ship has made it out, understand?"

The crew complied immediately, and the Twins went around collecting the discarded weapons.

"This is *our* station," Prann said. "We *earned* it."

"Hey," Han said, "what's your name?"

"Erli Prann."

"Erli Prann. Can't say as I've ever heard of you. But Prann?"

"Yeah?"

Her father's fist suddenly lashed out, cracking the butt of his blaster against the side of Prann's head. Prann dropped as if Han had used the business end of the weapon.

"If you ever touch my daughter again, I'll kill you," he said.

When he looked up, Prann's crew was staring at him.

"Well?" he thundered. "Don't you all have something to do?"

They jumped back to their tasks as if they'd been working

for Han Solo all their lives. The lasers and ion cannons started firing once more, covering the Alliance fleet as it gathered speed for hyperspace.

"And somebody get me the code to these stun cuffs!" he demanded.

The Dreadnaught was suddenly receding instead of getting closer. So were the other capital ships.

"Well, look at that," Wedge said. "It worked."

"They think we're overloading our core, don't they, sir?" Cel asked.

"Yes, Lieutenant, exactly," Wedge replied. "But they won't buy it for long."

He turned to the pilots. "Hard about. Point us toward that space platform. And get the shielding efficiency back up in the power core."

"Sir, the interdictor is down," Cel noted.

"Brilliant. Control, order all ships to lightspeed."

The Yuuzhan Vong shook off their uncertainty pretty quickly when they saw the *Mothma*'s drive turn their way. They gave chase like a pack of voxyn.

Up ahead of him, he had the satisfaction of seeing the rest of his ships vanish into starlight.

"We can ramp up to lightspeed ourselves, General," the *Mothma*'s commander said. "Shall I give the order?"

Wedge's lips pinched in. Jaina and everyone else on the battle station were doomed if they left now. Not a good reward for what they had done, but if he attempted an evacuation, the crew of *Mon Mothma* might join them.

He sighed. "Prepare—"

"Sir, I've got an incoming message—priority one, from *Millennium Falcon*."

"Put it on."

A few seconds later, Leia Organa Solo spoke over the channel.

"Wedge," she said, "can the *Mothma* make the jump?"

"Yes. Where are you?"

"In the docking bay of the Golan Two. Wedge, I'll explain later, but we're okay here. We'll cover you on your way out."

"That's good enough for me," he said. "Commander, take us out of here."

So long, Bilbringi, he thought. *If I never see you again, that'll still be two times too many.*

"It was easy enough slipping into a berth, after we lost the skips," Han explained. "What with all the shooting going on, I guess nobody was watching the dock."

Jaina, her mother and father, and Wedge Antilles were sitting around a table in the refectory of the Alliance-commandeered Golan II Battle Station, currently occupying an orbit in an uninhabited system with what remained of Wedge's ships and Admiral Gilad Pellaeon's fleet. A few Yuuzhan Vong ships had followed their vector on the jump, and had paid dearly for it.

Now they were awaiting orders on how and where to disperse to. Prann's people were in custody, waiting to be charged, and the near-system lookouts hadn't spotted anything that looked like an imminent Yuuzhan Vong attack. The combined fleet remained on high alert, but there was time for a little relaxation.

Wedge poured another round of Corellian brandy.

"If this station had lips," Wedge said, "I'd kiss it. Since it doesn't—Colonel Solo, I'll drink your health instead."

"Hear, hear," Leia said, and they all raised glasses.

"We really have Prann and his people to thank, in a way," Jaina said, after the toast was over. "I mean, it's not like they *intended* to help, but if it weren't for them—"

"Yes, if it weren't for them we would have all died," Wedge said. "Even as it is, we lost way too much here. Pash

Cracken, Judder Page . . ." He shook his head. "Old friends, young people I never knew."

He looked up at them, and to Jaina he seemed suddenly old. "You'd think I would be used to it by now."

"You don't get used to it," Han said.

From the corner of her eye, Jaina saw a flash of uniform, then an aging human face with an iron-gray mustache. She came quickly to attention.

"Grand Admiral Pellaeon, sir," she said, saluting.

The others at the table came to their feet more slowly, Han slowest of all.

"Please," Pellaeon said. "At ease, Colonel Solo. After what you've been through, you deserve a rest."

He turned to Wedge and saluted stiffly. "General Antilles, I've come to offer my apologies. Captain Devis's man found us, but we hadn't had time to prepare the fleet for lightspeed before you arrived here. I should have joined you regardless, but when our communications failed—"

"You did exactly as I would have done, Grand Admiral," Wedge said. "The battle plan was explicit. It simply didn't take into account that all our communications might fail."

"That's very generous of you, General Antilles. I hope if I were in your situation I could be as forgiving."

"Has anyone heard from Admiral Kre'fey?" Wedge asked.

Pellaeon nodded. "The couriers Captain Solo dispatched established communications between us, a bit belatedly. It seems, General, that the ships that initially jumped from Bilbringi when you arrived there encountered Kre'fey's fleet. They engaged briefly."

Jag? Jaina thought. Had she sent him into a firefight?

"Admiral," she asked, "do you know if Colonel Fel reached Admiral Kre'fey?"

"I do not, Colonel Solo, but I shall make inquiries."

"I'm sure he's fine," Leia said. "We'll find him."

Wedge cleared his throat.

"Grand Admiral," he began, "I wonder if you would care to join us for a drink. I believe the brandy is from your home province."

Pellaeon hesitated. "I would very much enjoy that, General Antilles, but at the moment, duty calls. I—I was wondering if I could make an inquiry of my own. Captain Devis hasn't returned to his command. Do you know his whereabouts?"

Han shuffled a bit. "I'm sorry, Admiral, he, ah—didn't make it. He died helping to take down the interdictor."

A strange expression passed over Pellaeon's face like a cloud, and like a cloud it was quickly gone. But Jaina caught something in the Force, something unmistakable.

"I see," Pellaeon said.

"He said to tell you he did what he thought was right."

Pellaeon clasped his hands behind his back and looked at the floor. "Well, yes, that sounds like him," he said. He glanced at Han. "He was a great admirer of yours, I believe, Captain Solo, despite the fact that in Imperial holos you are most often portrayed as something of a villain. Or perhaps that's *why* he admired you."

He clicked his heels together. "Ladies, gentlemen—until I have time for that drink."

He saluted and left—almost in a hurry, it seemed.

"Villain?" Han muttered. "Maybe I need to see some of these holos."

"That was a little odd, don't you think?" Leia asked.

"Yeah," Han drawled. "Devis was a good guy, sure, but—"

"Is the Grand Admiral married?" Jaina inquired.

"No," Leia replied. "They say he's never made time for it. Why do you ask?"

"Because," Jaina said, remembering what she'd just felt in the Force, "I think Devis was his son."

They were all silent for a moment, until Han raised his glass.

"To all of our sons and all of our daughters," he said, "be they with us or beyond."

"I don't know," she said. "It's not like my contact with them has been all that strong, but I felt them, especially Luke and Jacen. Now it's like—they're gone."

Han suddenly felt very cold.

"You mean dead?"

"No, not like that. I would know it if they died—I know I would."

"Then I'm sure they're fine," Han said, uncertain whether he believed that or not.

"Yes," Leia echoed. "I'm sure they are."

Tahiri looked up at the heavens and shivered straight to her bones.

No world should have hyperspace for a sky.

After the jump, *Jade Shadow*'s instruments had gone strange, and Mara had settled the ship in a protected ravine until they could sort things out. No telling what would happen to the atmosphere when they reverted.

If they reverted.

She drew her attention back to the conversation.

"Jacen and I had both sensed you for some time," Master Skywalker was saying. "But fitfully, and we couldn't get a sense of where. Sekot sensed something, too, but couldn't find your ship—it was hidden somehow."

"We came in a Sekotan ship," Tahiri said.

"With a few Yuuzhan Vong spare parts," Corran put in.

"That might explain it," Luke said.

"It certainly explains it," a new voice said.

They all turned, and Tahiri gasped. Nen Yim was standing there, whole, alive.

"Nen Yim!" she said.

Nen Yim shook her head sadly. "No. This one has passed on. I found her attached to my memory—her, and much information concerning her technology—and the ship that brought you here. The modifications she made to the ship are—interesting. I may experiment with the design, should we survive this."

"Tahiri," Jacen said, "this is Sekot, the living intelligence of the planet."

"I—" What did one say to a world? "I'm pleased to meet you."

"And I you, Tahiri," Sekot said gravely.

"*Should* we survive?" Luke asked. "What happened, exactly?"

"I was infected with a virus designed to corrupt the information-transfer system that links my consciousness to the hyperdrive. I believe the intended result was a core explosion. I managed to prevent that, but was unable to stop our jump to hyperspace. I have excised the virus and am regaining control as we speak, but it is difficult."

"Do you have any idea of our destination?"

"None," Sekot said. "The jump was blind. Eventually we will pass close enough to a gravity well to be pulled out."

"Our friends in orbit," Luke asked. "Do you know what happened to them?"

"They did not make the jump with us," she replied. "Whether they were destroyed, left behind, or pulled off onto another vector, I cannot say."

"I'm sorry," Tahiri sighed.

"Sorry?" Luke asked.

"Yes. I brought him here. I argued for it, and now everything's ruined."

"Tahiri, you weren't the only one who thought it was a good idea," Corran said. "Everything always looks clearer in hindsight." He put his hand on her shoulder. "You came here for all the right reasons—to end the war, to somehow find common ground between us and the Yuuzhan Vong. I thought we could handle the situation. I was wrong."

The figure that resembled Nen Yim smiled ruefully. "I

will not say I am happy to find myself sabotaged and in danger of destruction, and yet what you brought with you—the shaper and her knowledge—are of great importance. I do not entirely understand, and will not speak of it now, but I suspect the questions raised are the most important questions I shall ever have to ask myself. Now—if you will excuse me, I must return my full attentions to preserving us all through what is to come. I suggest you find sturdy shelter in the caves."

"Thank you," Luke told her, "and may the Force be with you."

"More than ever," Sekot said, "I believe that it is."

And on that enigmatic note, the image of Nen Yim vanished.

Soon after, the stars returned, spangled on a night sky.

The wind began.

EPILOGUE

Han was sitting on a shingle of a beach on Mon Calamari, silently enjoying the sunset with Leia, when Lando Calrissian came calling.

"They said I'd find you down here," Lando said. "I didn't believe it."

"Well, you know," Han said. "The wife likes this sort of thing."

"Is that Jaina?" Lando asked.

Han glanced off in the distance, where Jaina and Jag were exploring the tide pools below an ancient reef uplift in rolled-up trousers and windbreakers. Jag had shown up with Kre'fey a few days before, and Jaina and he had been annoyingly inseparable since then.

"Yep. I convinced her to take a little leave," he said. "What's going on? Still charging military prices for your courier service?"

"Hey, I'm just doing my part," Lando said. "I only charge enough to keep me from looking foolish. Anyway, my businesses won't run without communications, either. And there's plenty of competition—the Smugglers' Alliance loves this sort of work. Appeals to the romantic in them."

"Did you just come down here to fill me in on your good deeds, or is something up?"

"No, I'm just stopping in to say hello and good-bye before I head back out. But I thought you'd like to know some of my people caught one of the things that made such a wreck of the HoloNet."

"Really," Leia said. "What was it, exactly?"

"A dovin basal, basically, grafted onto some sort of living guidance system. They follow HoloNet signals to their source and then collapse the relays into singularities. The Vong must have released a million of them—they're everywhere. Some of my people think they're even multiplying."

"Wonderful," Leia said. "So even if we rebuild the relays, as soon as we use them one of these things will catch the scent, and good-bye relay."

"That's about the size of it. I've been building some compact new relays, though, and mounting them on retrofitted corvettes. If they're mobile, it'll be harder to find them."

"Sounds expensive," Han said.

"Yeah, but think how useful one of those would have been at Bilbringi."

"Good point. I guess the military will give you a good price for those, too."

Calrissian smiled. "Eventually. I'm going to give them the first few as samples. I have to think about the future, after all. Well, I'll leave you two alone, now. Places to be, and all that."

"Thanks for stopping by." Leia said. "It's always good to see you."

"I'm sure it won't be long before we see each other again," Lando replied.

They had finished watching the sunset and were walking back to the apartment when Leia suddenly stumbled. Han caught her.

"Hey," he said, "you know you don't have to act all clumsy to get *my* attention." But then he felt how tense she was. "What's wrong?"

"It's Jacen, and Luke—and Tahiri, they—"

"Are they all right?"